TOTAL ENHANCEMENT

A MINA KANE NOVEL: BOOK ONE

AMANDA CARLSON

CIU Agent Mina Kane has her lamella gloves full in the year 2105.

Mina Kane has been on assignment undercover for eighteen insufferable months trying to box up a sticky-fingered hacker. She's eager for this op to be finished—not only because the boredom of telework is literally draining the life out of her, but she's desperate to be rid of the fresh-faced rookie. Agent Adams is driving her straight into the stratosphere with his wide-eyed enthusiasm and lack of sufficient training.

Luckily for Mina, her next case is a solo classified. Someone at Total Enhancement Pet Center, where pet owners pay for their furbabies to be pampered, is using their access to attach encrypted data to animals. Mina's job is to uncover who it is. But what she discovers at Total Enhancement goes much deeper than just encryptions. The plan changes from passive to action faster than a world currency coin can spin on its edge.

One thing is for sure—catching bad guys is 2105 is never boring.

Other Books by Amanda Carlson

Jessica McClain Series
Urban Fantasy
BLOODED
FULL BLOODED
HOT BLOODED
COLD BLOODED
RED BLOODED
PURE BLOODED
BLUE BLOODED

Sin City Collectors
Paranormal Romance
ACES WILD
ANTE UP
ALL IN

Phoebe Meadows
Contemporary Fantasy
STRUCK
FREED
EXILED

Holly Danger
Futuristic Dystopian
DANGER'S HALO
DANGER'S VICE
DANGER'S RACE
DANGER'S CURE
DANGER'S HUNT
DANGER'S FATE

Mina Kane
Futuristic Thriller
TOTAL ENHANCEMENT
PERFECT PLANT
CUPID'S BOW

"NAME AND DESTINATION please." The young woman was enclosed in a tall, skinny booth outside the transpo hub on level twenty, lenses over a pair of diffracted cornflower-blue eyes, canal phones lodged in both ears. Her bright dandelion hair was piled on top of her head, and elaborate jangles as long as Mina's forearm dangled from her lobes.

Mina wondered if the noise coming from the ornamental links distracted her. Didn't seem like it, which was impressive. She reached up to her own printed stones, which sat up close and personal with her skin with no noisemaking opportunities whatsoever. Just the way she liked them. "The name is Mina Kane. I'm not taking public. I'm awaiting private transpo."

"In that case, take a seat over there." The woman gestured idly, her bright eyes flicking back and forth as she dealt with other issues, clearly not bothered by the cacophony coming from her ears. "If your cuff doesn't beep, someone will alert you when your ride touches down. Have a nice day."

"Thank you."

The Spire could've easily stuck a bot in here to handle all transportation orders, but as Mina had already noted, this building seemed to employ a fair number of air breathers. For a structure this size, that was a rarity.

If everything went according to plan, she'd have a new residence here by the end of the day. Her very first home in a megascraper. She was looking forward to it.

Mina entered the ample waiting area and rested her compucase on the rigid polymolded seating next to an expansive sheet of glass in full view of the hub. Her ride would be here momentarily.

Her cuff buzzed. She tapped the screen, and a tiny holo of her best friend—and fellow agent—Kaylee Poston popped up, hovering a few centimeters above her wrist. "Hiya," Kaylee said. "Just calling to tell you I can't make it over to see your place tonight. I have to take Dag to the vet. He's getting vacced, and he's always grouchy after. But call me once you're settled. I'll see it, with my full drool on, through your enormous brand-spanking-new wall-to-ceiling screens, you lucky comet streaker you. I can't believe they're authorizing megas now. I'm eligible in two, so I'm right behind you."

"A lucky comet streak had nothing to do with it. They finally figured out how to bypass the mega's internal biosystems. At least, that's what I was told when I put my option in." Mina shrugged. Federal agents were required to live in places where they could have integrated tech—

like a weapons printer, which required internal valves—and specialized security, like smudgers and retinal scanners. It was mandatory. "I'll miss your in-person critique, but Daggie comes first." Mina adored Kaylee's lovable mutt. "The mover bots are all set. I just have to deal with the mega rep, which is always an ordeal. She has no idea the unit has been altered already. But protocol is protocol."

To maintain discretion, one had to follow the rules. Or at least appear to.

"It takes a certain...panache to be a rep. But they do work hard for their borrow credits, so I'll give them that. In other fun news, is your op finally going down today?"

"Damn, I hope so. I'm so close it's painful." After five hundred and forty-two dismal days of posing as a teleworker trying to bring an elusive currency launderer to justice, Mina was praying hard it would end today. "There's a chance he moves funds tomorrow. Tuesdays are his usual syphoning day. But I'm feeling lucky."

"Well, he won't get very far in puffboots, so there's that."

Mina giggled. "The dude's got a pair in every color."

"The last time I wore puffs was in level-three schooling. We pretended we were 'etiquette poofing,' because the air shots were too discreet to sound like the regular blasters that came out of our tiny behinds. It was a hoot for age sixers. I'm sure the instructors wanted to chuck them into the nearest grinder and make us wear comfort slides. I honestly don't know how they endured."

"I never had a pair. Even as a child, I knew they were childish. The fact this launderer, with his stupid puffers, has eluded me this long is insulting."

"I thought you might retire in telework."

"Very funny." It'd been Mina's longest-running case since she was hired as an agent with the CIU six years ago. "He's tricky. He's not using standard coding. If he was, we would've netted him a long time ago. But a trap has been set. Once he starts syphoning, it'll trigger a cascade, then we'll catch him with an imprint. I have to hand it to the rookie. He's the one who figured it out. It's a brilliant scheme, overall." She had to give credit where it was due. Even if it hurt a little.

"That's high rookie praise indeed. Once this is over, your future will be The Wrong Lee-free, so that's pretty exciting." They'd christened the rookie The Wrong Lee, since Kay*lee* was the *right* Lee.

"Yes, being Wrong Lee-free will be worth every single boring day of telework drudgery." Almost. Maybe. Close enough. Outside, a hoverbus crested into view. Mina watched it slowly putter into place, bouncing twice on an air cushion. A second later, Mina's cuff beeped, flashing a quick arrival message in the form of a blinking craft and the number five. Eight o'clock. Right on time. "I have to go. My ride's here."

"Okay. Good luck. And don't be too hard on your mega rep. Remember, they're trained to be, well, you know, precise and reppish. Not entirely their fault."

"Precise and reppish. Got it. See you later." Kaylee disappeared and Mina stepped in front of the field doors.

They slicked open, and a cyclone of wind hit her full-on. Her long brown hair whipped around her shoulders as she closed the gap, the door of the craft rising. The transpo was fully automated, and even though it was a government craft, it was bland gray instead of an icy steel blue, with no obvious symbols or markers decorating the exterior.

She boarded, placing her finger in the helix slot to give her customary DNA sample. The female sim all but purred, "Good morning, Agent Kane. Your destination has been locked. Do you wish to make any changes?"

"No."

"Travel time to Cullen Industries will be four minutes, thirty-two seconds."

"Disengage voice commands, keyword civilian to reinstate."

"Order activated."

Once the craft was airborne and skimming across town, Mina flipped open her compucase. After her computer engaged, she ordered, "Show me the whereabouts of one Ricky Cantrell." The screen instantly coalesced into a detailed map of the city, homing in on a two-centimeter avi, complete with limp hair and a sleazy smile that didn't come close to reaching a pair of dull-pewter eyes.

Mina leaned back. Ricky wasn't running. His avi remained static at Cullen. He wasn't even worried. If this launderer thought for a moment his telework cover had been blown, he'd be scouring himself for possible implants—like the one she'd managed to place on the back of his neck. It'd taken a few choreographed giggles and some shy eye-blinking gazes over the course of eighteen insufferable months to get it there. But there it was.

She couldn't wait for this op to be over. The best thing about it would be walking away from telework for good. The second-best thing would be dumping the unseasoned rookie, who had caused her more headaches than she'd thought possible. It was going to be sweet icing on a printed cake to lose them both.

In her real job, Mina was in the business of eliminating corruption at the highest levels, so actively participating in fraud by chiseling a borrow out of some unlucky bastard in exchange for a nonexistent prize had been tedious. It was a dose of irony she was ready to part with.

But before any of that could happen, she was going to roboclean the floor with Sticky Ricky. It would be the first time that simpleton had been scrubbed to the bone in years.

Cullen Industries was a standard no-frills printed hunk of concrete in a banal area a few kilometers outside city limits. The squat four-story structure had just enough clear polycarb to make it feel like you weren't *actually* incarcerated.

There was no lure for commerce out here, just a few meal-printing kiosks for the lunch crowd and a small office supply store that carried printed merch.

Mina exited her ride at the same time as her

quasipartner, Lee, exited his. She refrained from exhaling the long, tired sigh sliding its way up her trachea. How Lee had been recruited into the Corruption Investigation Unit, or CIU, was beyond her. If he was tagged on Mina's next assignment, her director was going to receive some A-level arguments, chock full of as many colorful words as she could get away with without getting fired.

Lee fell into step beside her, nudging her. Mina grunted, trying her best to ignore the misguided rookie, clasping her hands in front of her so they didn't accidentally slip round his neck.

"Day's almost here," Lee said. "Do you think he knows his time is up?"

"No." Or he wouldn't be here. Mina hadn't shared that she'd managed to get a subderm on Ricky. Her reasoning was that she and Lee weren't "officially" partners. Not in the traditional sense, anyway, as telework wasn't a "team" job.

A large set of doors encased in corded steel provided the only public entrance into the building. Four shiny boxes were affixed to the jambs on each side. As they approached, the automated sim announced, "Please insert your DNA of choice. Hair, fingernail, skin, or saliva is accepted. Use the appropriate receptacle. Don't forget to complete your retinal scan once you enter. Thank you and have a nice day!"

Cullen Industries certainly had a lot of security steps for a business whose primary objective was to persuade people to forfeit their borrows for a nonexistent visit to paradise.

Mina stuck her finger in the appropriate receptacle, choosing a micro-skin scrape. It was the most hassle-free way to go. Lee, predictably, went for the hair, trying to yank a strand out of his scalp and managing to get four. Mina shook her head, her eyes front and center.

Her bioread at Cullen would identify her as Monica Lake. Lee Adams was Larry Fortman.

Once the lights switched to green on the receptacles, the doors powered open at the speed of an elderly person piloting an airchair.

They stood and waited.

The sim voice followed them inside. "Please step in front of the nearest retinal scanner. Place your forehead against the lever. Scanning takes only a second."

As they completed second-level identification, a security bot stepped forward. "Welcome to Cullen Industries. You're cleared for level two. The tubes are this way."

"Yeah, we know," Mina muttered as she hip-checked a thick, titanium bar. It *thunked* forward then fell back into place as it realigned. Cullen should really change up its bot greetings more than once a year. Hearing those same words every day was getting old.

She and The Wrong Lee made their way toward the fric-free pneumatic tubes that would whisk them up to the second level in less than two secs.

"Do you think he'll make a move today?" The rookie couldn't help himself. Lee's dirty-blond hair was tufted and uncombed, tumbling around his forehead, giving him that just-risen look. His nondiffracted hazel eyes were filled with anticipation. Mina had never seen them another color, even though diffracting was the norm in their appearance-conscious world. Her pseudopartner was young, likely not older than twenty-one or -two, but Mina had never asked. Being young didn't excuse idiocy. After all, Mina had only recently crossed into her twenty-sixth year, but hadn't been Lee-clueless since she'd named herself after a popular screencast character at the age of three. Lee bounced on the balls of his feet. "He's going to panic when the data bounces back."

"Yeah, he will. And when he does, we'll be waiting," Mina answered stiffly, not wanting to discuss this inside a tube, or anywhere within a seven-kilometer radius of this area. Thankfully, the doors slicked open. "Be on your toes, Lee." He already was. Literally. "I'll send an alert if I need you."

With that, Mina stepped out and into the spy game.

Chapter 2

THE ENTIRE LEVEL, all five hundred square meters of it, was densely packed with cloned workstations. They were clustered together like trees in a branchless forest. The semicircles boasted floor-to-ceiling curved crystalline, a clear work surface affixed at sitting level, and a single polymolded chair. The options for interfacing with a subscriber were lenses or screen.

Mina detested lenses, even though they were made of a comfy biomaterial that molded to the eye. She preferred working on a larger surface, rather than having the data so close to her eyeball she could seemingly scatter it with an ill-timed sneeze.

The automated semis could seal up, but most of the time, they stayed open, which Mina preferred. How else would she have spied on Rick the Rat all this time? She was lucky he usually kept his open, too. Unless, of course, he was busy stealing money.

Then he locked himself in like the rodent he was.

At the moment, Rick was shut in, a serious look on his face, his shoulders hunched over his personal compucase. His puffboots were a blaring yellow today, his limp hair tied back in a tail, which hung like a skein of unraveled yarn between jutting shoulder blades that stuck out like a couple of clipped wings. It's a good thing rats couldn't fly.

Mina deposited her compucase on the floor behind her chair, sliding off her navy suit jacket to reveal a yellow shirt beneath. She hung it on the hook provided, out of sight if a subscriber chose to vid chat in person. Thank goodness most preferred voice-only.

Before Mina could organize herself to face the monotony of yet another day of telework, Gerald appeared, his personal board cradled in his arms like a newborn. "Let's make today a better day than yesterday, Monica." Her manager's voice was filled with snark. His particular brand was painfully nasal, like wind whistling through shriveled leaves. His precisely manicured fingernails, dyed an unflattering shade of puce, fluttered over his clear tech, which he flourished in front of himself like a showy prize. His short black hair was slicked back in a popular style that Mina felt made the wearer look like an otter. All that was missing was a tasty morsel of kelp clutched between two pucy fingertips. "Your numbers are abominable," Gerald wheezed. "Only one subscriber borrowed in the entire week. Another few days at this level of failure, and you're out of a job."

It was the same holo dance they shared every week, sometimes more than once if Mina was feeling extra sour.

"I'm sure today will be much better, Ger," she replied sweetly. "Now, if you could be so kind and move on, I'd appreciate it."

Gerald folded his board back into a loving embrace. His head angled to the side, channeling more otterlike tendencies, his diffracted fig-colored eyes narrowing. Without his beloved square of crystalline, he'd be lost. He wore not one, but two cuffs. Some people hoarded tech. "You know," he said, "many would kill for this job—*any* job, for that matter. I realize it's not wild and exciting to be a teleworker, but in our automated world, there are very few positions available that require a real human touch. This is one of them. You're lucky to be employed here. It's best not to forget that."

"If by 'human touch,' you mean the wherewithal to manipulate an elderly person out of their borrows, then you're correct. Bots can't handle this job, Gerry, because they aren't programed to lie. It's a human trait. Lucky us. So, if you'll excuse me, I've got some defrauding to do, which I can't do with you lurking next me like an overlord in search of innocent outcasts to devour."

Gerald stiffened, temporarily rendered mute by Mina's snark. He sniffed loudly, flourishing his baby again as he made exaggerated motions. His keratin-enhanced nails clacked on the clear crystalline, the ultrahaptic material used for almost every screen on the planet. "I'm marking you down for that." His voice shook. "That, coupled with your piss-poor performance, should be enough to expel you from this company by this time tomorrow. You've never truly appreciated working here. Why they've kept you on for so long is beyond me. A badger could get more borrows than you."

They've kept me on because I've played my part well enough. But no need anymore. "If a badger could do my job, a nonsighted, nonaural mouse could do yours. Now, shoo." She swept her hand at him with a flick of her fingers. "I've got people to chisel, and you're wasting my time."

His eyes widened. They were surprisingly clear of any lenses, odd for a tech hoarder. Thinking better about engaging, Gerald stalked off, likely to wheeze about her backtalk with anyone who would listen, which was basically everyone who wanted to avoid doing their meaningless, soul-draining job.

Mina glanced at the semi next door as she sat in her uncomfortable chair, plugging the irritating canal phone into one ear so she could hear the depressing life stories of these poor folks Cullen swindled each and every day.

Ricky hadn't moved, still hunched over his compucase.

Immediately, a sim voice intoned, "Next call in five seconds."

The screen in front of her flashed a photo of an elderly woman, likely in her hundreds, going by age lines alone. Her white hair—no dye, thin, and sparse—was styled a little recklessly around a plump, oval face. Mina didn't detect any recent enhancements, likely because she was short on borrows. She had a full set of teeth, either hers or enameled filler. Not everyone did. The only giveaway to possible intelligence was a set of piercing eyes boring into Mina, daring her to commit legalized deception.

Her name was Geneva Zante.

More information ticked below: one hundred seven years old, lived alone, ten dependents.

The perfect candidate.

"Who's there?" the old woman tottered in Mina's ear. "Why won't the video load?"

"Hello, Ms. Zante, my name is Ms. Lake, and I'm calling on behalf of Cullen Industries to offer you the rare chance at acquiring a real vacation of your dreams." Mina relayed the standard spiel in a bored tone devoid of any feeling. She could've easily been a bot. "If you prefer a face-to-face vid chat, I'm happy to accommodate. We block video at the start because we don't want to intrude."

"Did you say vacation?" Geneva snorted, her voice cracking predictably. Most of the time, the elderly echoed like they were stuck in a zoom tunnel. "Why in the *hell* would I need to take a vacation at my age?"

Mina perked. A fighter.

"Well, Ms. Zante, you subscribed to our network, indicating you would absolutely adore taking a physical trip to a tropical destination of your choice, complete with full spa treatments, complimentary facial and skin enhancements, all transpo and meals included. Is that something you're still interested in?"

"Is this a joke?" she snarled. "Who subscribed me? It's illegal to subscribe a person to one of these scams without their knowledge. I want to speak to your superior!"

"Indeed, that is illegal." Mina grinned. Though, there were a trillion and one ways to circumvent those laws.

"According to our records, one Zara Zante entered your name. Because of your age, she has power of decision over your debt accounts." Another sad result of their money-grubbing world. This woman's daughter had control, because she and the rest of the Zante children would have to repay Ms. Zante's debts over a two-year period when this nice old lady departed the world.

Mina should've substituted the word *borrow* for *debt*, but she couldn't bring herself to do it.

"Always been a fool, that girl," Ms. Zante grunted. "A sucker for those high-end enhancements. I barely recognize her anymore. She doesn't even look like a Zante! She looks like one of those low-end screenstars with the overplumped lips and exaggerated eyes. She even had pupil enlargements, for heaven's sake. She can barely see out of those things, always bumping into walls and feeling around with those claws of hers dyed all kinds of crazy hyperglo colors, blinking on and off like she's trying to hail a drone. Throwing me to the vultures probably got her a minimum of two credits back on her borrow. Barely enough to print a new lamp. Shameful! Take my name off this list immediately. It's my right to have it expunged."

It was.

Mina was already plugging the appropriate directives into her board by hand, smiling like a fiend, even though she was forced to continue Cullen Industries' standard lines. "Are you sure we can't interest you in taking the vacation of your dreams, Ms. Zante? The cost is only two hundred and fifty standard world currency. The odds are in your favor to win. Let me remind you, that price gets you—"

"Fraud! Lies!" Geneva was becoming increasingly agitated, which Mina wanted to avoid. "I don't have to listen to this for one second longer."

Mina lowered her tone to conspiratorial. "I hear you, Ms. Zante. And I couldn't agree with you more. Let me assure you with the utmost certainty that your name is now expunged from our list. I have the deactivation code here, if you're interested." After a small pause, she added, "I'd also like to give you the number to the government complaint department. I'm certain they'd love to hear from you." Mina had given out that restricted number only a couple of times. When Gerald had found out, he'd nearly lost his faculties. Mina had avoided repercussions because she'd only just started her job at Cullen Industries and feigned that she hadn't understood the rules.

Their sweet, always-there-for-the-people government didn't want to hear complaints, but when they received them, they were required by law to file an inquiry.

"You're going to give *me* the number to the official complaint department?" Geneva all but growled. "I've heard that one before. Each time I've ever received one of those numbers, all they do is buzz and buzz and buzz."

"I assure you this one will work," Mina replied with confidence. "Set your device to record, and I'll give it to you." Mina held on while the nice woman tried to deal with her handheld. The elderly couldn't cope with cuffs for the most part—they were too small and required precise finger movements to work without voice command.

Ms. Zante swore a few times. Mina suppressed her urge to giggle.

It was a good start to the day. One she hoped would end with Rick in a box.

"This thing is too many years old," Geneva complained. "Zara won't let me get a new one. I should just buy one anyway. With those pupils of hers, she'd never notice if the thing was shoved right in front of her face." A few more grunts. "Okay, I got it on record. You better not be lying to me. If you are, and this call doesn't go through, I'm puttering down to your doorstep to lodge the complaint in person. My airchair is a lot newer than this thing."

Mina had no doubt Geneva would do just that. The woman had spunk. Average life-spans topped out around one-twenty. Mina hoped Geneva had a few more years left in her. After relaying the number, Mina added, "I hope you have a very nice day, Ms. Zante. It was a pleasure chatting with you."

"Find yourself a new job," Geneva offered in parting. "A nice girl like yourself should be selling printed sweets, not defrauding those who have very little to spare."

If only Ms. Zante knew.

Mina's eyes flicked over to Ricky. He hadn't moved, other than his fingers rapidly skimming over a keyboard he had hidden in his compucase. He never used voice command when he did his swindling. "Don't you worry, Ms. Zante. I'm planning on leaving this job very soon. I hope everything works out for you. Have a nice day."

Mina ended the call.

As soon as the connection was severed, the sim dinged. "Next call in five seconds."

Instead of taking it, Mina dislodged the receiver from her ear, effectively shutting down the program. She peered at Slick Rick through hooded eyes. He was oblivious to anything going on around him, as per usual.

Suddenly, he stood, so visibly rattled that his compucase nearly tumbled to the floor. He managed to catch it by his fingertips, his wiry knees knocking together a little at the top, causing his ridiculous boots to shuffle together. His semi was closed, so she couldn't hear their breathy puffs for help.

Looked like her call with Geneva Zante would be her last in telework. It'd been satisfying, but what was about to go down would be so much more.

CHAPTER 3

RICKY'S SEMI SLID open with a soft *schick*. Perspiration dotted his forehead like he'd been misted by coolant. Mina leaned half in, half out of her own area, her arms casually crossed. "Hey there," she called as he ventured out like a blind mole rat detecting sunlight for the first time, nose twitching.

He darted a glance her way, startled that someone had addressed him. His compucase was clutched in one hand. On par with his boots, it was a glossy orange that should've been outlawed by the color defense squad long ago. The case itself was thin and lightweight, just like Mina's, but it shouted *dickwad* instead of *working professional*. "Hey there, Monica," he started. "Good to see you. I'm...I'm just going to take a quick break."

Mina didn't point out that they'd all arrived at work less than fifteen minutes ago, and it wasn't time for a sanctioned break.

He took off toward the meal room, but Mina knew he'd opt for the staircase.

She tapped her cuff as she pursued. She had the local authorities programmed for a single alert. If the PPF received a call from a government agent, the code was always the same, and their participation was quick and mandatory.

They'd be here in five.

Duncan McAllister, her director at the CIU, would be proud that this was going down quietly, which was always a top priority for an agent in their department. Standing orders were to stay under the radar, and that usually wasn't a problem.

Just as Icky Ricky passed the waste rooms, Lee stepped out.

Mina was both relieved and irritated to see him. As she watched, Lee collided with the launderer, his hands shooting out to steady him, gripping his shoulders. "Sorry about that, man," Lee said. "I didn't see you there."

Ricky did his best to shake him, likely feeling the same way Mina felt about Lee, trying to get away without actually engaging. Lee didn't let go.

"Step aside, freak," Ricky yelled. "I'm trying to get somewhere!"

Lee held on. "Oh, I apologize. Here, let me help you." Then The Wrong Lee yanked Ricky down, his hands still firmly locked around Ricky's shoulders, and bounced him off his knee.

The scamming weasel collapsed, gasping for air in a confusing pile of limbs and outdated yellow footwear.

During the ruckus, Ricky's compucase shot out of his hand and spun down the hallway in a neon-orange blur before crashing against one of the walls outside the meal room, right as Gerald exited to see what the commotion was about.

The manager's shrill gasp could've hailed a thousand drones. "What's going on here? Larry, what are you doing? Get off of him!" Gerald rushed forward, one arm waving, the other shielding his tech against his body.

Mina shook herself out of the haze Lee had just created by bringing down the perp on a single bended knee. She reached into her pocket for her e-restraints. Pantsuits were an excellent all-around choice for this kind of work. E-restraints were made of millimeter-thick aluminum wire and once connected would produce a sizable charge. If Rick the Rat tried to break free, he'd get sizzled. Not enough to kill him, but definitely enough to stun him and make him soil his baggy, black activity pants. Who wore activity clothing to work, anyway? A child, that's who.

Lee stood over Ricky, the sole of one of his sensible mocha ecoslides placed squarely on the perpetrator's back, pinning him in place. He grinned at Mina as she approached. "I brought him down."

"Um, yes," Mina replied. "You did good."

Gerald came to a spittle-filled stop as Mina crouched next to the ratty launderer. Gerald eyeballed the situation, deciding immediately whatever had happened here was Mina's fault. "You're not only fired, Monica"—an exaggerated signature sniff huffed out—"but I'm reporting you to the local authorities! You're not only bad at your job, you're a *menace*."

"The police have already been alerted, Ger." Mina barely gave him her attention as she tugged a resisting Ricky into a single restraint. Thwarting her excellent progress, Ricky flopped suddenly, fighting for control, spinning like a guppy newly flung onto land knowing that his oxygen was about to be all used up. He jerked upward, knocking both Lee and Mina off-balance as he scrambled away, the unconnected wire dangling off a single wrist as he darted toward the stairs.

Mina wasn't going to let Lee have all the fun. Before Ricky could tug open the door, Mina rushed forward, grabbing him by the pathetic hair skein, and yanked him back, vowing that this was the very last time—in the history of the universe—she would ever have to engage in skin-on-skin contact with him.

As he spun around, a complaint formed on his lips right before her fist landed. "What the hell, Monica?" Ricky cried, reaching up to stem the blood now gushing from his nose. "You can't just—"

She struck him again. This time she timed a precise chop to the neck just like she'd fantasized about for eighteen miserable months.

He crumpled at her feet, as people often did when their airway was compromised. Mina secured the other restraint, then walked over to pick up Ricky's compucase. The metered pulse of multiple sirens sounded in the distance. She and Lee had managed to make this a spectacle after all, instead of keeping it covert.

It was time to slide out.

Mina grabbed Lee's arm, tugging him along, ignoring Gerald's gaping, stunned expression.

As they rushed back to their semis, trying not to cause any further disruption, Lee gave Mina a lopsided grin. "That was fun."

"Yeah, yeah," Mina muttered. "Grab your stuff. Meet me by the tubes. We have to get out. No need for civilians to pick up on anything else."

"Where do you think you're going?" Gerald had come to his senses, clomping after them, highstepping in his custom euroboots with the square toes and platypus heels. "You can't just leave him lying there! Passed out on the ground…and bleeding. What's happening? This has to be a bad dream. Or else we're on one of those laugh-teaser screencasts. My early-rise biotic intake was too low this morning. I must be having a hallucination." A small audience had gathered between the closest stations to the ruckus. Gerald sneered, waving his free arm. "Get back to work! We're losing money with everyone loitering here. Go! Go!" They scattered back to their seats.

Mina grabbed her jacket and slung it over one arm, then picked up her own compucase. She met Lee by the tubes and found them immobilized and the door to the staircase locked. The security bots must've activated a lockdown. Likely an order from the PPF.

"Stay right where you are," Gerald ordered, his head back in the game, on their heels like an irritating, yippy mutt with square paws. "You can't just ignore me. When Mr. Cullen gets wind of this—"

Mina marched forward, happy to get up close and personal, invading his carefully cultivated personal space with the kind of joy reserved for little children celebrating a new birth year. Gerald arched his head back rather than be sprayed by her spittle. The boot was firmly on the other foot. "Open this door. Now." She adjusted both cases to one hand and grabbed the front of his shirt, dragging him even closer, making sure her hot breath flowed right up his flaring nostrils.

"What are you doing?" Gerald sputtered, almost dropping his board, which elicited a scream and a quick arm reconfig.

"That sleazeball"—Mina shot a nod down the hall at Ricky, where she could see he was still passed out—"has been embezzling money on Cullen's orders. He will be charged, as well as anyone who knew anything about it. Minimum jail time for hacking, embezzling, and defrauding the government out of taxable currency is twenty. Abetting is ten. You wouldn't happen to know anything about that, would you, Ger?" The man in front of her paled like a printed mushroom. "Just what I thought. Now it's time for you to pull your slick-haired head out of your ass and unlock these doors. All of them."

She let him go, and he stumbled backward, smartly keeping his retorts to himself. He brought one of his cuffs up to his lips. "Engage master. Keyword walnut. Override door locks." Then he positioned his overpriced crystalline in front of the locking mechanism. A satisfactory click sounded.

"Good job." Mina depressed the lever, ushering Lee

onto the landing in front of her as she addressed her beleaguered manager. "When PPF arrives, Ricky's DNA will give them everything they need to know. And things are looking up for you, Gerry." She flashed a toothy grin. "Cullen Industries will be shutting down, effective immediately, and if there's any justice in the world, this will be the last time we ever have to set eyes on each other. So it seems, in a rather deliciously ironic way, you're the one who's fired." Mina took off down the stairs.

At the bottom, she and Lee entered the lobby. The quickest way to exit this fecal stain of a building was by the front doors. Several security bots had amassed, and multiple steel-blue-and-white-striped PPF craft were landing outside the entrance. Mina walked briskly toward the security bot that welcomed them each day with the same three lines. She engaged her cuff, her badge hovering in holo off her wrist. "My name is Agent Kane. You need to let us through." She indicated the doors.

The bot dutifully zeroed in on her ID. It took only a second for him to digest the graphic. Then he glanced at Lee. Mina made an inpatient gesture for Lee to produce his credentials, swallowing her frustration but allowing for a tiny eye roll.

"Oh, right. Sorry." Lee's holo badge blinked on, and the bot scanned it.

"Right this way, Agent Kane and Agent Adams."

Before they could reach the doors, the local authorities rushed in, several security bots gesturing them toward the tubes. One officer slowed, coming to a stop in front of them. "Did you call this in?" he demanded. "I'm Sergeant

Bailey, PPF, 21st Borough." His badge flashed out in front of the microcam fastened to his lapel. It recorded everything the police did and said, as dictated by law.

Mina stuck out her hand. "I did. I'm Agent Kane, and this is Agent Adams." Sergeant Bailey gave her hand a firm shake. "The suspect is restrained upstairs. Full name is Richard Francis Cantrell. Case file listed under his DNA, third level. My department representative will get a hold of someone in your department within the day. Any follow-up will be done via that representative. This is as far as we go."

Sergeant Bailey's eyes wandered to her ID, still hovering above her cuff. "What agency did you say you're with?"

"I didn't," Mina answered. "That information is classified." This was one of Mina's favorite parts. She almost dared Sergeant Bailey to argue, giving him a look—a single eyebrow slowly arching toward an impressive peak. Some officers pushed, which got them nowhere. Even if they insisted on a DNA swab, which she would consent to, her rank and affiliation with the CIU were nowhere to be found. Other than her general identity and the fact she worked as a government agent, nothing else existed.

Sergeant Bailey seemed like he might press the issue, but then thought better of it. He hadn't made sergeant for nothing. "We'll wait to hear from your representative." He took off.

As she and Lee exited the building, Mina began the process of summoning her craft, but stopped short when, surprisingly, Lee's government ride was already grounded, passenger door lofted.

Lee appeared sheepish. "I, um...I took the liberty of calling us a craft when I went to use the waste room. I noticed that Ricky was making his move, so I decided it was a good time."

Mina tried her best to cover her shock and liked to think she almost succeeded. "Okay, nice going. Thanks." They headed toward the ride, a literal carbon copy of the one Mina had rode in earlier, panel for panel.

"I figured we were both going to the same place now that the op is over," Lee said with more enthusiasm than necessary, stopping at the door to allow her to board first.

Mina made a face, unsure what to think, but got in and made room for her pseudopartner. They both entered their DNA. This time, Lee had no choice but to use his finger.

The sim announced, "Welcome, Agents Adams and Kane. Your destination is logged for headquarters. Do you wish to make any changes?"

"No," they both replied simultaneously.

"Your travel time will be six minutes, twenty-seven seconds."

Mina told Lee, "Sorry," meaning it. "I'm not used to sharing my ride."

"That's okay. I don't mind." The craft took off smoothly, shooting toward the city. After a few minutes of awkward silence, Lee announced in a sincere tone, "I just want to let you know that I've really enjoyed working with you. I know I'm new and all...but I'm trying to become a better agent. I'm taking some classes—"

"No need to share." Or overshare. Mina lifted her hand, cutting him off, feeling somewhat embarrassed for the kid. "It's been nice...working with you, too." She hoped he didn't pick up on the lie. "What's important is we apprehended our target. We did our job. He'll do time, and the currency will be recovered. I'm sure your next assignment will be much more interesting. Telework sucks."

"Yeah, talking to those old people every day was a real downer," Lee agreed. "I felt bad taking their borrows. Gerald threatened to fire me almost every week."

"Me, too. I think he would've actually succeeded this time."

"I managed to give some back, so that was good," Lee added proudly.

"Give some of what back?" A kernel of alarm rang through her.

"Well, I...I kind of...hacked the system." Lee fidgeted in his seat, jamming his fingers together in a little thumb dance. "It wasn't hard. The program they run is fairly simple, no more than a Class VII. I just pretended subscribers called back to lodge complaints. Then I formulated call times and transcripts, autogenerated, of course." Oh, of course. "Once the complaint was filed, their borrows were transferred back into their accounts." He shrugged. "Nobody found out."

Mina's tongue was in jeopardy of tumbling out because her mouth had creaked open so far. "You...

hacked the system...at Cullen? To give old people their borrows back?"

"Yeah, it's probably against procedure, but I couldn't help it."

Probably? Try *illegal.*

Lee bowed his head like telework had beaten every last tiny gram of dignity out of his body. "Cullen Industries is making money on business practices that should, by all accounts, be illegal. That's why we joined the CIU. To protect people against crime, not perpetuate it." His expression turned bright and hopeful, a hank of hair falling over a hazel eye. "It was the right thing to do." He shifted in his seat. "At least I think it was."

Mina nodded absently, her brain ten steps ahead of her now firmly closed mouth. "Lee, can I ask you a question?"

"Of course," he replied. "That's what partners do. Well, they do other stuff, but they also answer questions."

That hadn't been their routine until this point. They'd shared very little personal backstory due to the fact that Mina had spent almost zero time with him. Now a bloom of guilt crept through her like fungus ripening on a rotted log. She wondered if she should've pried deeper sooner. "Are you a computer specialist? I mean, did the CIU recruit you out of PPF, where you specialized in tech? Or somewhere else?" It wasn't unheard of for agents to be recruited from other areas, but it wasn't the norm.

Lee smiled widely, lightly enhanced teeth gleaming. "I didn't go through specialized training. I was a hacker—*am* a hacker. Level XIII. I never broke the law.

Well, not on purpose," he added hastily. "I tried to help people, like altering unfair bank borrows for friends and family." Highly illegal. "I only got caught because this guy I teamed up with was sloppy. He was only a Level X. I should've known better, but my friend was in a mess, and the banks were about to cut him off. The agency gave me a solid. Said I could come work with you guys or spend time in a box. Since I was already fighting the system on my own, I agreed. It was a no-brainer, really. Working with you is my very first assignment." Mina thought Lee's cheeks might flex off his face he was grinning so hard. He'd never looked younger.

You don't say, Lee.

Mina swore several times inside the safety of her own brain, picking lots of colorful words that would make a nice kid like Lee blush. Not having bothered to delve deeper into Lee's file was on her. It was likely all there. Mina had just figured he was a rookie, and not a very intelligent one. Spending time performing a lifecheck on him had seemed like a waste of time.

But that didn't excuse her director for not telling her Lee's story when she'd complained about his lack of training. McAllister knew exactly how green he was and had stuck him with her anyway.

Mina cleared her throat as Lee gazed expectantly at her for some kind of response to his bountiful admission. "If you were a hacker before this," she started, "how did you learn that move? The one where you broke Slick Rick over your knee?"

"Oh, that was from a VR program one of my buddies

wrote. It didn't work that well at first, but I've been practicing." He puffed out his chest. "It was amazing I got to use it."

Amazing. "Okay, Lee." Mina closed her eyes, angling her head back against the gel-rest. "Thanks for letting me know." McAllister was going to get an earful in the form of a mild rebuke in a calm—*okay, calmish*—tone.

As the craft drew closer to their destination, an unwanted thought crept into her brain about as subtly as a kitten pouncing on unprotected toes. Because McAllister hadn't trusted her with Lee's ultra-unseasoned status, Mina had failed miserably as his caretaker. She'd effectively let a toddler run loose in her house—even though said toddler had figured out, if in a highly illegal fashion, how to reimburse innocent people—instead of making sure he received the training he needed to become a decent agent.

Had she actually been *asked* to mentor Agent Hacker, would she have done it?

Maybe. Possibly.

Probably not.

A tired breath of air issued out of her mouth in a predictable end-of-op kind of way.

"Did you say something?" Lee asked.

She shook her head. "No, Lee. I didn't."

Chapter 4

"It was negligent," Mina argued calmly. More or less. Calm enough. "You dumped an untrained agent in my lap and didn't tell me." Mina was pacing around McAllister's office, exerting four steps in any one direction before she was forced to turn and tread back the other way. The room was no wider than a utility closet in a derelict rental, containing four stark, unadorned walls and one serviceable wall screen.

The entire place had been updated sometime during the last century, when they'd installed a basic fiber floor covering that was now a scuffed charcoal but had possibly once been black. There was only enough space for a printed desk—one adequately mimicking wood grain—and a chair the color of a bad sunburn.

Once upon a time, the counter that ran the entire length of one wall had been shiny. Now it was dull and chipped, holding an ancient meal printer perched precariously on three legs, along with a few other supplies, such as a reusable coffee mug and some utensils. The printer probably only dribbled out coffee and a few snacks. Mina had never been in McAllister's office long enough to be offered anything from it.

Agents in the CIU didn't have offices, nor did they venture into headquarters very often. They worked from home or directly from their op. They gave reports by screen. It was more covert that way, and that's what this agency was all about. Secrecy. Staying below the radar. Hiding in plain sight.

That meant sacrifices, which were in full effect in McAllister's outdated cube. The only extraordinary thing about the room was a single floor-to-ceiling solar-catch window featuring a totally spec view—a wide swath of water coupled with a generous slice of Atlas Park. The newly designed public park had been installed on top of the massive concrete enclosure that surrounded the lower end of the city. The much-needed barrier kept the ever-rising sea at bay. The recent addition of greenery made the infrastructure necessity much less of an eyesore.

"It wasn't negligence." McAllister sat behind his desk, hands folded. "It was a calculated risk. You wouldn't have taken him on had I told you he'd recently been recruited with only basic training under his cuff."

"The last time I checked, you give the orders and I follow them." Mina was aware she was grumbling, and felt childish, but she soldiered on. "I lodged several complaints about his ineptitude over the past year, and you never said anything. Placing him undercover on a lengthy job for his first assignment wasn't calculated, it was risky. Honestly, he's so wet behind the ears, I'm surprised his collar doesn't leak when he turns his head. It was a constant battle keeping him from compromising the op. Not talking is covered in security training on the first day. *No unnecessary vocal communication at any time.* Full stop. If you'd told me, at least I could've amended my tactics with him, tried to give him some pointers. Tried to..." She trailed off. They both knew she would've kept him further out of the loop so he wouldn't have compromised the mission even more.

"That may be true, but according to the report you just gave," McAllister countered, "Lee Adams, the sopping-wet rookie, brought Ricky Cantrell down efficiently and without much fuss. All told, it took you no longer than ten minutes once the altercation began before you both were exiting the building. He even had a government craft waiting to whisk you away. Not only that, he was the one who came up with the code to infiltrate the syphoning data." Her director was kindly leaving out the dustup they'd created, which Mina had dutifully recounted. Not the finest CIU op that ever went down. It wasn't even in her top ten. "I had my reasons for not telling you," he went on. "The biggest was the job itself. Telework is drab and boring. It was a good way to start his training. I wanted to see how he handled himself without interference. He needs work, but overall, I'm satisfied with how it went."

Mina had omitted the details that Lee had hacked the system at Cullen and refunded borrows. That was for the rookie to tell. Coming from her, it would've been tattling. Kind of. But really, it was on him to divulge or not divulge. Or so Mina had convinced herself. It wasn't going to be on her if a reversal of Lee's actions drained those poor souls of their borrows after all.

She dropped into the rickety chair, running both hands over her face. It was time to get back to reality. Feeling sorry for her Lee troubles was officially over. "Truth be told, this was a painful op, with or without Lee. Eighteen months was much too long to pull that creep in. Ricky was slippery, and his programming was on par, but it should've been handled quicker. I'll take the hit for that. I knew it was him, I just couldn't prove it. I'm glad it's over. I'm looking forward to doing something that isn't telework."

She glanced at her director across his sparse desk. She'd never answered to anyone else. Duncan McAllister had been here from the beginning, appointed as head of the newly formed CIU ten years ago after two decades of undercover work with the Federal Bureau of Investigative Crime Abroad, or FBI-CA.

McAllister had spent a good part of his career executing numerous critical overseas missions. It went without saying that the government excelled at tracking down violators afar and handing them over to the World Council with aplomb. They failed to do the same at home, where it could affect their monetization and greed.

Director McAllister was a decorated officer of distinction. His moral compass was on par with a certified aid worker helping the disadvantaged.

Those not in the know about the CIU—which were many—figured Director McAllister had fallen on hard times when he'd taken what appeared to be an administrative job handling a handful of petty agents who did nothing more than chase after street criminals.

Appearances were deceiving. Mina leaned back, crossing her arms. "Has my new op come in?"

McAllister grinned, one gray-flecked eyebrow cocking upward. "It has."

Seeing her boss smile was a bit off-putting. It was an odd look on him and didn't go with his precisely shorn hair, untypically undyed, or his square jaw that never carried a hint of stubble, or the patrician nose he often stared down when looking at subordinates.

"Are you going to tell me what it is?"

"I will now that you've taken a seat," he agreed, unclasping his hands, his cuff catching a ray beaming in from the best part of the room. A newer model than Mina's, the cuff was thinner and ten times more powerful. Nothing on the open market was comparable. Cuffs in general could set a person back a couple thousand borrows, but one as fancy as McAllister's would be considered a lux item, costing borrows in the five-digit currency range.

A cuff pretty much ran your entire life. Without one, performing mundane tasks would take much longer than the average human had become accustomed to. Everyday survival was integrated inside that one small, sleek-looking, easy-to-wear bauble. Several companies had tried eyeglasses, some had experimented with ear wraps and rings, and one company had even flirted with a choker. Lenses tried to compete, and people did use them, but they weren't good for running everyday things.

Mina wore a government cuff, but it was a recent retrofit of a high-end consumer model, not the techies' wet dream like the one dazzling on McAllister's wrist.

"I'm enjoying the delay," he said.

"I can see that. That's not exactly…normal."

McAllister remained coy.

"The last time you were this gleeful about one of my ops, my job was to pose as a coin dealer in the outskirts."

"Yeah, that was a good one." Her director actually snorted. So strange. "You snagged a big-time illegal-goods runner in under forty days. And don't forget, we installed a sleeping pod and a security bot inside that shack. As things run, I think that was pretty gracious of us. A handhold because you were just starting out as an agent in this department."

"Handhold, my backside. That *shack* wasn't anything more than a few pieces of corrugated steel tethered together with some carbon fiber. And that rent-a-bot would've been dismantled and traded for parts in a nanosecond if anybody had figured out it was in there with me. No one came to my sorry excuse of a door because they didn't dare. I played the role of a blow-your-brains-out-first, ask-questions-later outskirt like I'd been birthed in a greasy hovel." Mina grinned. "And if I remember correctly, I snagged that trafficker because I had a literal hoverbus full of physical coin at my disposal. And he liked my eyes. Or so he said. He was exceptionally strange."

Not to mention highly dangerous. Mina had enjoyed taking him off the streets. He'd gone by the name of Barker, and he was doing time in a box for the next thirty. That assignment had been quick, but dirty. Heavy on the grub. Living in the outskirts put your life up for grabs, literally. Mina had gone in heavily armed, which wasn't the norm, dressed head to toe in black syn leather, and with an attitude to do damage. Luckily, the locals had bought it. The outskirts reeked of desperation and was controlled by criminals and swarmed by down-on-their-luck souls with no borrows left to their names. Everyone there was hanging on to life by the slimmest of filaments.

It was a sad, treacherous place. She'd been happy to leave it.

"Before you hear about your next assignment," McAllister told her, "I'm going to preface this by telling you that you're the perfect candidate for this particular op. And even though it might sound somewhat trivial, it's important." He tapped a button, and the underside of his desk revealed a high-tech board, another government gadget. Mina couldn't see the screen because it was blocked by the replicated polycarbonate wood grain separating them. Her boss read over the notes, smiling to himself. He finally looked up. "You begin work at Total Enhancement Pet Center tomorrow, nine sharp. You're booked as a temp replacement for a worker who had the good fortune to win a last-minute physical vacation to the Colonies of the Bahamas, paid for by the US government."

That was more than Cullen Industries had ever given anyone.

Mina scooted forward. "Are you talking about a place where they pigment dog fur, dye claws in flamboyant colors, and give poor, unsuspecting creatures bioblasts that make them light up at night?"

"Yes, the very same. This facility also specializes in deep-tissue massage, walk therapy, and various spa treatments. Apparently, animals in general don't get outside enough to have their needs met, or so claims the center's holosite."

"Walk therapy?" A quick image of herself trying to control five animals at once as they dragged her along the newly installed Atlas greenway found its way into her brain. She winced. But at least she'd be outside, rather than stuck inside a concrete wasteland. Mina's eyes focused sharply. "Wait. Is someone doing something to these poor creatures? And while it's an unusual post, I don't hate it. But why am I the right person for the job?" Mina was an animal lover and enjoyed walking. Who didn't? But this seemed like a no-brainer op that any CIU agent would be intelligent enough to figure out.

Well, maybe not Lee.

"Pets from this particular center have been found to be carrying high-level encrypted devices from point A to point B," McAllister explained. "And you're the most qualified because you're the best body-language expert we've got. If someone darts a glance in the wrong direction, you notice. Someone in that shop is physically attaching microdata to these animals, and it could be happening during any step of the process. It's probably a quantum drive of some sort. We'll have that information shortly, as we've just intercepted one. What we know for sure is that these pets have been spotted in the location of a known trafficker."

"What are they trafficking?"

McAllister's expression went from amusement to wrath in the space of a millisecond. "Pleasure. Young girls."

Mina whistled, easing back. "The CIU doesn't usually take on sex crimes." The pleasure industry was extremely lucrative, as well as highly regulated. It was a booming industry for banks and borrows. Pleasure workers, as long as they were above a certain age, could get licensed. Pleasure emporiums, with fancy VR rooms to cater to every sexual fantasy, were numerous. A government-approved pharma called Plush had recently hit the market, supposedly enhancing the overall sexual experience of the user. Plush had taken off with the masses like meal printing had in the 2040s. Everyone was doing it.

Because the industry was so big, lots could go wrong, and laws were broken frequently, which was why the government had created its own department to deal with it, the Federal Pleasure Investigative Unit, or FPIU. Nicknamed the Sex Squad by anyone in the know.

Even though the pursuit of pleasure was up front and center in their world, that didn't mean trafficking didn't happen. Unfortunately, it did.

"The FPIU is handling it," McAllister said. "But they've recently discovered this ring reaches up to the highest levels. This is no low-borrow operation. The participants are government officials, bureaucrats, and bankers."

Mina whistled again. Once the ring was exposed, it was going to be a hot, sticky mess. Would every individual caught go into a box? Unlikely. But she was glad the Sex Squad would see it to the end. She'd do her best to aid them and the innocents—especially the innocents.

"We won't be involved with the case once it breaks," McAllister said, "but they've requested internal help locating who is doing the encrypting. Not from our department directly, of course, but word got to me. They know we're sending an agent in, but not from where. You'll have no contact with anyone else on this, unless specifically directed by me. Your profile is level ten and so low to the ground you should see the skin pattern on a flea." Fleas had skin? "Under no circumstances are you to expose yourself. If approached, you deny and disappear. You enter as a temp and leave as one. No arrests. We just need to know who's applying the encryptions and what animal will be wearing the microdata next. These chips contain detailed information in the form of a buyer portfolio, DNA identities, images, ages, everything needed to track these girls down. The buyer makes a choice, and the girl is delivered." Horrific and revolting. "You find the source, posing as a keen-eyed pet enhancement worker, and the men and women in FPIU will shut it down. Then we can get those girls back where they belong and stop any more from being snatched."

Mina nodded. "Got it. I'll report first thing in the morning. Dog enhancement sounds...interesting."

"It's not just dogs. You'll be dealing with cats, rabbits,

pigs, and anything else that can legally be registered to a personal residence. I think they draw the line at reptiles, but I'm uncertain, not being a pet owner myself. My wife is allergic. She's tried many remedies and even had some biochem alterations done, but nothing has worked, much to the disappointment of our children."

Many people owned pets. They were considered necessary stress relievers and, if properly registered, could accompany their owner just about anywhere.

Mina stood. Now that she had her next assignment, it was time to move. Lee was waiting to give his report, and she had an appointment with a certain mega rep. "What's my identity on this one?"

"Marjorie Wilcox. Out-of-work linguist from the Dalton Temp Agency. No prior credentials needed. They'll fill you in as you go. Your DNA cover is set in that immediate sector for the length of five days." McAllister slid his board back into its concealed position inside his unassuming desk. "After that, the permanent worker is due to arrive back. Arranging mechanical issues on her supersonic transpo home can give us another day, if needed. I'm hoping you'll wrap this sooner. Keep me informed if you run into any issues. I'll expect regular screencast reports."

Mina knew the drill. "On it." She made her way to the door, which was all of two steps. "Anything else?"

"No. Are you heading to your new residence now?"

"Yes. I was able to reschedule an earlier appointment." Mina glanced at her cuff. "The rep has no idea the place is already mine. Mover bots and drones are packed and ready to hit the air once I swipe my DNA and seal the deal."

"Check your utility room. A weapons printer has been installed behind the east wall. Panel is fingerprint-sensitive. Use it sparingly. We can't circumvent the elemental hoses integrated to your mega like we can in the smaller buildings, so settings are listed. If you order up a plate of spaghetti, you'll get a handgun and so on. It's equalized by weight. If you surpass your monthly carbon allotment, it'll trigger the local precinct's monitoring system, and they'll send a squad to do a sweep. Use it for emergencies only."

Printing any kind of weapon or destruction device was against the law and was monitored as much as it could be—by ordered item and carbon weight. Weapons tended to be heavy. One had to have a special permit to print things that didn't come standard on a preprogrammed unit. If you were caught making weapons, prison sentences were lengthy. It's a good thing Mina had a badge.

"Will do." She turned the knob, surprising herself as she added, "I think Lee has potential. With the right training, he'll make a good agent. Go easy on him."

McAllister's eyebrow rose as Mina walked out the door.

Chapter 6

"HELLO AND WELCOME to The Spire, the tallest, most-integrated megascraper in the city." The woman cradled a clear, voice-activated board no bigger than an antiquated piece of paper in the crook of her arm. She was giving Gerry a run for his borrows. "My name is Suzanne. And you must be"—she squinted down at her device as though her luminous eyes, diffracted the same shade of violet as her one-piece suit, had suddenly decided to play tricks on her—"Wilhelmina Kandy Kane?" A small snort escaped despite her otherwise unruffled façade.

Her hair was an elegant twist of platinum, silver streaked to give it a subtle sparkle under the ultra-lights spaced evenly across a lobby large enough to house a sports arena. Her cheek shapers were almost undetectable, save for the fact the upper portion of her face stayed firmly in place each time she smiled. "Wasn't that the name of a children's screencast back in the day?

It was a quest program, wasn't it? *Wilhelmina Hoover & the Candy Cane Adventurers.* They hid items in hologram episodes, and kids had to find them. It was before my time, but I know it was popular."

Extremely popular.

Mina already had her identity chip out, passing it to the woman between two fingernails that were glossed rather than dyed. Mina wasn't an anti-enhancer, but she wasn't remotely close to diamond status like this rep. "Yes, it was the number one screencast twenty-three years ago." Mina's birth name was forever an embarrassment, and luckily needed only in times of verification, like this one. "I went unnamed my first three years to avoid accumulating interest."

The loophole had been discovered by new parents in the spring of 2079. No name at birth, no debt number assigned. The error had been closed almost as soon as it had been detected. But being able to avoid accumulating debt during those early years had been amazing luck. Though Mina had never understood her parents' indulgence in allowing her to self-name. Wilhelmina Hoover had been a heroine to an inquisitive young girl. So why not become her? At age three, it had made perfect sense. Now, not so much. "I go by Mina Kane. The identity chip reflects that. Please change it in your system."

"Will do," Suzanne replied, her violet-creamed lips curving as she tapped the chip against the edge of her board before handing it back. "I've come across a few like you before, but none with such a colorful moniker. You were certainly lucky to avoid accruing that interest.

I'm sure if I'd had the chance, I'd be named something like TinFoot Tooty." She tinkled with laughter, her perfectly aligned, blindingly white, micro-enameled teeth flashing. When Mina didn't join Suzanne's chiming giggles, the rep gathered her composure, resetting herself back into professional mode with a capital P. "It says here you're"—her precisely drawn brows, no thicker than a single carbon thread at any given point, furrowed—"a trilinguist?" She glanced up at Mina for confirmation. "That sounds...interesting."

"It is," Mina replied comfortably. "I teach holo courses for those completing their advanced-degree cycle." It was her standard backstory. If Suzanne decided to quiz her on her specialty, she would pass. But she assumed the rep wished to espouse on the megascraper's many selling points, rather than probe her on the finer points of linguistics. "Does this scraper come equipped with holo-integrated virtual offices?" Mina asked, helping her along.

"Oh, yes." Suzanne made a sweeping gesture, her nails contoured to perfection, dyed in purple hyperglo that blinked intermittently as her hand swished. "The Holo Centers occupy the four corners of the structure. We have no less than eight hundred and forty cubicles, all individually programmable. The cubes come with airmelds, so integration with any other tech is not a problem. Some of the bigger offices can accommodate twenty holo guests at a time." She took a breathy pause, then leaned in. "Honestly, you can't get any better without going private. You can book a cube day-to-day or reserve regularly. The fee is fifty world standard currency for a two-hour block and can be easily attached to your monthly borrow. It only takes a DNA swipe to unlock."

"Good to know." Virtually *anything* could be attached to your borrow, a soft term banks had established in place of the word *debt* a few years ago after a massive outcry. The average person carried debt of nearly five million in standard world currency across their lifetime, starting at birth, with no hope of clearing it.

Mina glanced at her wrist, tapping her cuff. Suzanne noted the data check and suggested, "Let's get going, shall we? Time to visit the upper floors." Turning on a blade-thin heel, Suzanne briskly clacked over the gleaming marble floors toward the nearest group of tubes.

Mina had done intel on this building over the past week, choosing this mega over the other four located in the city center because it was the biggest and busiest. The bustling mini mecca held thousands of people, each of them scurrying to and fro at every hour of the day. It was just what Mina needed to keep a low profile and blend in.

As they walked, Mina took in the water feature the size of a small lake, with not one but two cascading waterfalls tumbling off clear polymer sheets three stories high. Pedestrian traffic was routed efficiently around it, diverting potential customers to specialty shops staffed with retail bots ready to serve a consumer's every whim. Food-printing stations with crisp green awnings were situated every ten meters, offering hard-to-find trace element options, like ginseng tea, oysters, and exotic nuts.

"The Spire is a fully enclosed system," Suzanne offered. "Everything is ground and recycled by atomic weight to twenty-second-century standards." She didn't so much as blink as she rattled off the rest. "Our Zine rating is two, the lowest of any other building this size in the city. We have mingling stations, enhancement centers, integrated spas, large-scale 3-D shops specializing in expertly designed custom items. We even have a real gemstone jeweler. She's the only licensed dealer in the entire city." She tapped a hyperglo nail to her earlobe, highlighting what looked to be an amethyst. Her salary must be excellent for her to afford real stones. "We're even lucky enough to employ two authenticated print-free restaurants with *actual* chefs using grown-from-soil ingredients." Her voice bubbled like it was pumped full of carbon dioxide. A real meal would cost triple a printed one. The ultimate lux way to borrow. "It's such a treat to have real food after such a long era of print-on-the-go, dontcha think?" She gave Mina a wink and dipped her voice to her preferred conspiratorial tone. "We even have an entire level devoted to pleasure. Those suites book out in advance and come with sensory nodes, floor-to-ceiling screens, and access to Plush if you have a prescription. Use your residential calendar to schedule those dates as soon as possible."

"I'll be sure to do that."

Once they reached the bank of tubes, Suzanne's custom sling-backs, likely printed from home to get the color exactly perfect, tapped to a stop as the pad of her finger lightly brushed over her board, her lengthy nails barely getting in the way. "It says here you're preapproved for anything in the gold sector, which spans floors two hundred to three-twenty. I have seventeen units available in that sector. Are you interested in a home health pod? It comes with a small monthly borrow, but overall it'll save you time and money. I have one and adore it."

This was the tricky part. Mina had to finesse it just right. "I'm actually interested in one specific unit. Three-twenty-eight, to be exact. No need to see any others."

Her precise and reppish rep didn't mask her surprise, her eyes narrowing as her gaze fluttered back to her board. "Have you been here before? If you have, you're required to sign on with the same rep at all times. It protects all of our interests and saves time and repetition." Her finger worked double time. "*Hmm*...it doesn't look like you've been assigned to anyone else. Not under your legal debt name or your identity. That's odd."

Mina faked a good-natured chuckle as she swept her long hair, free of any sparkle, behind her shoulders. "This is my first time visiting, don't worry. I've just been perusing your holosite. The real-time graphics are superb."

"The graphics are good," Suzanne agreed, "but nothing compared to seeing the units in person. Show me unit three hundred and twenty-eight," Suzanne ordered her board. She'd been making good use of her fingers, but they must need a break. The hyperglo was already starting to lag. A moment later, a low, satisfied growl came from the back of her throat. Her commission would be hefty, which changed everything. "Three-twenty-eight is an excellent choice. It's fully loaded, upgraded just this week. It's one of the only units with floor-to-ceiling screens in every room, surface charging throughout, a state-of-the-art meal printer, and a new spacious platform sleeper. This unit also comes with that home health pod we talked about"—Suzanne blinked rapidly, like something had gotten in her eye—"but it states here that it's an X600." A hand snaked up her chest, settling over her heart. "That's strange. As far as I know, 600s are military grade. I've never seen one in a mega before." She frowned, her cheeks unmoving, finger back to tapping. "Yes, it looks like this is the only one. It also has a soaker and several custom printers that are larger than usual. Because of that, your monthly elemental utility borrow will be higher." Suzanne met Mina's gaze, nipping the edge of a shiny plum lip, flashing a corner of extra white. "And with the recent reno and upgrades, it's not on our holosite yet, and it's actually over your preapproval range because of the X600. If you want it, I'll have to get upper-level permission." Then she surprised Mina with a chuckle and a small wink. "But who knows? After those three years of interest savings, maybe you can afford it after all."

"I'm sure it won't be a problem," Mina responded smoothly. "Contact your supervisor."

"You're a food printer, not lifesaving tech," Mina complained to her meal printer, refraining from giving the controls a solid whack. She was starving after a long day filled with getting Rick into a box and moving. She hadn't done any of the heavy lifting, but her appetite begged otherwise. The mover bots had been quick and efficient, relocating her few personal items into her new lux unit in under an hour. In Mina's world, when you could print anything, recycle it, and print something else, prized possessions were few and far between. She had clothes, of course, and a few basic have-to-haves, like a hairstyler and a tooth polisher, but other than that, her place had come fully stocked, including this top-of-the-line, fussy meal printer.

"I swear, if you don't print the food I ordered, I'll resort to physical violence." Violence toward inanimate objects hardly ever made things better, but it felt great while it was happening.

The female sim with the plucky British accent Mina had programmed to run her residence purred through the high-tech aural system. "Perhaps you could try, *May I please have a turkey sandwich on rye?* Or, *Please make me fish and chips.*" Mina had named her Veronica and had set her on Casual so she could interact with her without being prompted.

"I shouldn't have to say please in my own residence," Mina muttered as she eyed the shiny buttons daring her to give up and go hungry. "Eggie, print me a BLT on sourdough, standard plate, no cutlery." She intoned clearly, adding a quick, but pained, "*Please.*"

Eggie replied succinctly in a formal male sim. "I'm delighted to make whatever you desire within the Standard Elemental Diet. If you would like to add rare trace elements, please connect the appropriate valves. Would you like to hear some delicious suggestions?"

Mina moaned, "I know you heard me, or you wouldn't have responded. Why can't you make a BLT? It's been around since the dawn of time. Even small-time printers can handle an order like that."

"Order received. Printing ziti and tea. Would you prefer herbal or green?"

The machine began to hum, vibrating like drone props as it processed her order.

"Herbal," Mina replied, giving up.

At least it was finally giving her food.

Veronica announced, "Incoming vid chat request from Kaylee Poston. Would you like to accept or decline?"

"Accept, display in living room, visual at one hundred percent, both directions." Mina took a seat on one of her new stools, spinning toward the seemingly innocuous white wall that was about to morph into a two-way virtual conduit, and spread her arms wide. Her best pal, and fellow agent, appeared at full scale a second later. Technology never ceased to amaze. "Tada!"

"Whoa, fancy schmancy," Kaylee crooned, getting up from her chair. "Thanks for pumping up the view."

Visuals at one hundred percent meant the entire room was on display. Mina had also placed the vid chat at one hundred percent because she wanted to test her wall size.

She'd never had a screen this big. Her friend looked like a giant.

"Your cameras are excellent. I can't even see the mountings. Holy shit, is that a Magnito meal printer? Their meals are supposed to taste better than anything on the market. Or so say the food snobs. Lucky girl!"

"Yes, it's a Magnito. I named him Eggie. So far he hates me." Mina got up to check on her food. "I asked for a BLT, and he's making me ziti. But if it's good, I'll forgive him."

On cue, Eggie beeped, followed by, "Meal completed. Please slide back the screen to receive your food." A pretty plate of tubular pasta in a red sauce smothered with cheese awaited her inside the compartment. It smelled amazing. Next to it was a white cup full of steaming tea.

"You didn't print any cutlery, Eggie. I'm going to need a fork."

"Order received. Printing pork—"

"No!" Mina cried as Kaylee unabashedly howled behind her, watching the scene unfold.

"Be firm with Eggie," her friend suggested. "Show him who's boss."

"Cancel printing, Eggie," Mina demanded. "I don't want any pork. I need a *fork*."

"Printing in progress. Please wait."

"I guess you're eating pork and ziti with your fingers." Kaylee sat back down on her comfy, well-worn chair in front of her screen. Kaylee had lived in her nicely appointed adapted high-rise for the last five years. "*Daaamn*, but that's a sweet setup. That view outside those windows is incredible. I've never lived up that high. Your furniture looks like Castile & Co., those froufrou designers from Paris. They do all the shiny chrome with the puffy white cushions you can barely get out of. It's their sig."

Mina carried her plate and cup to the lounge area, setting them on the glass table with the stylish chrome legs situated between all the puffy cushions. "I'm not sure if it is. I didn't ask." Two end tables flanked a wide lounger, accompanied by shiny lamps adorned with blindingly white shades. It was all high-end and arranged in a tasteful, conversational way, with a soft, shaggy-pile floor covering. "Hope you don't mind if I eat while we talk. I'm starving."

"No problem. Have at it. You look beat. Long day?"

Before Mina could actually sit and enjoy her ziti, Eggie beeped, announcing that the food she didn't order was ready. She padded over to the printer. "Yes. I wrapped the Cullen op early, thank goodness. I'm so glad it's finally over. The launderer went down with a thud. His puffers definitely didn't make for a smooth getaway. Then I had a face-to-face with McAllister. After, I finalized this place and literally just finished organizing everything. I'm worn out."

"Yeah, moving into all that lux would make anyone tired."

"Ha-*ha*. Moving *is* stressful. The precise and reppie rep said there are sixteen other units in this sector. I hope you can be my neighbor at some point." Mina was pumped to see a fork sitting next to a plate of what appeared to be a pork chop slathered in some sort of cream sauce. Maybe she'd wanted pork after all, and her new meal printer was a psychointuitive genius. Instead of taking the risk of accidentally ordering more food, Mina said, "Veronica, cut power to Eggie."

"Cutting power."

Kaylee let out a snort. "You named your house Veronica? Is that a tribute to that waitress we used to see down at the Scoot? She was efficient. Talked too much for my taste, though."

"No, I named her Veronica because I thought it sounded dignified. This kind of a high-end borrow needs stature, don't you think?"

Kaylee shrugged, her jet-black hair, perfectly cropped in a severe line just above her shoulders, swished back and forth uniformly. "Don't ask me. Kevin would work just fine over there. Wouldn't you, Kevin?"

A male sim with a Southern twang replied, "How can I be of service, ma'am?"

Both women hooted with laughter as they always did when Kevin displayed his efficient Southern charm. He was a perfect contrast to Kaylee, who was a city girl, born and bred. Her porcelain features and slightly upturned nose were in direct contrast to her bash-you-in-the-face, talk-later attitude.

Mina took a bite of her ziti. "*Mmmm.* Good grief. You're right. The Magnito is wonderful. This is better than anything I've had in a long time. It's like..."

"Gourmet?" Kaylee helpfully supplied, leaning forward. "That's what they used to call high-end food made by actual chefs back in the day. I wish I could smell it. The texture looks spot-on. Try a mushroom next. Even without the proper trace, I bet the Magnito could make it passable. It's almost worth a ride over to grab a taste, but I should stay home with Dag."

"How's the pup?"

"Oh, he's fine. Just a big baby when it comes to air pens. They make a popping sound, and it's like he's been shot. He sulks around for days."

Mina giggled. "Poor, Daggie."

"Even if he was fine, I honestly don't have the energy to do much. I'm hip-deep in this assignment, and I can't catch a break."

"The forger, right?" Mina asked between bites.

Kaylee stood and began to pace. "Yeah. This guy is good. He sits at his big bank desk every single day like nothing's wrong. I swear he has liquid mercury for blood. I managed to link to his board with a stealthy air-override, which he hasn't picked up on yet, so I know when he's interfacing with his clients. That, and his face gets all serious and constricts like this." She mimicked someone taking a big gulp of freshly decomposing biomatter and trying unsuccessfully to swallow it. "Then I link in, and I can't find any communication. It's like it doesn't exist. And if I can't find it, I can't trace it. This guy is forging identities, the works—full DNA profiles and chips."

"Maybe it's time to bring in some specialized help?"

"Oh, yeah? What do you have in mind?" Kaylee wore a similar outfit to Mina's, but the cut was trendier, shoulders capped and slightly angled in the popular flight style. The color was moss green with a sheen, so each time Kaylee moved, there was a flash of contrast. The pants tapered slim, ending in tuck points over the tops of her feet, which were currently bare, her toenails dyed to match the suit. Kaylee took more time on her appearance and spent more borrows on clothing, and it showed. Mina would be envious if she'd cared more.

"Not what, but who." Mina ventured a bite of her pork chop, but because she didn't have a knife, she had to tear into it like a predator attacking prey. "Shit, this is good." She was forced to wipe some dribble off her chin with the end of her sleeve. "The texture is fab."

"Watching you eat that thing is going to give me nightmares. Get back on topic. Who are you referring to?"

"Lee."

"The Wrong Lee?" Kaylee sat down in her chair, tucking her feet under her petite frame. "You can't be serious. You're recommending I take *Lee* on assignment when all I've heard from you over the last year and a half is how incompetent he is? Is this a birthday prank or something?"

Mina gave up on the chop. It was delicious, but eating like a wild animal in front of her friend was beyond her abilities at the moment. "It's not your birthday and it's not a prank. I recently discovered something." Mina got up to hunt for a cloth for her face. A meal prep area this stocked had to have one, likely a stack. "McAllister didn't specify it was classified, so I can share."

"What? Spit it out. You're killing me."

"Lee's a hacker. Level XIII." Mina pressed her fingertip against various smooth, sleek surfaces, hoping to find a portal that would hook her up with something to wipe her face that wasn't her shirtsleeve. "They didn't recruit him out of training. He got busted, and they gave him a double-down." Indenturing hackers was not completely unusual. Good ones were worth their weight in real gemstones and essential for combating hackers on the outside.

It was either a job or a box, and they usually chose the job.

"Shut up. That cherub is a Level XIII? I never would've guessed."

"He's not even close to cherublike. He's a pain in the ass and as green as they come. *But* the guy knows his way around tech. He'd be an asset."

"That kid is seriously adorable. You're just jaded and couldn't see it because you were so irritated by his ineptitude."

"He *is* inept." Mina shut a cabinet that had popped open, containing useful items such as a robovac and a small cooling unit for those unique times when she'd feel like saving her food for later. "Where are the cloths? There have to be some here. It's an essential item, and my rep said this place was positively stocked with essentials." She stopped, hands on hips. "Listen, Lee sucked at regular agent duties, but he hacked into Cullen Industries to give old people their borrows back. I know my way around a system, and I admit I looked into doing the same thing, but there was no way I could penetrate their blocks. They were at least eight levels thick. The way Lee described it, it was like a skip through a VR park while eating a printed treat. He'd be an asset on your project if you could get him to keep his mouth shut. Full lockdown, not allowed to speak about anything but the weather." Mina threw her arms in the air. "I can't find the damn things."

"Try the island unit. I bet there's a drawer under there somewhere."

Mina bent over the edge, and sure enough, there was a long, skinny drawer. She placed a single fingertip on it, and it ejected, containing enough clothware for a dinner party. "Sweet." She took one out, pushed the drawer closed, and went back to her food.

"So you're telling me The Wrong Lee is actually The *Right* Lee." Kaylee hooted. "That might be the most ironic thing that's happened to us in a very long time."

"He can't be The Right Lee, because you are. But I will begrudgingly admit he might not be The Wrong Lee after all. How about we call him Hacker*lee*?" Mina took a bite of ziti. It was still warm and yummy.

"And blow his sweet cover by mistake? Not a chance. Let's call him Jubilee, because now he makes us happy."

Mina snorted. "He doesn't make me that happy. Let's just stick with Lee. I'm not sure what McAllister has in store for him, but you could submit a request. A hacker is what you need to nail down this forger."

"I'll think about it. What's next for you?"

"A classified." Mina finished the last bite of pasta and took a few sips of tea. It was slightly floral with a peppermint aftertaste. It's like Eggie already knew her deepest desires.

"Seriously? It's been years since I had a classified."

"Me, too." Mina rose, gathering her plates. She still had a million things to do before bed. She carried her recyclables to the grinder. "Hold on. It's going to be loud for a sec."

"You better keep that fork if you know what's good for you," Kaylee ordered. "Put it in the drawer with the cloths for the next time Eggie flakes out on you."

"Good idea." Mina palmed the fork, setting her plates and cup inside the basin and tapping the button on the wall. A safety shield engaged, muffling some of the noise as the grinder consumed the contents, sending the particles down to the bowels of the building. Mina would be reimbursed a small monthly elemental borrow based on atomic weight. The credit wouldn't equal the consumption, but at least it was something. "This is the quietest grinder I've ever had. I think I'm developing big love for this place."

"Who wouldn't? It's lux personified." Kaylee's dog, Dag, ambled into the frame. "Come here, you big lug." Kaylee made kissy noises, ruffling the canine's fur under the ears. He was a mix somewhere between a Labrador, shepherd, and mastiff, which made him enormous and lovable. "Say hi to your aunt Mina."

"Hi, Daggie, glad to see you're better," Mina offered. "Who's a *good boy*?"

Predictably, Dag barked, and Kaylee giggled. "Do you have to do that each and every time?"

"Dag deserves a treat. Being a good boy is hard work." Dag barked again. *Good boy* was his cue to be fruitfully rewarded.

"Okay, I'm going to go give this pup a treat and take a soak. Does that place have a soaker? Wait, don't answer that." Kaylee held her palm up to the screen. Her hand was as big as a drone. "Of course it does. That place has everything. I'm coming over sometime this week to see it in the cold, hard flesh. And look, I'm wiping the drool." She mocked sliding a finger over her chin.

Mina laughed. "Looking forward to it."

"I'll bring some real wine. I've been saving up the borrows. Good luck on your classified. See you soon. Kevin, end vid."

The last thing Mina heard before Kaylee disappeared was Kevin saying, "I'll get right on that, darlin'."

Mina chuckled as she padded toward her bedroom. She was ready to hit the platform sleeper hard.

CHAPTER 6

THE WINDOW SHIELDS disengaged a second before Veronica chimed, "It's seven forty-five. Time to start your day." Mina groaned as her cuff vibrated, letting her know that Veronica was on point in her wake-up. Light speared through her newly unshaded windows, blasting her eyes. Thank goodness for pupils that still constricted. She tossed an arm over her face. "I'm awake. No need for a reminder," Mina mumbled.

A few seconds later, she began the arduous task of exiting her enormous platform. She'd stiffened the contour foam by lowering the molecular excitation factor, but it was still too soft. The sheets, the color of shimmering, melted gold, were exquisite, though, like a silky kiss against her skin all night long. She'd slept like the dead. "Veronica, display newscast, simul sleep room and shower room, forty percent."

Screencasters tended to be excited in the morning, so no need for a full display.

A moment later, Melissa Socorro's upper body flashed at the foot of Mina's bed. Forty percent was big, but doable for this space. "Expect delays today all over the city, both air and land," Melissa intoned with her usual grounded seriousness. This screencaster could talk about puppies like they were breaking news. "It's messy out there. Some say it's because of a surprise visit from the imperial leader of Unified Asia. But until we see his hat, that gossip is circumstantial."

Melissa was dressed in an ensemble Mina guessed she'd been harnessed into. It was skintight, the color of spring leaves, with fourteen crisscrosses over a single shoulder. She wore her long, dark hair slicked back in the otter style, but somehow it worked on her. Two diamonds the size of perfectly printed blueberries glittered in her ears. They had to be real. Melissa was the top caster in the city, which meant she might be one of the lucky ones able to earn out their borrows.

Mina padded into her shower room. It was enormous. And so was Melissa. "Drop screen twenty percent in here, lower decibels by five. Lights on low." Melissa shrank as the ultras came on at a nice, easy-on-the-eyes brightness. Mina chuckled because now Melissa looked like she was taking a dunk in Mina's soaker, the top part of her body positioned perfectly along the ledge of the gently curved stone.

Directly across from the big-enough-for-two soaker sat a double sprayer, nozzles aimed in a three-hundred-and-sixty-degree arc. Next to the soaker was an elaborate drying stall with fans and jets. A littler farther in, her X600 gleamed seamlessly in the corner, ready for all her home health emergencies. On the other side, two personal sink stations jutted out of a wall with a beauty printer and grinder integrated above them. The entire back wall was mirrored.

A door was inset to the right, which led to a private waste unit.

Mina leaned over one of the vanities.

It appeared she'd lost an altercation with her pillow during the night. Her hair was a spiral of brown tangles, more or less the color she'd been born with. A few light strips were intertwined, which her beauty rep, Cami, referred to as "streaky sunbeams." Sleep caked her extra-long eyelashes, which had been the result of a permanent enhancement her teen self had insisted on. She'd contemplated removing them on more than one occasion, but it would hurt like holy hell since they'd been derm-inserted more than ten years ago. She'd wept like a baby once the pain blockers had worn off. But they did accent her eyes without the need for much daily enrichment, so they stayed.

Her lashes rimmed cool gray eyes, a color unusual enough that people often asked her for the diffraction number. There was none to give, so she usually said fifty-seven. She'd later learned that fifty-seven was the color of a ripe apple, but it hadn't stopped her from using it.

Shrugging out of her sleep gown, Mina bent over the sink and splashed water on her face. "What do I wear as a pet enhancer? Regular clothes, I guess, but nothing too upscale or trendy." She had a few couture options in her closet. Like, two.

Veronica replied, "Would you like me to access my database and provide a description?"

"No." Mina walked into the sprayer. "I'll figure it out."

<hr>

Mina overshot. Her dark pinpoint ankle slacks and scarlet pullover with the flow neck made her look like she was visiting royalty rather than ready to do the grimy job of washing and scrubbing animals.

"Um, sorry." Mina cleared her throat as she addressed the plucky young woman behind the counter. The granite countertop was a mix of yellow and orange swirls with slashes of chocolate throughout. Low-hanging pendant lights with frosty shades hung intermittently above it. "Looks like I'm a little overdressed. It's my first time working as a pet enhancer. I'm Marjorie Wilcox, the new temp from Dalton, sent to cover for Pauleen." She did her best newbie impression, flashing a sweet, embarrassed smile, hands clasped in front of her, eyelids slightly lowered.

"You're fine. Everybody wears a uni anyway. They're provided for you in the back." The woman's name—Babbettlyn—was printed on her high-necked crisp black shirt, but Mina wasn't sure how to pronounce it, which was more the norm than not. It was polite to wait for an introduction. "Pet work is messy, but gratifying on most days. Unless you get bit." The woman giggled sweetly.

Her innocent smile produced a pair of inset dimples. Her hair was the color of a vibrant pink rose, secured off her shapely face with trendy mag-clips, her eyes diffracted a pale sky blue. Her enhancements were artistically drawn, not too many bold lines, but not too soft either, with just enough contrasting elements. She set the tone for the image this center was trying to achieve—quality at an affordable borrow.

The main reception desk flowed into a nearby waiting area, accented with four different kinds of seating options, from chairs to loungers, each containing body cushions in jewel tones. Greenery was splashed here and there in the form of large potted plants highlighted by warm-glow lamps with massive oval shades. Three of the walls were coated in soothing caramel, the textured resin meant to relax. The back wall was one large screen, currently displaying an array of slowly moving orbital dots in similar tones as the rest of the room and in sync to soothing music issuing out of hidden speakers.

Several early customers sat waiting for their appointments, their animals appropriately contained.

The setting resembled many of the human spas Mina had frequented across her lifetime. The only indication it catered to a four-footed clientele was the subtle indent of a pawprint on the wall behind the desk that this nice woman was situated behind.

"By the way, I'm Babbettlyn. You can call me Babs." She smoothed two hands down her sides, then up to her hair to catch any wispy stray hairs—there weren't any—straightening everything. It was a natural movement, one she must perform multiple times a day. "I check in our furry friends, escort them back, and then fetch them once they're done. I'm one of the three desk admins. We prefer a human touch here at Total Enhancement. You'll enter right through there." She gestured to an integrated door covered in the same print as the walls. "Ruth will give you your assignment. Hope you have a wonderful day!"

"Thank you." Mina's critical eye roamed the interior as she moved toward the door. Everything was in its place. Nothing was over the top, yet it was high-end enough that, as a consumer, you'd figure your pet was going to get a thorough treatment for the borrows you were about to spend.

Once Mina's foot was close enough, the door slicked open.

The lighting directly inside was the same as in the waiting room, comfortable and dim, but as soon as Mina cleared the short distance and rounded a corner, things changed dramatically.

She pushed through a door with a small glass circle at the top. The room she entered was cavernous, dominated by industrial apparatuses. Hoses and cables hung from an exposed ceiling full of girders and plenty of steel. Netted utility lights illuminated dozens of individual workstations, each enclosed on four sides with glass or a good polyacrylic copy. Each station contained all the gadgets needed to perform whatever task was at hand. Mina saw some workers beginning to douse animals with large spray nozzles. Others used clippers, fur flying. Some had a variety of colorful pots containing dye colors lined up on shelves and were busy with brushes.

The noise was incredible.

Barking, grunting, screeching, meowing, oinking, and howling all mixed together in a concert of sound. As Mina moved forward, she spied a long wall separated by more glass—likely plexan—and behind it stacks of kennels. The animal holding area took up one entire wall, with large dividers every tenth crate. There were at least two hundred animals by her estimation. The dividers, it seemed, were in place so similar animals didn't mingle with different species.

McAllister had been wrong about the reptiles. Mina spotted several short enclosures containing some. She'd never handled one before and didn't relish the thought of it. But she was here to do a job.

Resolute, she ventured farther.

The smell was akin to soggy, waterlogged fur. Mina resisted the urge to shield her nose. The acoustic-canceling firewall between here and the graceful waiting room, where owners sat unaware of what awaited their pets, must be top grade. Mina was positive customers weren't allowed back here. The illusion that their beloved Scruffy or Pookie was being escorted into individual spa rooms was in full effect as long as they didn't venture this way. It seemed this pet enhancement center had an underbelly.

But Mina wasn't entirely sure, since this was the first one she'd ever seen. Maybe they all operated like this?

Project a certain image up front, then get down to no-frills business behind closed doors. Mina had owned a pet as a child, her beloved Cotton Candy, a curly-haired mild-mannered mutt who'd crossed the Rainbow Bridge when Mina was seventeen. Being a child, she hadn't paid attention to any of Cotton's care and maintenance and had doubted her parents had ever treated her pet to this level of service.

"You must be Marjorie Wilcox." A middle-aged woman, with a halo of wiry auburn hair styled in no particular fashion around a sturdy face and wearing what was quite possibly a perpetual frown, walked up to her. "I'm Ruth." Mina got that from her name tag. No trouble there. "You're late. Don't make it a habit."

Mina replied in a flustered tone, "I'm so sorry. I decided to walk, because I heard there was a traffic delay, and I don't live too far."

It had turned out the congestion wasn't due to a visit from Unified Asia, but because of a visit by the head of the French Protectorate, Ambrose Bernard. Melissa Soccoro hadn't been kidding about the traffic, though. The streets and air had been jammed. Bernard was an elite eligible bachelor, after all, and people went out of their minds for that kind of thing. "The sidewalk movers stopped for a few blocks. It won't happen again."

Mina was doing her best nice-cooperative-worker impression. She'd actually arrived five minutes early, but had taken time to chat with Babs. She'd be ten minutes early tomorrow. All the better to sweep through this place.

"I'm starting you off on sprayers." Ruth remained steadfast with her upside-down smile. "It's our most common booking. Clean them up, get 'em out. We spray three hundred animals per day. Most get dropped after work and picked up twenty-four hours later. Or else we wouldn't be able to get to 'em all. They go home smelling sweeter than they came. If the animal is scheduled for another enhancement after the sprayer, it goes to another workstation. You just get 'em wet. Once you're done, you ding a transfer, and a bot picks 'em up. We'd use bots all the time—they're cheaper and less hassle than air breathers—but most of them don't know their own strength. After a few injuries with the smaller breeds, the owners were forced to hire people." Her eyes raked over Mina, widening just enough to express her doubt that Mina could actually perform a grueling day's work based on her fit-for-royalty outfit.

Mina should've let Veronica do a little research. There was very little you couldn't find out in the world today with a simple search.

"Animals come in with a tag, you scan it, you complete the process. It's as simple as that. If you mess up and slow us down, you're out. Head to that room." She gestured to a plain steel door. "Bot behind the counter will get you a uni. After, head to station sixty-seven." She'd rattled this off without the aid of a board or anything remotely technical. Mina couldn't help feeling impressed.

She headed in the direction Ruth had indicated. On the other side of the industrial door was a long, boxy room lined with full-size personal security lockers. She stepped up to the desk, a long stretch of printed poly, not the fancy printed granite like in the waiting room. The LiveBot manning it had shoulder-length black hair and average features. She gave Mina a bright smile. "Hello and welcome to Total Enhancement Pet Center. If you'll step this way, I'll have you select a security locker. Indication light will be green to show availability, red when in use. Once opened, place your personal items inside." Mina followed the bot to a section midway down. "To program the locker, simply insert your finger."

Mina stuck her digit in the appropriate slot. The skinny metal door popped. "Is this required each day?" Mina asked conversationally as she hung her shoulder bag inside. She'd opted to leave her compucase at home and instead had packed a few gadgets she'd thought she might need in a black carbon fiber bag, such as a DNA hair strand helix masked as a simple status reader and a few amplifiers disguised as hairclips. She would bring more once she assessed the situation.

"Yes," the bot answered helpfully. "Uniforms are to be left inside the security box overnight. This is standard procedure."

Mina glanced around for a place to change that wasn't exposed. "Where can I put on the uni?"

"Right around the corner. Choose one of the printing stations. After you undress, step into the machine, insert DNA, and press the green button. Once your exact measurements are taken, the door will release. Your uniform will be printed immediately. Don the new articles and return here, placing your regular clothing in the security locker."

Sounded simple enough.

Mina returned in less than five minutes, wearing the standard black shirt and slacks with the name Marjorie stitched in the upper-left corner. She was back on the floor heading to station sixty-seven exactly a minute later.

Her glass cube was located in one of the rows farthest from where she'd entered, which allowed Mina to get her eyes on the space. Most of the workers hardly glanced her way as she passed. About half the cubes were occupied. Adhering something to wet dog fur probably wasn't the ideal time to attach an encryption, so Mina focused her attention on the other stations, primarily the ones where workers were clipping and dyeing. After a few moments, she realized no one was performing a massage of any kind. McAllister had specifically mentioned massages. The pets being worked on were standing or sitting in industrial-sized tubs, like the one inside her own stall, to catch all the drippings and droppings. No comfy beds or platforms in sight.

Mina turned, feigning only casual interest in her new surroundings, spotting a row of doors on the other side of the room from the kennels. If workers were massaging animals behind those doors, it would make her job harder, but not impossible. Being alone with an animal was the perfect time to plant something. If she were a smart criminal whose primary directive was to avoid detection, she would do anything to secure a job inside one of those closed environments.

However, that didn't mean this criminal was particularly smart. Mina had run into her fair share of stupid ones. After all, they'd gotten caught. Smarter ones tended to elude law enforcement.

Ruth appeared, seemingly out of the air itself, frowning harder. "Time to get started. Your first spray client will be here in less than a minute. I'll give you a quick demonstration of how the nozzle works. Then you're on your own."

Mina stepped aside, thankful the overall perfume of the place had ratcheted down a few degrees as her brain had gotten used to processing the smells. The cubicle itself held the scent of astringent, which was preferable to anything on the outside. But Mina knew once the animals got wet, she'd be in for some more interesting olfactory experiences.

"I hope you have some prior animal expertise," Ruth grunted as she manhandled the nozzle dangling from a long curly cord affixed to a brace next to the tub. "You're getting a doozy of a first guest."

Mina detected a hint of glee in the woman's voice. Her new manager was happy the animal would be a challenge for her. What was it with managers and power trips? It never changed. "I have some. I owned a pet until I was seventeen," Mina replied.

"You had a family pet, and you think that's enough experience to do this job?" Ruth's voice held a challenge.

"I guess," Mina said. "I washed her at least once a

week." Mina had had to coax Cotton into their family sprayer by enticing her with treats. Same thing. Kind of.

"We'll see about that."

Mina raised an eyebrow. There was no mistaking that this woman was daring her to mess up. Mina couldn't afford to lose this job, so it was on.

She was about to become the queen of the sprayer.

Chapter 7

THE LIVEBOT WHO approached Mina's station toted something akin to a small horse on a short leash. Mina's eyes widened. This bot had wavy brown hair clipped just below her shoulders. Her features were delicate, decidedly on the pretty side. LiveBots were so humanistic, sometimes it was downright creepy.

Mina pushed open the door with some hesitation, resting her hip against it as the bot entered.

"Hello, I am Candace, and this is Morty. He's a seven-year-old Great Dane." The bot tugged the white-and-black-speckled pony into Mina's cube. The animal took up almost all the space. "I'm not allowed to handle the pets directly," the bot informed her cheerily, handing Mina his leash.

Mina glanced at the industrial-sized tub, then eyed the beast.

The container was steel, with high sides. How in the hell was she going to get this massive canine inside?

She looked up and caught Ruth smirking at her from several stations over.

The bot, sensing Mina's hesitation, likely by detecting her increased pulse rate, told her, "Morty is very well trained. He won't give you any problems."

"Thank you. I'm sure I'll be fine." Mina turned her attention to Morty the Monster. "Hi there, good boy. Are you ready for a spray?" No bark. Not as well trained as Dag, it seemed. Although the dog did wag his hank of a tail, the action producing echoing bangs as it hit the basin. If its owner wasn't careful, that tail could unseat a small child. Morty's tongue lolled out.

The bot stepped forward. "You must scan Morty's collar and then my cuff." She held out her arm. Her cuff was old and worn. They didn't overspend on these bots, Mina mused.

She glanced around, wondering what to use to complete the task. Ruth had omitted this helpful information. "Candace, can you please inform me how to do that?" Mina gave the bot a smile. She'd learned over the years that if you were nice to machines, they responded in an eager-to-help way. Likely something hardwired into their system.

"Certainly. The scanner is located on the digi readout. The button is here." The bot indicated a shallow indent on the floor.

"Got it." Mina hit the spot with her foot, and a skinny piece of steel rose. The top was crystalline with a small, thumb-sized scanner attached to one side. Mina plucked it off and proceeded to scan Morty's collar and the bot's cuff. Once both were entered, a green check flashed on the screen.

Underneath, instructions for Morty scrolled in big, easy-to-read letters. He was scheduled for something called a lavender-scented premium soak with extra bubbles. Pet owners, it seemed, had gone over the deep end since Mina and her parents had owned their lovable mutt.

Candace prepared to leave. "When Morty's done, tap the screen, and I'll get an alert. Good luck!" Then she was gone, the door clicking shut.

Mina pondered the dog. "Are you ready for this, big guy?" Morty cocked his head, but remained silent. "Be a pal and tell me how I'm supposed to get you into this tub?" The dog rotated his massive head. "It looks like you're trying to figure out what I'm saying, and I appreciate that, I really do. But I've got a timeline to exceed, and I can't do that without getting you inside that basin. I'm not getting fired on day one." She knelt in front of the pony. "This is a very important op, you know. It would be nice if you gave me some intel." When the dog did nothing but slobber on her, Mina stood, tugging his leash, trying to coax him closer to the tub. The dog must have known a spraying was in store, because he stopped in his tracks, refusing to set one paw closer. After a few more pulls, and Morty not moving a single step, Mina gave up. "Okay, so you're going to make me lift you in? At least you seem nice and not bitey." Mina bent over, bracing her back as best she could, sliding her arms under the dog's belly, and hoisted him up. She turned, panting and straining from his weight, finally managing to settle the hairy beast in the tub, his feet skittering for purchase. "Good grief," she huffed. "What the hell are they feeding you? Hunks of printed ham hocks glazed in bacon grease?" After a brief catch of her breath and a few minor internal curses, Mina grabbed the sprayer and got to work.

At twelve o'clock on the dot, an automated sim boomed around the large space: "Break time for section A workers starts immediately. Section B workers please remain in your rooms."

Mina swiped at a line of perspiration on her forehead. She was just finishing up with a golden mix of some kind that wouldn't stop licking her. She'd sprayed and scented a total of thirty-three animals: twenty-eight dogs, four adorable miniature pigs, and one angry feline. That cat wasn't going to forgive her anytime soon, and she had several scratches to prove it. The owner must be sadistic. Mina had kept the spray time short, trying to spare the poor thing. Now Mina was sopping wet and exhausted.

Was she an A worker or a B worker?

Yet another thing Ruth had neglected to tell her.

Her astute manager had milled around outside Mina's cube a few times, watching her, but had never ventured close enough to chat. Regardless, Mina recognized the grudging acceptance forming in her eyes. She'd earned that, one hoisted dog at a time.

"What do you think, Rexy? Am I an A worker?" The sweet dog nuzzled her hand. "Almost done. I promise." Mina was eager to get out and stretch her legs and survey the rest of the space. She'd tried to keep an eye on the other stations throughout the morning, but the spraying and dousing of these animals was fairly all-consuming.

Mina depressed the appropriate button on the nozzle, and clean water tinted with the essence of roses sprayed in a full arc. It was warm and comfortable for the dog.

Once she was finished, she tapped the screen and engaged the mini dryer to make sure the dog wasn't dripping once she lifted him out.

Less than thirty seconds later, a bot arrived at the door to retrieve the pet. This bot's name was Elsa. She looked exactly the same as the others. Mina had now counted at least eight identical LiveBots. The only distinguishing features were the lengths of their hair and their name tags.

"Hi, Elsa," Mina said, grunting as she lifted Rexy out of the tub. "Do you know if I'm an A worker or B worker?"

Elsa smiled brightly. "Unit sixty-seven is an A worker." She proffered her cuff, and Mina dutifully scanned it. Then the bot was on her way to take a happy Rexy to a full drying station before his next treatment.

Mina stepped out of her cube, unsure where to go. This was a mealtime break, and Mina hadn't seen any meal printers in the uni room. She walked down the aisle, spotting a few workers weaving their way toward an opening on the opposite side of the room. She followed.

A long, wide hallway led to a break room large enough

to hold at least fifty. A dozen round tables with six to eight chairs apiece were spread throughout the space. Two counters ran on either side, stocked with printers and ready-made drinks.

Mina got in line.

These weren't voice-activated printers, or it would be chaos with everyone ordering at once. The woman in front of her turned and asked, "Are you the filler for Pauleen? That lucky bitch. I've never been on a real vacation, only a VR. Not even once." She selected her choice on the middle printer, punching the button with a little extra finesse. "The first two printers are savory, last one sweet. Sandwiches, soups, plate of pasta, cookies, ice cream, pretty basic. Not much of a choice."

"Thanks." Mina came to a stop in front of the sandwich printer. There were three options: turkey croissant, ham and cheese, and meatball sub. No BLT. Mina chuckled.

The woman a step behind her chuckled along. Mina noted the woman's hands were covered with splotches of purple and orange. "I think these printers are hilarious, too," the dyer snarked. "You'd think a company that took in all these borrows from people obsessed with their pets could splurge on better options. But no. We work ourselves to the bone and get rewarded with dry, crumbly sandwiches for our efforts. Don't waste your time. Go with a soup or a basic plate of marinara. The texture of the sandwiches is terrible. Not nearly enough elements. They skimp on everything around here."

"Thanks for the warning," Mina replied affably. She moved to the next printer and punched the button for cream of tomato soup. The disk stuck a little, so she had to tap it again. The soup was ready in fifteen seconds, piping hot in a basic white bowl. Mina was happy to see a spoon sitting next to it. She grabbed a drink next, some sort of green juice, and waited for the dyer to finish her order. "Can I sit with you?" Mina asked. "I'm filling in for Pauleen. I don't know my way around yet."

"Sure." Her name tag read Kelly. She had honey-blonde hair and a homey face with no visible enhancements and a few comfortable laugh lines. "I usually sit with a few other dyers. Come this way, and I'll introduce you. Pauleen worked with us often enough."

Two women were already seated, one with pasta, one with soup. Kelly announced, "This is Greta. This is Robina, and I'm Kelly."

Mina took her seat. "I'm Marjorie. Nice to meet everyone. I'm filling in for Pauleen for a few days."

"You can call me Robs," Robina told her. She was the sturdier of the three, with ginger hair in a short, easy-to-manage hairstyle with a few highlights. Her lip cream was light nude and her eye dye a sedate caramel. She struck Mina as a hard worker who was used to paying her way. "Is this your first time working at a pet enhancement center?"

"It is." Mina tested the soup temp with her lip before consuming. Lots of printers produced food that was way too hot. After a couple bad burns, you learned to check. It wasn't sear-her-tongue scalding, so she took a spoonful. The soup was average, if that. At least it tasted mostly like tomato. "I'm enjoying it. It's pretty physical, but the animals have been really sweet. I'm an animal lover, so it's a good fit."

"Yeah, the pets who repeatedly bite are banned." Robs took a scoop of her pasta. "Going to give dyeing a try? We do full-body, fur tips, claws, and bioblasts. The blasts are undetectable until nighttime. Owners like it if they walk their pets in the dark. Makes it easier to see them or chase them down if they get away." The group of women laughed knowingly. Runaway nighttime pets must be a niche problem.

"I'd like to give everything a try, if I can," Mina answered after another taste of soup, wondering how Eggie would do with this basic fare. "Do you rotate job stations on a regular basis? Ruth didn't exactly give me a rundown."

Greta snorted. She was a petite brunette with a trendy blunt cut framed with forehead fringe and bright pink lip cream. "Ruth likes to assert her power wherever she can. If you don't buckle, you'll be fine. Usually, we switch around every few days or so, so nobody gets too bored. You've got one of the easiest jobs. Spraying them down and sending them out. Sprayer does most of the work. Pretty basic."

Mina's voice was light and conversational as she asked each woman a little bit about herself. Then, very casually, she asked, "What's behind the doors on the far side, across from the kennels? Is that where animals get massages?"

Surprising her, Kelly tossed her head back and chortled. "Those are the *prime* jobs. Everybody fights for them. Basically, from what we've heard, you sit in there with the animal and pet it the whole damn time. Mood lighting, screencast of your choice, cushy place to relax. It's good work if you can get it."

Robs shook her head. "Never been in there, but each day I keep hoping Ruth will finally assign me."

Greta added, "Some think bots do that job, since none of the A workers have ever met the B workers. The Bs are the ones who get the massage jobs. You'd think a few of us"—she gestured to indicate the entire room—"would have had that rotation, but no one has."

Mina's ears perked. No one had ever seen a B worker? Or held a massage job?

"Ruth told me they don't employ bots for direct animal work because they're too strong," Mina said, "and could hurt the animals."

"That's a bunch of crap printed on a cracker," Robs growled. "Something happened. I know it. Before we all got jobs here, something went down, but they won't tell us what. They had a mass human hire about a year ago, and they're real careful about the bots they get now. Total overhaul. Gossip floated around, rumblings about malfunctions or some such thing." She took a large bite, smacking loudly.

Finally, Mina was getting to some interesting tidbits. "Has Ruth been here the entire time?" She scanned the room, taking note of each person. "Before the human workers were hired?"

Kelly took her last spoonful of soup. "I think so. She was here when I got hired, and I was one of the first.

She seems to know what's going on. We've never dealt with anyone else. She can be a hard-ass, but she's fair if you work hard."

"She's not *exactly* fair," Robs complained. "She picks her favorites and lets everyone else rot."

"And who"—Mina pretended to be engrossed in the last bit of her soup—"are her favorites?"

"The B workers, that's who," Robs griped. "I bet they get better meal-printing options, too. But nobody knows for sure, because we're all back in our cubes when they get their break." It was clear Robs didn't think the B workers were bots, since bots didn't need to eat.

Mina glanced up. "Do you regularly ask to get the massage rotation?"

They all nodded. "Not exactly regular anymore, because we get denied so often, but we do still ask," Greta said, standing. "I'm going to get some ice cream. You guys want anything?"

Once she left, Robs leaned forward. "Some people say Ruth takes bribes. But we've got nothing of value to give her, so we keep doing the grunt work, mostly dyeing since the three of us have gotten good at it. We go over our quota most days."

"You seriously have never seen a B worker?" Mina wanted to be absolutely certain.

"Never," Kelly said. "They come in at a different time and take their breaks separate from us."

Things were getting interesting.

Chapter 9

"THERE'S A GOOD chance the adhesion process for the encryptions is happening in one of these rooms." Mina stood in front of her screen, submitting a report to her director. "I ruled out a few workers I lunched with as possible suspects for the time being, as well as several others. They gave no indication of stress and spoke freely, most of them grumbling at the unfairness in the division of job duties. Anyone tied up in a large, illegal ring would likely display some sort of nervousness when chatting about the inner workings of the company with a stranger." There were exceptions, of course, but Mina was listening to her instincts for now.

"Getting stationed in a massage room alone won't do you any good," McAllister pointed out. Her director's image was at thirty percent and positioned at eye level, so he looked fairly normal rather than like a giant specter as Kaylee had. "You'll need to witness the perpetrator applying the drive or identify an animal immediately following adhesion. If you're alone, you won't have eyes on who is doing the deed. I'm working on getting you a gadget to detect this particular encryption device, which was indeed a quantum, but it has to be coded to detect exactly what we're looking for, or it will go off in the vicinity of any drive, which would be counterproductive."

Mina's stomach made some grumbling noises. She was hungry after her long day of spraying animals, but she'd contacted McAllister as soon as she'd arrived home, as classifieds were top priority. "I have voice amps. If I can get into a few of those rooms before the other workers arrive, there's a possibility I can eavesdrop while I work."

Five days on an op was skinny by anyone's standards, even the most skilled of agents. Time was an issue, and there were six rooms, which would be difficult to cover at once, since she had only two ears.

"That might work, but it's doubtful our perpetrator is going to announce what they're doing. You mentioned those rooms have screens inside. If they're on, it would dominate your feed."

"That's true, but there's not much else I can do while I'm trapped inside a cube. Working those animals is completely engrossing." And exhausting. Mina rubbed her lower back. "Since I have no other leads, bribing Ruth to get inside one of the rooms to get a look around will be primary. Once I'm in, I'll try to infiltrate the others. There's a high likelihood they use the doors on the other side to come and go, which from my visual surveil on my way to the meal room is down a separate hallway. If I'm discovered, I'll use my temp status and say

I got lost. I'm itching to get a look at these mysterious B workers, see if anything gets my hackles up."

McAllister nodded. "You'll know when you see it."

"I have to figure out how to bribe this woman. Ruth is an enigma. Not a beauty enhancer, so no borrows to spas. Doesn't look like much of a sports fan. I'll figure it out, but right now I'm going to take a long soak and scrub this dog slobber off of me."

"How was the work itself?" McAllister asked.

Mina shrugged. "Getting the animals in and out of the tub was the most strenuous part. A few of them weighed well over fifty kilos. The sprayers were automated, but not tough to handle. All I had to do was choose the right button. Water and suds came out, then water and scent came out. Over the course of the day, I doused sixty animals. That should be enough to earn Ruth's trust." And several kinks in her spine. "She actually gave me a smile when I left. Well, it was more like an upturned snarl, but I'll take it." Mina yawned, even though it was barely six thirty. "I think you should try a pig."

"Excuse me?"

"For a pet. You said your wife has allergies. But pig dander is different from dogs and cats. I had a few adorable squealing clients today. These mini breeds stay small, and they're incredibly smart."

McAllister's gaze turned contemplative. "I'll consider it. Thank you."

"I'll contact you tomorrow around the same time."

"Good work today, Agent Kane." McAllister nodded. "I'm sure you'll have this wrapped up in no time. Screen end."

Her boss disappeared off her wall, and Mina decided to save fighting with Eggie until after her soak. Even though she was hungry, getting clean was essential. Her muscles were screaming for release. She made her way down the hallway, disrobing as she went. "Veronica, fill soaker, ninety-two degrees. Mood music, decibels low. Lights dim. No scent."

Mina had had enough smells for one day.

"Completing tasks."

Water began to splash into the tub as Mina took a detour into her utility room. This space between her bedroom and the living area was generous. She tucked her clothes inside a cleaning pod, and as she shut the lid, it engaged. Upon completion, her clothing would be washed, dried, and folded. *Folded* was a loose term. Some machines nailed it, and others made it seem like the items had been tended to by a drunk panda. Mina would have to wait and see what this one would do. Odds were in favor of them looking fairly decent. This was a lux residence after all.

Once her clothes were mixing, Mina placed a fingertip on the hidden panel modified by government workmen last week. Once it popped, she checked her weapons printer. It was bigger than the Magnito, but instead of voice-activated controls, there were a dozen pre-programmed buttons. Each weapon was based on the weight of a comparable food dish. A roast turkey would get her a full automatic. Mina didn't have a lot of ops where she needed a firearm, but she did from time to time. Once she was finished using a desired weapon, she would simply grind it up and recycle it. In the safe next to the weapons printer, Mina kept her gem laser.

Those couldn't be printed, as there was no way to print the gas-filled vacuum chamber required to produce a small, precise, high-powered laser. It was her weapon of choice, even though it had a finite range. It was clean, quiet, and burned an accurate hole—the size of her choosing—through anyone who deserved it. And the goal wasn't to kill perpetrators. A nice hole through the leg stopped them from running. A tear through the arm and they dropped their weapon.

"Shall I play your messages for you now?" Veronica asked as Mina made her way to the soaker. The calls had come through to her cuff, but since she'd been busy at work, they'd diverted to home.

"Sure."

"First message," Veronica announced, followed by the sound of Mina's baby brother's voice. "Hey, sis, it's Quinn. Just wanted to let you know I got a job mixing drinks at Primal. It's totally spec. You should come down. I'm working three nights a week, starting tonight. Be sure to bring your hot friend Kaylee." He chuckled, ending on a snort.

Her brother was in the process of completing his degree cycle. He'd chosen metallurgy, which would serve him well. The advent of amorphous alloys had opened infinite new material combinations due to atom manipulation. It was a hot field and good work if you could get it. Mina adored her baby brother. He was the all-around family favorite and her only sib.

"Not tonight, little bro," she muttered as she stuck a single leg into the hot water, moaning in pleasure.

"Would you like me to relay that back to Quinn?" Veronica asked.

"No," Mina said. "I'll hit him back later."

"Second message," Veronica intoned in her comforting English lilt. "It's Kaylee," her pal announced. "I took your advice and contacted McAllister. Lee's joining me tomorrow. Wish me luck that it doesn't implode on me like a fiery hydro-bomb. Let's get together soon. I'll fill you in. And if this kid sucks, I'm blaming you. By*eee.*"

Mina sank up to her chest, *oohing* and *aahing*.

Her last place didn't have a soaker. They were a rarity these days, only recently making a comeback. Mina's parents' generation had been all about creating no-nonsense efficiency, and they'd been astonishingly good at it. That specific era had been credited for many valuable upgrades, such as fully recyclable sprayers and dryer stalls, print-on-demand for just about anything a human could want or need, integrated voice command everywhere, atomic grinders to streamline recycling, and so much more. The entire world had benefited—and was thankful for—their contributions. But somewhere along the way, her parents' generation, nicknamed The Makers, had lost their ability to sit back and enjoy the simple pleasures. Mina's generation, The Doers, were in full stampede to bring that back. One awesome soak at a time.

"Send this message back to Kaylee," Mina instructed Veronica. "I'm in agreement. Let's go out tomorrow after work. Quinn landed a job at Primal. I'll meet you there at eight."

"Audio conveyed," Veronica said. "Beginning message three." The voice coming through Mina's speakers wasn't instantly recognizable. It was male with a low, on the verge of growly cadence. "Hi, Mina, it's Vince. It's been a while." A hesitant chuckle followed. "It's a little out of the cosmos me contacting you, but I ran into your mother today. She gave me your tag because she thought you and I might enjoy catching up. I hope you don't mind. I'm back in town for a few nights. I live in Western Europe now."

"Veronica, pause."

Vince, Vince. Mina tried to place the name and the voice. Then recognition hit with the force of a meteor crashing into earth. "Oh, *hell.* Vincent Kramer. It has to be." She sat up suddenly, water lapping up the sides, almost sloshing over. "Why is he contacting me?"

Mina had grown up with Vince. He was the son of her parents' friends and had lived in her neighborhood. They'd attended different base education programs, but had seen each other often at social events. They'd generally hung around together, palling around, as kids did. It'd been at least seven years since she'd had any contact with him. They'd both gone on to their advance-degree cycles and lost touch. If she remembered correctly, Vince had gone into international business, specifically banking.

"Veronica, continue message." Mina slid back down in the tub, nibbling a corner of her lip.

"Anyway," Vince continued. He sounded like a man now,

not a cracked-voice teen, which was throwing her. "I'm hoping you're free tonight. I wish I could've given you more notice, but I'm slated to leave the country tomorrow. I thought it would be…" He paused, inhaling a small breath before he continued. "It'd be fun to reminisce about old times. Chat me back if you're interested. Hope all is well."

"End of messages," Veronica concluded.

Mina edged down so the hot water rose high enough to tickle her ears. It might actually be nice to catch up with Vince. She remembered him fondly. Back then, he'd been a semigawky kid with a tousle of black hair covering most of his forehead and all of his ears. He'd had an easy smile and a nice way with people. Her parents must not be as close with his anymore, or Mina would've heard more about his whereabouts through the years.

Because of Mina's choice of career, she wasn't on any large networking sites—and there were literally *thousands* of them, all focused on different aspects of life. You could hook up with people from your schooling years and social programs, people looking for partners, people with kids, people without kids, people with various hobbies, every interest you could think of. Mina had once seen a site for people who enjoyed sharing pictures of their toenails. Social sharing was a mass addiction and had been for over a century. People enjoyed interacting and keeping tabs on each other all day, many of them contacting each other daily via hologram or vid chat groups. Honestly, it sounded exhausting.

Mina preferred staying out of the mix. She valued privacy, which came in handy, as her job required it. Couldn't very well go undercover if she was on a dozen networking sites chatting about everything from hydro-gardening to personal craft repair. She would also run the risk of people recognizing her out and about. Hobbies overlapped in this great big world. Plus, doing something like taking pictures of her toes all day would be tedious, not to mention so, so gross. When the urgency to eavesdrop on someone else's life reared its head, she slipped in under her brother's screen tag to take a look around. But that didn't happen very often.

If Vince had asked Mina's mother what she did for a living, her mother would've told him she taught holo language courses. Occasionally, people like Vince from her past reached out, interested in catching up, but it was a rarity. Her main go-tos were Quinn and Kaylee, and she was fine with that.

What to do? What to do?

Mina hadn't planned on going out tonight, but it'd been a while since she'd done anything spontaneous. "I think I'm going to go," she mused. "I mean, why not? I don't have anything else to do except fight with Eggie for my dinner and watch a naturecast."

Mina never tired of being up close and personal with rainforest monkeys or pods of dolphins dancing through the waves. On her new huge screen, the images would be spectacular. The industry had perfected integrated wildlife bots with three-hundred-sixty-degree cameras. It was a worldwide phenomenon.

"Shall I send word to Vincent Kramer you accept his offer?" Veronica asked.

"No!" Mina sputtered quickly. "I'll contact him when I get out."

Then she sank under the water.

"This is not at all weird," Mina muttered to herself as she glanced at the other diners, who were happily enjoying their real, nonprinted meals, trying not to check her cuff again to see the time or if she had any messages.

Busy servers rushed by, balancing large silver trays with plates of food that looked and smelled amazing.

This was the first time Mina had eaten in a restaurant with real food since her parents had taken her to less technically advanced countries when she'd been a teen.

À La Carte was situated inside The Spire, one of the restaurants the mega rep had told her about. Suzanne hadn't been wrong. It was the epitome of lux. The interior gleamed with glossy chrome accents, just like her froufrou furniture. Flickering candles set in elaborate crystal holders fashioned in the form of blooming flowers were situated on smooth, square table linens in stark, unblemished white. Elegant stemware and real silver utensils were placed in exacting sequence around a plate of the thinnest porcelain she'd ever seen. The lighting was dim and conversational, splashed here and there via custom curved leaf-shaped pendants.

It was a jarring juxtaposition to print-to-order places,

which were full of bright colors, geometric designs, and stations where you lined up to order your food before carrying your own plate to a shared table bare of any adornments.

When Mina had spoken with Vince and told him where she'd recently moved, he insisted on meeting her at this particular restaurant. Apparently, where he lived, food grown from dirt and fed by the sun was valued above printed. He couldn't believe it'd been so long since Mina had tasted the real thing.

According to her home calendar, this restaurant had been booked out for months. But Vince had pinged her back not five minutes later and told her he'd snagged a reservation. Now he just had to show up.

Because Mina didn't have much experience with this kind of thing, she had no idea how much time to allow for a no-show. He was already ten minutes late. She'd give him five more.

A server whisked by her table with a large plate of some kind of meat still on the bone sitting on something green and spongy. This place was going to *cost*. A small plate of something called *carrot puree in au jus* was more than fifty world currency. Mina could book an entire holo office for two hours for that amount.

Honestly, she wasn't *that* hungry.

Well, maybe she was, but spending that many borrows on an orange vegetable Eggie could print seemed all kinds of wrong. If Vince didn't show, Mina was going to slink back upstairs and order something edible and fairly delicious at the cost of an elemental utility borrow.

The waiter came to the table for the second time. "May I offer you a drink while you wait, madam?" he asked politely. "In addition to our real wines and champagnes made from vine-ripened grapes, we have cow's milk, juiced fruit over ice, and a variety of fermented teas."

"Oh, no, thank you." Mina tapped a finger, flicking off the holo menu. It disappeared like it'd been sucked inside the tiny holocam, which it had. "I'm just waiting for my companion to show."

A commotion erupted by the entrance, and both Mina and the server glanced that way.

A man wearing a French Protectorate uniform—a sleek, dark gray ensemble with deep-red stripes, complete with a sweeping overcoat with a French flag affixed to the lapel—had entered the restaurant. He was flanked by two guards in similar duds.

Mina wondered for a moment if he was Ambrose Bernard, musing that the women here would likely lose their minds if that were the case. Exotic government officials were the biggest heartthrobs there were, even more so than royals residing in what was left of the scattered monarchies.

The restaurant began to buzz like a hive of endangered bees.

The French Protectorate kept Paris and the other French provinces safe. Europe had broken apart into eastern and western sections based on global commerce, instead of cultural lines, at least forty years prior. Each section contained a large military force, but the provinces had established their own guard. The French Protectorate was well-known and highly regarded.

The man in the uniform stalked toward her. His dark hair was styled away from his face in comfortable waves, a little longer in the back. It wasn't a style worn in the States, but it worked for him. His chin was square and strong, cheeks prominent, nose slightly sloped, his lips full. He was tall, over two meters by her estimation.

As he neared, Mina's eyes widened.

No. Nope. It couldn't be.

The waiter stepped back, bowing at the waist like a servant of yore. "It's a pleasure to see you again, Colonel Kramer."

Mina stumbled up from her chair, suddenly unsure how to move all her body parts at once. *Holy crap.*

Now what?

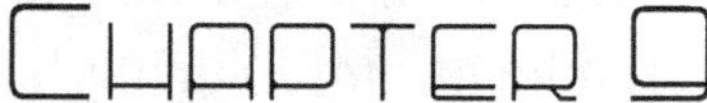 CHAPTER 9

WAS MINA SUPPOSED to shake his hand? Did she give him a quick hug? What was protocol for a long-lost friend turned colonel of the Protectorate? Mina had no earthly idea. All this ran through her mind as she awkwardly scrambled out of her chair, thanking the heavens that the sleek chrome hadn't clattered over in her haste, making her look like a fawning klutz.

Luckily, Vince bridged the gap, placing a featherlight kiss on each of her cheeks. Very European. "Please sit," he offered as his guards went to a nearby table to watch over them. Vince waited for her, the server aiding Mina with her seat, which only added to the continued awkwardness. Once Vince joined her at the table, he smiled, leaning forward with a wistful expression. "I take it you didn't know I hold a place in the French Protectorate?"

Mina cleared her throat, an errant hand snaking toward her neck before she redirected it back to the table.

She grasped the stem of her water glass, needing to focus on something other than the mystery man in front of her. "Um, no, I didn't. But I'm thinking it would've been a helpful thing to throw out during our dinner-setup convo." She brought the glass to her lips, relieved as the cool liquid splashed the back of her throat. It grounded her, giving her what she needed to get a hold of herself. She set the glass on the table and sat back, finally remembering she was a government agent and could handle a surprise like this. She assessed him with a cool stare. "To be honest, it doesn't look like you're *in* the Protectorate. It looks like you *are* the Protectorate." She gave a breathy chuckle. "I can't believe I didn't know. How am I just learning about your career path?"

Vince flashed her a dazzling smile. He was the picture of comfortable elegance, his handsome face wreaking a little havoc on her internal organs, flustering her in ways she didn't want to think about. Mina detected the boy she'd known in there someplace, but the man who'd evolved in the years since was a leaner, more angular version of the kid she'd once played holo seek with.

"This wasn't actually my chosen profession," he admitted. "Unlike you, who enrolled in the PPF right out of programming, I earned my degree in international finance. I actually had my heart set on becoming a banker, if you can believe it." When the waiter approached, Vince imperceptibly flicked his wrist, sending the guy skittering off. Mina refrained from arching a brow. She wasn't used to ordering staff around, but clearly he was. "My first job was at a large bank in Paris, but it didn't last long. When I moved to Western Europe, my parents decided to join me. I was their only child, and they wanted to see the world. Unfortunately, a short time later, they were killed in a craft collision."

Mina gasped, surprised and saddened by the news. She'd always enjoyed his parents. They'd been grounded, funny, and seemed to enjoy life to its fullest, even when their generation had been more interested in practicality. That explained why her parents hadn't mentioned Vince in recent years. She wondered if her parents even knew what had happened to his parents. It wasn't likely, or they would've shared.

"I'm so sorry to hear that. Your parents were wonderful people."

"Yes, I miss them very much. After their deaths, my life changed drastically, as you can imagine. I felt rudderless and unsatisfied with my chosen path. On a whim, I enlisted as a guard in the Protectorate. I went through the rigorous training and worked my way up, starting as a private. After a few years of hard work, I found myself promoted to colonel, and here I am." He spread his arms, an easy smile on his face.

A memory of the two of them together flashed in her mind—his tenth-year celebration, where he'd made a similar gesture when he'd gotten a particular gift he was certain he'd receive. She couldn't recall what it'd been, but she was comforted by the image.

Several women in their immediate vicinity sighed loud enough to make themselves heard.

Yes, indeed. Here you are.

"Again, my condolences," Mina replied. "I remember your parents being warm and affectionate people. It must've been agonizing to lose them." She took another sip of water, unsure what to say, studying this enigmatic man over the rim of her drink.

Her radar was fully engaged. He was nothing like she remembered, yet echoes of the past lingered in familiar gestures, a twinkle in his eye, the way his lips curved to one side. He was confident in the extreme, bordering on cocky, which automatically upped her radar to critical.

"So, you're a colonel." He'd reached that position in a very short period of time, possibly only three or four years. Not unheard of, but unusual. "Where does that place you in the rank and file of the Protectorate?" Mina was extremely familiar with French protocol. Her line of work required her to know all the ins and outs of each regime. But she wanted to hear it straight from the colonel's mouth.

"My official title is colonel-in-arms."

A rank that was even more unusual to ascend to so quickly. Mina kept her expression neutral. She watched as Vince signaled the server, apparently deciding now was the right time.

"I'm the third-ranking official under Ambrose. My job is to protect him and see that his orders are carried out." The server hurried over, his breath visibly hitching, even though he'd been lingering only a short distance away. Vince shot him a wry look. "We'll take a bottle of your vintage bouquet champagne and an order of mignonette oysters." He inclined his head across the table. "If the lady agrees."

Mina's attitude went from slightly irritated at the presumption of him ordering for her, to flustered in the space of a simple head tilt. She had no baseline which to compare this experience. Vince was intriguing and charming. They had history together. "The lady agrees," she decided.

The server hurried off.

"It's such a treat to have real oysters," he told her. "In France, they're considered a delicacy. I've never had a single printed one that tasted right, even from a special-order kiosk."

"It's hard to get the quantity of trace selenium perfect." Mina smoothed the starched napkin across her lap. It resisted being molded, too lux for its own good.

"True," he agreed. "But I'm a firm believer that some things will always be impossible to recreate with manipulated atoms alone. Even with all the correct elements, the ratios are a delicate balance and have to be just so, something nature gives us automatically. But we don't have to worry about that here."

He eased back in his chair, seeming content. Mina had to admit he was incredibly nice to look at. She was trying hard to remember if he'd ever caused a spark of anything in her before, but came up short. He'd just been somebody to pal around with, nothing more.

"So, tell me about yourself, Mina. Your mother says you're a linguist. *Parlez-vous Français?*"

"*Oui,*" she replied easily. "*Mais je ne parle pas couramment.*" She'd never been more relieved *not* to be fluent in French, which was what she'd just informed him. She wouldn't be able to fool this man, with his eagle eyes the color of the raging sea—no need for enhancements there—that she was a master of the French language. She was keenly aware he was analyzing every move she made. She was doing the same with him, but hoped she was pulling it off a little more subtly. "My focus is obscure languages, actually." For this very reason. Mina rarely came across anyone who even knew a few words in her three chosen dialects. "Portuguese, Greek, and Polish."

The server came back with the champagne, toting a tall, shiny pedestal topped with a bucket filled with neat ice cubes. He opened the bottle with a flourish, and the cork released with a resounding *pop*. Mina thought the room might burst into applause and was relieved when she heard only a few twitters. She darted a quick look around, noticing that no one else had a champagne pedestal. Very few tables even had a bottle of wine. The borrows were too steep.

Another server set down two elegant flutes, which were promptly filled.

Vince took his glass first, swirled it, and took a sip. "Very good. Thank you."

Mina followed suit as the server who'd poured waited for her to take a taste. She'd never imbibed real champagne before and found it to be far bubblier and tarter than anything printed. She smiled. "Thank you. It's very nice."

The servers disappeared.

Vince seemed intrigued by what Mina had told him

about her career, almost like he might try to quiz her, but instead he said, "I thought your dream was to be an officer in the PPF. What happened to change your mind?"

Mina was used to fielding this question. It came up frequently for anyone who'd known her once upon a time. "Well, much like you, my life took a turn." She was careful to shift a shoulder and express mild amusement. It was important to keep natural appearances going. It was an act, but one she'd honed well. "I realized fairly quickly that catching bad guys wasn't where my expertise lay." Not remotely true. Her finger hooked a swath of hair behind her ear, widening her eyes slightly as she chuckled. "Learning languages was something I adored growing up. I'm sure you remember, since I always made you watch *Wilhelmina Hoover & the Candy Cane Adventurers* with me in a different language. My mother deserves the credit for that. She's the one who made it mandatory. Later, she told me it was because she couldn't stand listening to the same screencasts over and over again." Mina let out a tinkle of laughter and picked up her champagne, taking a small sip. "So, Quinn and I, by the time we were five and eight, had watched just about every single episode in multiple languages." She shrugged, setting down the glass. "After I figured out criminal work wasn't my forte, I made the easy decision to pursue my real passion and enrolled in a specialized-language-degree course. It took two years." If anybody dug, the trail would be there. "I've been a practicing educator for three years, teaching holo courses all over the world. It's very satisfying and rewarding."

"I can imagine. It sounds ideal." A small quirk played on his lips. It was hard to believe this was the same kid who used to eat noodles with his fingers. "Speaking of Wilhelmina Hoover. I absolutely adored that show, mostly because of you. It was a highlight of my week when we got together to go on those quests. But no matter how many times we did those challenges, you always won. You had unbelievably keen eyes. You used to tell me you took cues from the characters in the story. But they were digital creations. I tried to do the same, but it never worked in my favor. You insisted that whoever made the show put tells in them unconsciously. A stray look here, a foot pointed there." He shook his head wistfully. "I never saw them. You kicked my ass every time. I thought for sure you'd be an officer right now, tracking down criminals, adding them to your bounty of Candy Cane Trophies."

Mina hadn't missed the challenge in his words. She was a trained officer after all. She was about to reiterate her passion for linguistics when the server flourished a plate of oysters on the half shell drizzled in some sort of yellow-tinted sauce with an abundance of green specks. The dish smelled divine, citrus mixed with butter and herbs.

On the menu, the borrow price had been left off.

A little guilt swept through her as she scooped one up and placed it on a dainty plate that had replaced the bigger, more formal one at some point. The server then set a shiny silver fork with three prongs, the length of her index finger, to the right of her dish.

Who was she to be treated to a meal like this? It felt insanely extravagant.

But as she forked the small, oval bite into her mouth, all guilt was swept away as a rush of flavor exploded on her tongue. "*Mmmm.* Oh, my." She placed three fingers over her lips so nothing escaped by accident. "This is exceptional. That oyster literally melted on my tongue. No weird texture or lumpiness at all."

Vince took his own taste, his eyes fluttering shut, head angling slightly toward the ceiling as he swallowed. After a good savory-relishing moment, he agreed. "I would get in trouble for saying so at home, but this might be the best oyster I've ever eaten in my entire life." Vince addressed the waiter, who had stayed within reach, hands clasped, ready to spring into action at the next finger curl. "Please give our regards to the chef immediately. This is a meal fit for royalty."

The poor man took off at a run.

Mina almost snorted, but masked it with the back of her hand as she scooped another oyster onto her plate. She leaned in, whispering, "You're kind of like royalty to them, but you know that already."

"I do." He pretended a whisper, but it came out husky. "But honestly, I find the whole thing extremely silly. This entire infatuation with governments and the people who run them should cease. People should go back to idolizing screenstars, like the olden days. Not people like me."

Mina took another bite and barely refrained from moaning. As she politely swallowed, she considered her response. "Wilhelmina Hoover, even in her heyday, or any other screenstar pretending to be someone else, can't hold a laser point to what people are seeking from the real world these days. Times have changed. And honestly, can you blame them? Every single one of us is in search of happiness. For the majority, that means the elusive dream of being free from the banks, free of borrows, and finally having the chance to earn and save. We all want a life where debt doesn't cut deep grooves into our backs. When they see you, and your upper-government ilk, snuggled up tight with rich-pocketed bankers, they envision you as knights who can ride in and make their wildest dreams come true—and possibly, somehow, fix what's gone wrong with the system. It allows them the kind of hope that only comes around once a century. It's an illusion for the most part, but a necessary one, in my opinion. Once people in power choose to make our lives better, everyday humans can go back to the quieter life of idolizing screen and sports stars and saving up for that special vacation they've always dreamed of. Until then, you're it."

He sat back, contemplating her. Or possibly dreaming of his next taste of delicious oyster. His eyes smoldered as he gave her a look she wasn't sure she was qualified to interpret. "Well, if I'm a knight, does that make you my princess?" Reading her reaction accurately, Vince arched forward, amending his words quickly, a hand coming up in front of him. "I'm sorry. That was the exact wrong thing to say. I've been known from time to time to speak without a filter, and it usually gets me in trouble."

Mina didn't choose to respond or give him an out.

Instead, she waited, somewhat amused, to see how he would go on.

After a lag, he continued, "But you're completely right. People need to believe in something. I agree whole-heartedly. I just…I just wish it wasn't me. The entire being-on-display thing makes me uncomfortable. As to my earlier comment, depending on your definition of a fairy tale, if I'm the knight in shining armor, then by default you'd be a princess." He admitted defeat as he slumped back in his chair. "It was a dumb thing to say." He gave her a tight smile, shaking his head, apparently thinking he'd blown it with her.

Whatever *it* was.

Was there even an *it?*

It seemed like there might be an *it,* which was completely surprising on so many levels.

Mina took her time, bringing the cloth up to her mouth, very slowly clearing the nonexistent butter off the corners of her lips with a stiff end. She made a point of setting it back in her lap before she spoke. Then she leaned forward, elbows on the table, hands clasped. "Just to be clear, I never said knight *in shining armor.*" Mina fought back a grin. Under normal circumstances, she'd be more irritated, but Vince looked so miserable, it was hard to be too offended. "To clarify, in my story you're a *dark* knight, no princesses in sight. Though, now that I think about it, there might be a kickass queen somewhere. But I digress. What I should've said was that you and your comrades in government—both knights and *ladies—* should show the public a little more sympathy.

They simply desire to have what you have. I see nothing wrong with that." Mina unclasped her hands, finally letting a grin form. "Unless I'm wrong, and you're actually like one of us. Completely under a deep, dark layer of borrows with no hope of ever resurfacing?" She refrained from flicking her eyes to the champagne pedestal or the oysters in front of them. "I, like the rest of the world, assume working for the French Protectorate allows you to live without debt. But feel free to clear that up if I'm wrong."

Mina immediately knew she'd hit a sore spot.

She'd both meant to and not. Really, she couldn't help herself. To be fair, Vince had no idea who Mina really was and that she worked her backside off every single day of her life to fight against a corrupt system of government for the good of the people. She felt a small twinge about holding Vince's feet next to a bucket of hot plasma, but not much. It was true she held a government job, but their career paths couldn't have been more divergent. You had to be a part of a *regime* to make the kind of income Vince did. Buy into it. Accept it. And prefer that way of life.

It wasn't just a job. It was a lifestyle.

Vince frowned. Then he quickly smiled, back in the game. His recovery was good, and likely practiced, Mina noted. "One of the reasons I moved to Paris in the first place is that their banking system is much better than anything we have here. It's a fairer system, and people actually have the chance to earn their way out of debt. That's probably why there's much less fanfare about what I do there. I completely understand people are struggling and searching for happiness. To you, I must seem ungrateful, but I assure you I am not. Far from it. I'm thankful each and every day, even with all the attention and fanfare I get here. I desperately wish the system was different, and I know a lot of folks who are working to repair it. But until it changes for good—by people more powerful than myself—each of us has to find his or her own way, and some of us trip on a luckier path than others."

Trip was an interesting choice of word. There was no way Vince *tripped* into any of this, but by choosing that single word, he'd told Mina something. Vince was likely a skilled colonel, but there was more to his story than pure sweat equity and hard work. She watched as he ran a hand over his face, choosing not to respond just yet.

"I'm sincerely sorry about the princess comment," he told her. "I think for a moment there, my mind zapped back to when we used to play make-believe. It's a lame excuse, I know. But if I remember correctly, you used to call yourself Princess Priscilla of the Poconos, and I was Sir Servant of Seville. I think my job was to deliver our printed lunch to the pod fort we built in the corner of your room. I apologize. I can promise you it won't happen again."

Mina leaned back, deciding to let this conversation go. It wasn't worth ending a long-standing friendship over. "*Ah*, yes, Princess Priscilla. That takes me back." Mina chuckled. "Since we're apologizing, I'm sorry about making you a servant. But hey, at least you got a spunky title.

I mean, it was only fair. Maybe those days of make-believe and role-playing were impactful, and without them you wouldn't be where you are now."

He grinned, worry easing out of his eyes. "Maybe so. Those were some of the happiest times of my life. There was no place I'd rather be than chasing the Candy Cane Adventurers or under that fort with our plates of oatmeal cookies and apple slices."

Mina lifted her champagne in a toast. "Thanks for inviting me out. It's wonderful to see you. And for what it's worth, I'm extremely happy for your success. You've achieved the dream, and here's to an even brighter future."

Vince raised his glass and clinked it against hers. "To the future."

Chapter 10

MINA WASN'T EXACTLY sure how another bottle of champagne found its way to the table. After their initial uneasy back-and-forth, she and Vince found a rhythm, focusing on stories of their youth. There'd been a lot of laughing, reminiscing. And a lot of eating. Like, a ton.

The food had been some of the most delicious Mina had ever tasted in her entire life. The carrots had ended up being one of her favorites. The lamb they'd eaten for their main course had fallen off the bone. Sensational.

Now it was late, and Mina had important work to do in the morning. Once she was upstairs and safety settled inside her residence, she'd have to fill up on some detox pills so she could function in the morning. Possibly even take a spin in her home health pod for a cleanse. That might be for the best. Thank goodness the X600 had an alcohol flush that came standard.

Mina set down her fork, leaning back, barely refraining from settling a hand on her extended belly.

She quietly exhaled a satisfied sigh. The last course had been a chocolate hazelnut confection presented in three delicious tiers, balanced on thin, crisscrossed strands of crystallized maple sugar. It'd been divine, the remnants still in front of them. She couldn't eat another bite, the sweetness still dancing on her tongue. "This has been so enjoyable, Vince. Thank you so much for the invitation. I feel incredibly spoiled. I likely won't be returning here for a while, but I'll remember the flavors and the company forever."

The alcohol had relaxed them both, there was no doubt.

Vince had one arm casually hooked over the chair rail, his coat long gone. "It was wonderful to see you, too, Mina. I've so enjoyed your company. And if you don't mind me saying, you've grown into a beautiful woman. I hope I can say that without offense, as I'm just stating the obvious."

Mina felt a blush blossom. She set a hand on the table so she could fiddle with her fork. "Thank you. You're not so bad on the eyes either." Not knowing what else to do or say, she slid her chair back, thankful the server wasn't there to aid her. They had practically closed the place down, all the other diners gone home. "I had a great time, and now sleep is calling. I have classes to teach in the morning, and it's late." How did it get so late?

Vince dropped his arm, easing out of his seat. "I'd be happy to walk you up."

"No, that's okay. Really," Mina insisted. "You've got a big day tomorrow." He'd told her over dinner that he was in town for an important meeting between government officials. Not only was Ambrose in town, but so was the Parisian president, along with a big contingency of guards. After the meeting, the entire entourage would be on its way back to Paris.

His big day wasn't the only reason she intended to leave solo.

Vince had been incredibly charming—over-the-top charming—and although she had no reason not to trust his intentions, Mina was a cautious creature by nature. She rarely made rash decisions, much less under the influence of champagne made from real vine-ripened grapes. She was an agent. Those habits were ingrained in her. Whatever this was—or wasn't—she was determined to take her time with it.

"Okay, then." Vince appeared a little lost as he came around to her side. "Would you mind if I contacted you in the future? Maybe we could vid chat from across the Atlantic?" Surprising her, he grasped her hand. "I need to tell you, this has been one of the best nights I've had out in a long time. Seeing you again, talking about the old days, has been a real joy. All those stories about my parents have made me so grateful I reached out. I'd love to continue reconnecting, if that's okay with you."

"Um, sure. That would be fine. Great." They stood together like that for a few seconds, hand in hand, which was exceedingly weird.

"Let me at least walk you as far as the tubes." Vince began to lead her toward the door, tugging her gently, his hand still firmly around hers.

"Thank you, that would be—" Mina came up short, pulling back sharply, snatching her hand back as she took in the crowd that had gathered on the other side of the glass separating the restaurant from the atrium. À La Carte was located on the third floor of The Spire's mezzanine. She could see the tops of the cascading waterfalls just beyond.

"Are those..." She gaped at the crowd for a moment. "Is that *Melissa Socorro*?" Mina squinted. She was having trouble comprehending the scene in front of her.

Vince gave a good-natured chuckle, his hand seeking hers again. "It seems the press has found us."

"The *press*?" Full-on regret that she'd imbibed so many glasses of champagne flooded through her like a typhoon obliterating everything in its path. *No. No. No.* How could she have been so foolish not to realize the colonel-in-arms of the French Protectorate would be pursued by the media? But in her defense, when he'd contacted her, she hadn't known that her Vince was *this* Vince. She never paid close attention to raggy screencast gossip. And even if she'd thought, for a single second, that childhood chum Vince Kramer was Vincent Kramer, the foreign heartthrob, she would never have met him here in the first place.

All excuses. And lame ones at that.

Nothing about this meeting had been low-profile. Once she'd realized his status, she should've excused herself. Mina had moved to The Spire to keep her profile *under* the radar, not fifty meters above it. If she walked out there with him, her face would be splashed across multiple screencasts tonight and likely all day tomorrow.

It was a risk she wasn't willing to take. Her director wasn't going to be happy about her error in judgment, but she could still fix it.

Maybe.

Probably.

"It's okay," Vince assured her. "We'll just power through—"

He reached for her again, but Mina darted away, taking several steps back, fumbling for the right words. "I'm sorry, Vince. I really am." She stammered a bit to convey her innocent unease. She was still capable of acting, even with a fizzy alcohol buzz clouding her brain. "I'm…I'm going to have to ask you and your guards to go first while I wait here until things cool down."

He looked at her like she'd just lost her mind, or perhaps left it on one of the half shells. His guards stood in front of them, everybody ready to go. "But…surely we can just—"

Adrenaline coursed through Mina's body in the form of a tidal wave of regret and thankfully gave her a boost, clearing the fog somewhat. "I have to be completely honest." She clasped and unclasped her hands, making sure his body was blocking her from any vid shots. "This is not my thing. I can see that you're used to the big spectacle, as it comes with the job." She gestured toward the waiting horde. "But I'm not. I like to retain my privacy." She added, "I mean, if that's okay with you." She put the onus on him, knowing if he said no, he'd look like an ass.

"Of course," he hurried, glancing around, seeming

desperate for another option. "What about the kitchen? I bet they have a back door. We could go through there."

Mina was going to do exactly that, but not with the French Protectorate in tow. The screencasters on the prowl would chase them down like lions on the scent of a herd of wildebeests. Melissa Socorro didn't simply *give up*. That woman was tenacious. Ultimately, they wanted a sound bite with him. They didn't care about her.

"No, you go," Mina insisted. "Once you're gone, everything will settle, I'm sure of it." She placed her hand on his arm, her face upturned, sweet and imploring, turning him slightly so his big frame continued to block her from any gaping glances. "And I'd prefer you not mention my name when they ask who you were with tonight. I meant what I said. I'd like to remain private."

He nodded. "Yes. I respect that. I'll just say I was with a childhood pal. That should satisfy them." Vince seemed genuinely sad to part ways. So he didn't get any ideas of planting any more cheek kisses, Mina took another step back. She was in deep enough already. Lips on skin captured on fire-fast digital was not happening. "It really was good to see you, Mina," he said. "I've missed your smile and keen eyes more than I'd realized. I wish you well in the future. I hope our paths cross again soon."

"Me, too," Mina said. "Take care of yourself, Vince."

Then he and his guards exited the restaurant.

Through the gap of the closing doors, Mina could hear the eruption of chatter and excitement. Bright lights began to blink so the viewership could get a better look at the elite bachelor who had just had dinner with a mystery guest. Once they found out she was just a friend, everyone would forget. At least that's what Mina told herself as she made tracks to the kitchen.

Her startled server happened to step through a pair of tall metal doors with two oval windows inset at eye level as she arrived. "Excuse me," she said, unruffled by his obvious discomfort at finding her standing here. "Can you kindly show me out the back? Or at least give me a place to shelter until the crowd out there dies down?" She gestured toward the front, where intermittent pops of light were continuing to go off.

The young man couldn't adequately shield his surprise at her request. He'd likely thought she and Vince were a couple, as did everyone else in the restaurant. Mina was certain that she'd helped perpetuate that viewpoint, since she and Vince had thoroughly enjoyed their time together. She'd giggled like a simpleton, completely oblivious to things happening right in front of her dumb face. Well, they had been technically *behind* her face. But had she excused herself even once to go to the waste room, she would've been able to make an escape before things had gotten out of hand.

"Sure. Right this way," he finally replied, snapping to attention. "I'm sure the chefs won't mind you leaving out the back."

She followed him through the door, weaving through food-preparation areas flanked by long steel countertops and stacks of shelving holding real ingredients, such as sugar and flour and everything it took to make a meal from scratch. No one stored food like that in their residences anymore. Why would you when your printer could produce a delicious meal in seconds? It looked as though only a thin portion of staff were still on duty. A few people gave her inquisitive looks, but nobody spoke.

"After all, letting you go through here is the least we can do," the young man began. "The colonel spent a record amount tonight. We only sell one of those bottles of champagne every few months. They cost—"

"That's okay," Mina interrupted, her voice coming out in a literal squeak. She felt vaguely sick, and not just from the alcohol swirling around in her belly. She didn't want to dwell on what this meal had cost. She'd offered to pay for half, but Vince had politely declined. What else was she supposed to do? "I really don't need the specifics."

The poor guy blushed to his hairline. "Of course. I'm sorry. Follow me."

***

"I saw you on the screen this morning!" Babs clapped excitedly as Mina stepped into Total Enhancement, a full fifteen minutes early. "You were with Vincent Kramer!" She clutched both hands over her heart, her extra-enhanced eyelashes fluttering, causing her bright blue eyes to glimmer. Mina realized with a shock that they were *actually* shimmering, swimming in what might've been tears mixed with awe. "What I wouldn't kill for a night out like that. He is just about the most gorg guy I've ever seen. You two looked so sweet together, too. I want to hear all about it." She leaned over the counter, hooked both wrists under her chin, a dreamy expression on her face, her pink hair orderly and perfectly contained. "I need all the goss. What's he like? What did you eat? Tell me absolutely everything!"

Mina braced herself. She'd gone over the screencasts again and again, both last night and this morning. The restaurant had been dim, and no one had gotten a perfect shot of her. Luckily, their table had been in the back. And although *she* could tell that the woman with Vincent Kramer was her, she'd hoped that no one else would notice.

McAllister had barked at her this morning to clean it up, and she was going to do this just that. "Huh?" Mina scrunched her face in confusion. "Me? You think you saw *me*? And who was I with? Vincent Kramer? Are you *serious*?"

Babs' expression fell, bottom lip, creamed a tulip pink, pouting forward.

"Man, I must have a doppelgänger," Mina continued. "Because I was in bed watching a naturecast by eight thirty and snoozing by nine." She casually leaned her hip against the desk, crossing her arms. "But I agree with you, Vincent Kramer is incredibly dreamy. Whoever he went on a date with is a lucky gal. But I'm sorry to disappoint you. It wasn't me."

Babs frowned. Confusion took the reins for a few more moments before her face brightened as she straightened. "I could've sworn it was you. Same hair, same features, same everything." She fanned herself with her hand. "But I did think to myself, what is a temporary pet enhancement worker doing out with Vincent Kramer?" She brayed, the tinkling laugh from yesterday gone. "That didn't make any sense. Now I'm wondering who it was." Her gaze slid past Mina and went glossy somewhere over her left shoulder as she peered into the next room. "Melissa Socorro said he was out with a childhood friend. But nobody really believes that. They'll find her. And when they do, we'll all know!" Her eyes snapped back to Mina's, dry and focused again.

"Well, I hope so," Mina retorted. "What will we do without...the knowing?" She smiled at the young woman, who was genuinely excited about the mere prospect of finding out who the mystery lady was. "I'm telling you," Mina intoned in an excited voice as she took a few steps toward the door that would lead her to the back, "I would've traded my entire night watching the humpback whale migration for a whirl with Vincent Kramer in a single heartbeat."

"Oh, me, too," Babs agreed readily, clapping her hands twice like a child receiving the best gift ever. "But I was watching *Win Big*, not nature. You know, the interactive screencast where you can win thousands of borrows if you answer the questions exactly right? I've applied to be on it, like, a hundred times. I'm sure they'll pick me sooner or later. The odds are in my favor!"

"I'm sure you'll get chosen in no time at all." Mina's foot hit the sensor on the floor, and the door swished open not a moment too soon. "Have a great day. Don't forget to let me know if they track down the mystery date. I want to know right away!" She waved for good measure.

"Will do." Babs waved back.

One down, hopefully no more to go. Everyone who worked here had seen Mina only one single time, and only a handful had had any interaction with her. Putting the blurry face on the screencast together with hers would take effort. And the screenhounds didn't have her name. And even if they got it, it would be Mina Kane, not Marjorie Wilcox.

After exiting the uni room, she was ready to get to work, hurrying on her way. She was moving so fast she almost collided with Ruth.

The woman wore a strange expression, her eyes raking Mina up and down, like a painter eyeing a canvas and about to dip her brush into some paint and go to town.

"It wasn't me," Mina declared, deciding to head off the discussion from the get-go. "I just went through this with Babs out front. In my dreams, I was out with Vincent Kramer last night. In reality, I was in bed watching a naturecast about whales, zoned by nine." When she'd checked, Mina had been relieved to have seen that one of the naturecasts she enjoyed had been replayed, providing the perfect alibi. But she wasn't going to let this woman who obviously thought she was lying and appeared to have something bitter stuck under her tongue get a word in. Mina settled her hands on her hips. "Can I ask you something? Why would a person who could go out with Vincent Kramer be a temp worker at a pet enhancement center? The answer: They wouldn't. I'm here because I'm desperately in need of borrows. My family's on the brink of a crisis. My mother's sick, and we can't absorb her debt, even for two years, let alone five." Mina projected her voice higher, gathering the attention of several incoming workers. Ruth's eyes darted back and forth. "If my mother dies, we land in the outskirts. That's how bad it is." Mina's voice shook with emotion. "So, if you can show me to my station, I would appreciate it." She took in a big gulp of air like she was barely holding in tears, the back of her hand swiping imaginary liquid away from her eyes. "I am *not* interested in losing this job over something as stupid as mistaken identity."

Ruth pursed her lips in palpable distaste. Instead of giving a verbal response, Mina's manager turned on a sturdy, printed-at-home comfort heel the color of freshly packed dirt and marched down the aisle in front of them. "Today you're trimming and dying claws. Same as before, bot brings 'em by, you scan 'em, and do what the instructions say. Unlike the sixty you sprayed yesterday, you need to do seventy today." She yanked open the door of the cube.

"*Seventy?*" Mina didn't think she'd heard her intrepid manager correctly. There was a possibility that the barking and general chaos going on around them might have occluded her ears. She'd worked her back to the bone to get her sixty in yesterday, and that had been pushing it. She'd have to work even harder today. Not that she couldn't. Her home health pod and the pills she'd taken had cured her of any aftereffects of the alcohol and late night, but still. This was getting into overworked territory, and there were laws to protect workers whose bosses treated air breathers like bots.

"Dyeing nails is automated," Ruth countered as she strode into the glass enclosure. "Insert the claws into this device." She yanked a boxy contraption out of a small workstation where it was connected with a curly cord. "Select the color, and five seconds later it's done." She nodded toward the tub. "And you could've done seventy sprays yesterday, no problem. The basin is automated. All you do is flip this switch, and it lowers to the ground on its own." She leaned forward, her fingers curving underneath a section on the rim.

Once activated, the tub sank into the floor, the end flipping open like a ramp, so the dogs could walk right in.

Mina unconsciously rubbed her back. The fact that she hadn't noticed how this contraption worked in other cubes was not lost on her. Nor had she asked her new lunchmates for advice. She was a body-language expert, not a workstation expert. But still. That was a low, painful blow. Even her home health pod hadn't eased all the muscle cramping.

"Good to know." Mina kept her voice even. Unfortunately, this was not the time to engage Ruth about getting a massage room job, but Mina had no choice but to ask, or it wasn't going to happen. As Ruth headed out, Mina casually asked, "If I do my seventy today"—she hitched a thumb toward the doors lining the wall—"any chance I can try a massage gig next?"

Ruth's gaze narrowed to slits, like a lion spotting a

delicious gazelle. Saliva might even have accumulated at the corners of her mouth. "Those jobs are for primary workers, not temps." She marched out, the door whooshing shut behind her.

Clearly, she would've preferred if it had slammed.

One couldn't have everything.

Chapter 11

By the time the automated sim cued A workers to take their meal break, Mina had already clipped and dyed thirty-six sets of animal claws, most of them canine, though a few had, surprisingly, been rodents. That had been an experience. Guinea pig claws were much tinier than canines', but Mina had found the magic dye-and-clip box could tell them apart just fine. There wasn't enough thanks to give for that. Trying to clip and dye a nail the size of a grain of rice would've been nearly impossible, not to mention doing fourteen of them.

Mina had done the work, while her brain had been busy sleuthing out what it was going to take to get behind those closed doors. She'd been here early enough to notice that no one had entered or exited the massage rooms, and no bots had taken any animals through the doors either, which was strange. Her cube today was closer, which made it easier to keep tabs.

Mina searched for Ruth, who was two aisles away

giving someone a dressing down, which included arm movements and finger-pointing. Generally, unhappy people could be bribed, and someone like Ruth seemed like a good candidate. People in her category tended to have a lower-than-average threshold. Meaning it wouldn't cost as much to bribe Ruth as it would someone with more, say, moral integrity. Mina just had to figure out what it would take. She was thinking good, old-fashioned credits streamlined into her account.

But even if Ruth remained steadfast and decided to take the high ground, Mina was going to see what was behind those doors. But first she had to find out if anyone was actually doing those jobs, because it seemed no one was. She would've detected some activity by now.

Mina hit the button to summon the bot, her fingertips tinted purple, the most common color requested. "Come here, cutie," Mina coaxed the small curly-haired poodle. "Don't your nails look nice?" The dog yipped as she lowered the tub. Mina attached its leash and walked it toward the door as the bot arrived. She had the timing down to a science.

Mina, scanner in hand, hit the bot's tired, scuffed cuff once. It beeped, followed by a green light. Mina handed her the dog's leash. "Thank you," the bot, named Heidi, told her. This LiveBot resembled all the rest except for her hair, which was cut in an oval around her face.

Once the bot led the dog away, Mina exited, following the other workers toward the meal room. She hadn't encountered anyone throughout the morning, other than Babs and Ruth, though she'd certainly noticed the glances and inquiring stares across cubes. More people than she'd thought had recognized her on the screen last night. She was going to have to quell curiosity about this Vincent Kramer thing, but she was coming in prepared.

"Oh, my upper stratospheres!" Kelly rushed up to her once Mina had entered the break room, her dyed-purple hands matching Mina's as they clutched Mina's shoulders, shaking her lightly. "Was that *you*? Please tell me that was you I saw on my screen!" She gave Mina another shake. "I've been dying to talk to you all day. Pun intended." Mina glanced over Kelly's shoulder, noticing the expectant looks on the faces of Greta and Robs from where the women stood in line.

Mina slapped on an expression resembling both curiosity and wonder. "You're the third person to ask me that today. I can't believe it!" she exclaimed, loud enough for anyone who was interested to overhear. "If only. Vincent Kramer is, like, my *dream guy*. But unfortunately, it wasn't me. I must have a doppelgänger out there, and she is one lucky girl."

Kelly was immediately crestfallen, dropping her hands. "Dang it. I was hoping against all odds it was you. Honestly, I didn't think it was. But that girl really looks a lot like you. I rewound it and magnified. Same hair, same height, same eye shape, even the same ears. Though this woman was wearing these gorgeous crystal drops. I bet they were real, too."

Mina felt like reassuring her they weren't. Totally printed. She'd been inspired by the girl at the transpo hub and had worn her only dangling pair on a whim.

But Mina was thankful she'd remembered to take them out, because Kelly was peering at her left ear like it might divulge a juicy secret.

Today, Mina's ears were adorned with printed opals. Analyzing ears hadn't even entered her mind. She had to hand it to these women—they were thorough. "I'm going to have to go back and rewatch it." Mina punched the button for tomato soup when it was her turn. She wasn't taking any chances. "Babs thought so, too. I wonder if this lucky girl is related to me. I mean, she could be one of my cousins or something. That would account for some of the resemblance."

"If she's a family member, wouldn't you know?" Kelly asked. "Man, if one of my cousins was dating Vincent Kramer, the family grapevine would be sparked *up*." Once they finished, Mina followed Kelly to a table, Greta and Robs trailing after them. "It wasn't her." Kelly sat dejectedly.

Mina had crushed any excitement life would've given them to know an *actual* person who cavorted with someone famous. "Sorry, guys," Mina said. "It wasn't me. I was in bed watching a naturecast. But I can tell you, I *wish* I was the lucky one who was out with him." She took a spoonful of soup, eyeing the group to gauge their reactions. "But did you honestly think a temp worker would be lucky enough to be asked out by Vincent Kramer? I mean, come *on*."

Greta's face was serene as she nodded along. But Robs directed a hard look in her direction. Mina knew skepticism and distrust when she saw them. They were written all over Robs' face as the woman's compressed eyes assessed Mina with open hostility. "I saw the screencasts. I think it was you. They said the woman was a childhood pal. That's not exactly a romantic dinner. Where did you grow up?"

Instead of seeming taken aback by the intrusive question, Mina feigned a cheerful expression. "I grew up in Cincinnati, Ohio. Suburban printed neighborhood, group programming, pretty much a normal, boring life. Vincent Kramer was *not* my childhood friend, though I wish he was." She giggled as she took another spoonful of soup. "Where did he grow up?" She pointed the question back at Robs, knowing the woman had done her homework. Robs most certainly looked up Marjorie Wilcox. There would be a number of them to go through, as Robs didn't have her DNA to make things a snap, but everything Mina just said would match the Marjorie Wilcox she was supposed to be.

"He grew up here," the suspicious woman grumbled into her meal, shaking her head. "I don't get how two people can look so much alike."

"Marjorie thinks it might be her cousin or something," Kelly added helpfully.

"Not any family member I'm super close with or anything," Mina asserted. "Now you guys have me curious. I'm going to have to look for myself. But I can't rule out a family connection. If she looks that familiar, there has to be a reason, right?"

"With all the enhancements people receive almost daily," Greta said, "I'm surprised we all don't look alike."

She chuckled like a friend trying to save another from falling into a deeper hole. Mina appreciated it. "I mean, anyone can look like anyone else with the proper work. I bet, right this minute, there's literally hundreds of women getting enhancements to look just like this girl. I mean, if that's what someone like Vincent Kramer is interested in, you can bet that look is going to become all the rage."

People were certifiable.

However, if there were more women who resembled Mina out there, so be it. All the better for her to blend in as one of many.

"Yeah, one time I saw this girl," Kelly added, "who looked so similar to me it was spooky. We both commented on it. I guess it happens." She shrugged. "But this time I was hoping I was right. I've always wanted to meet someone famous."

Mina needed to ease the conversation in a new direction. "Hey, remember yesterday when we talked about the massage rooms?" She took a bite of food, continuing on a lighthearted upswing, "I noticed today and yesterday afternoon that none of the bots take any animals in from our side. Why is that? I mean, why have those doors on the side at all if you're not going to use them?"

Greta shrugged. "They keep them locked on our side. The bots enter from the other side, but it's down a locked hallway. They tell us it's to protect the owners and make sure they don't wander back here."

"Yeah," Kelly added, "not only are the doors on our side locked, but they don't work anymore. They did some sort of a reno and blocked them all off."

It always baffled Mina when people believed exactly what they were told. She'd been born to question things, and had she been a worker here, she would've at least investigated the situation herself. Not one single bot had brought an animal down the hallway toward the meal room, and as far as she could tell, there was no other entrance to those so-called massage rooms. The only people who could get in unseen during the day were Babs and the other front desk workers she hadn't met yet.

It was time to see for herself.

"*Ow*," Mina moaned, hunching forward suddenly, hand flying to her belly.

The women stopped eating in unison. "What's wrong?" Kelly asked in the concerned tone of a mother to a child. "Are you feeling all right, sweetie?"

Mina pushed her tray aside. "My stomach is cramping a bit."

"No doubt it's the shitty food," Robs grumbled. "A few months ago, a bunch of people got sick all at once. Next day, they changed out one of the printers. That slurry stuff can go bad if it's not cleaned regularly."

"*Ew*." Greta pushed away her food. "We all had the same soup. I think my stomach is hurting, too." She ran both hands along her abdomen, concern blooming on her face.

Not what Mina needed. A group run on the waste room would hinder her plans. "No, I don't think it's the food. I've been having small pains all day, but now it's getting worse." She spoke firmly. "I bought an old meal printer from a reuse shop to save on borrows. The seller assured me the internals had been cleaned recently. Now I'm not so sure." She stood, making sure to keep her face pained. "I'm going to head to the waste room before I have to go back to my station. I can't afford to lose this job."

"Okay, that sounds like the best idea," Kelly said. "We hope you feel better soon."

"We'll tell Ruth if we see you're late," Greta said. "I'm sure she'll understand."

Mina slipped out, aware that more than a few people had been staring at her. This Vincent Kramer stuff was going to take a little more effort to stamp out. What a hassle. This flub might rank up there with Lee-type idiocy, and that was humbling.

Once in the main hallway, Mina slid a hand into her pocket. She'd brought a high-tech disengager, one that worked on any standard automated lock. These kinds of mechanisms were illegal for civilians to carry. Only law enforcement were allowed to have them. If the locks were standard, and not specialty hack-safes, she'd be able to gain entry.

There were five doors between here and the main workroom, two for the waste room on the right, one that she surmised led to the front desk, and two next to each other on the left. One had to be the entrance to the hallway to the massage rooms. She'd have to move quickly, before people finished their meals and the area got busy again.

Mina shimmied up to the first door, leaning casually, one shoulder braced against the wall as she placed the device into the seam next to the handle. A second later, there was a click.

She eased the door open and took a peek.

A supply closet chock full of sprayer nozzles, tubes, and other replacement items. She shut the door and moved to the next.

This had to be it. She did the same thing, and the lock popped. She slipped through, shutting the door quietly behind her. Since A workers were having their meal, she assumed that B workers would still be doing their jobs. But the hallway was dimly lit and smelled stale. No one had been back here in a while. Mina stilled, analyzing the environment. There was no movement coming from anywhere. No animal sounds or blaring screencasts. She tiptoed to the first door, settling her ear against it just to be sure.

Nothing.

She went to the next and the next. All rooms behind the doors were quiet. If there was anything happening, she'd hear it. At the end of the line, she placed the disengager in the appropriate seam of the final door.

No click.

She repositioned the gadget and tried again. Nothing.

Mina attempted to unlock each door as she made her way back. None opened. They'd all been retrofitted with hack-free locks. Someone was obviously hiding something here, but she was absolutely certain there were no humans, active bots, or animals behind any of these doors. That meant no one was adhering encrypted drives on fur in this area, but it also meant Mina had stumbled onto something else going down in this fine establishment.

Once back at the main door, she placed her ear against it.

A few voices passed and faded away. She had to make a move. People would be exiting the meal room in greater numbers now. She took a breath and ducked out, shutting the door firmly behind her in one movement, placing her back against the wall like she'd just been casually standing here, shoulders hunched, fingers pressed into her forehead.

Greta and Robs came from the meal room a moment later. Mina took several long, exaggerated breaths.

Greta rushed up to her. "Are you okay, Marjorie?"

Mina took a few gulps just to be safe, her hand reaching down to cradle her stomach. "I splashed some water on my face and was feeling a bit better. I got this far, but the cramps came back." She leaned forward, bending at the waist.

"You need to get some help," Greta said. "There's no medi-pod here, but there is one next door for emergencies. Ruth sends people there sometimes, like when they cut their hand or get a sore throat."

Mina eased her stance. "No, that's okay. It's already passing. I think I'll just go back into the waste room for a few more minutes. I'm sure I'll be fine. I can't afford to miss work. I'll be back soon."

Robs appraised her with a scrupulous eye. She'd make a good agent. "I'd do more than splash a little water on my face. Don't come out of that stall until you're cleared out. One way or another, that's the only thing that'll help."

"Got it," Mina said as she pushed her way inside the waste room. "Tell Ruth I'm on my way."

"We will!" Greta called.

Inside a stall, Mina tapped her cuff. Once McAllister's code came up, she whispered, "They're hiding something. I'm going to need a high-grade key-crack and imaging sensors, stat."

Chapter 12

Mina paced in front of her wall screen. "If we can't get a special key-crack," she told McAllister, "the imaging equipment alone might work to see what's behind those doors. But we're limited to tech I can carry in a shoulder bag, and most lidar imagers are bulky. Whatever they're hiding, they don't want anybody to find it. And even if we discover what it is, that doesn't solve the main issue of uncovering the perpetrator who's placing the encryptions on the animals, which is still my number one priority. Decoding what's behind those doors comes second." She took a seat on one of her comfy gel-cush chairs, crossing her legs, then uncrossing them. She was restless.

After she'd returned to her cube to clip and dye claws, she hadn't had a chance to do any more reconnaissance. The openness of the environment sucked for sneaking around. She couldn't be stealthy when everyone else could see exactly what she was doing. "None of the workers in my section seemed to be up to anything nefarious.

Nothing caught my eye. All side looks were aimed at me." She ran a hand through her hair, sighing. "This Vincent Kramer debacle is going to be harder to quell than I thought. I think we might need to feed something to the media."

"We'll get you a hack-grade key-crack, as well as imaging equipment," McAllister replied crisply. "You are correct. Finding the perpetrator is still your number one priority, but I want to know what they have behind those doors. There's a high possibility it's all linked." His expression was fairly grim. He was not happy with her, and she didn't blame him one bit. "What exactly do you have in mind to leak on the Kramer matter?" *The Kramer matter* was a nice way to phrase it, considering.

"We can't have people thinking Marjorie Wilcox was out with the famed colonel-in-arms." Mina held up her hand. "And before I get another lengthy speech, I was wrong to stay, and I take full responsibility for my actions. I didn't know who he was when he asked me to dinner, but as soon as he walked in, I could've made the choice to leave. I chose wrong." Mina stood. Everything around here was too soft for her liking at the moment. "If the press hounds believe somebody named Wilhelmina, no surname, was out with him, that should be enough to divert the suspicion away from Marjorie or any of my future aliases. Wilhelmina won't be a name Kramer will dispute or hopefully comment on. But if he's forced to, he'd have to agree. If they find my silly surname, so be it. My cover is as a boring linguist, who everyone will believe is only a childhood friend of Kramer's and nothing more. I never do ops under Wilhelmina, and most everybody in my casual life knows me as Mina. Good insulation all around."

Director McAllister considered, then nodded. "I guess that's as good as we've got. I'll see it gets to the media. But having your image out there, even if it's not fully in focus, is not ideal. As long as speculation stays clear of your operative covers, there will be no reprimand from above. Having intel inside the French Protectorate will be valuable to us in the long run. Cultivating an ongoing friendship with Vincent Kramer is an asset."

They'd already discussed this. Access to any regime was invaluable. Letting the press find her, however, had been a Lee-sized mistake. It wasn't going to happen again.

"Until you end this op and the fervor of potential celebrity sightings dies down, you will spend your personal time incognito. Hair, facial prosthetics, the works. I do not want a *single* civilian to mistake you for the woman who was out with Vincent Kramer. Starting tomorrow, you will take private transpo to and from the pet enhancement center. A craft will arrive at eight thirty, and all the tech you'll need will be waiting inside."

Incognito was a reprimand as well as a precaution. Mina deserved the reprimand, but it still stung. "Make it eight fifteen. I want to get there ahead of Ruth. Something tells me she arrives extra early. I want to know why." Her director was correct that it was likely all tied together somehow.

"Consider it done."

"I'm going to run a background check on those bots once we're done here and find out where they came from. It seems odd Total Enhancement would purchase eight of the same exact model. The only way I can tell them apart is by their hairstyle, name tag, and slight voice modulation. I'll cross-check the LiveBot manufacturer sell list with the names of the suspected government officials who have been confirmed in this ring, via the file you sent this morning. There might be a connection. Bots don't feel guilt and therefore don't give off guilty vibes, so they're easy to overlook. Their duties consist of shuttling animals from one place to another. Not much opportunity to attach the drive, but it's a possibility."

"It's a solid direction to go in, especially if you're not getting much from the other workers," McAllister agreed. "I'll expect more results tomorrow."

"You'll have them." At least they'd know what was behind those doors.

"I'm assuming you tried to get Kramer to discuss French politics at that dinner of yours last night?"

Mina hadn't had time to discuss the actual content of the dinner convo this morning with her director, as she'd had to get to work.

"Yes, of course. But he curtailed the topic numerous times. Other than telling me his general duties, each time I tried to veer the conversation that way, he redirected." Mina had even resorted to outright flattery to try to get her pal to speak freely, but Vince was remarkably skilled at avoidance. She guessed, not for the second or even third time, that he was good at his job.

"You said he requested further contact. Keep it up for as long as you can, but no more public meetups." Mina didn't need her boss to specify that. She wasn't going to forget anytime soon. "Vid chat is encouraged. There are rumblings up the chain about things bubbling over in Western Europe. Some sort of banking espionage that they're trying to keep a lid on. But once it blows, it's going to be big."

"Interesting. Vince didn't let on that anything was amiss. I'll do my best to gather more intel. He hasn't reached out again." It hadn't even been a single day. It was ludicrous to think he would have tried to get a hold of her already. But oddly, she felt a fluttering anticipation about seeing his face again. The sudden flavor of buttery oysters bloomed on her tongue like a delicious, edible memory. She cleared her throat and took a seat. "I ended things abruptly when I headed out through the kitchen, so that might've put him off. If he doesn't contact me in the next few days, I'll send him something. An apology of some kind. That should bring him around."

"Monitor yourself. It's unclear what tech the French Protectorate has access to and how good its hackers are, so make sure the conversation stays clean." McAllister shifted a bit stiffly in his seat. "Assume a dozen people are listening in at all times."

Mina nodded, suppressing a smile. "I will assume all communication with the colonel-in-arms, both private and public, is being recorded." Mina pondered. "I don't envy him his position. Living in the public eye is difficult. Everyone is constantly scrutinizing your every moment, interested in every move you make. Even if you offered me ten million in credit, I wouldn't do it. I'd never have another peaceful minute to myself again."

Duncan raised an eyebrow. "For ten million, almost everyone on the planet would do it."

—◆—

"If you laugh one more time, I'm going to knock you out of that chair, and you're going to wake up tomorrow unsure what happened to our beautiful friendship," Mina told her giggling friend.

She and Kaylee were situated at the bar watching Quinn mix drinks at Primal. It was a high-end club, catering to those who could afford real alcohol over printed, though they offered both. The space was covered in slick black lacquer, mirrored surfaces, and animal prints to give it that quasiprimal feel, whatever that was. A holo band was performing, and the dance floor was packed, lights blinking. A jumble of sweating bodies, drinks held high in the air, grooved back and forth. This wasn't a place Mina would frequent if it weren't for her little brother, who was smiling and waving at her from across the bar. But it was entertaining, she'd give it that.

"I can't help it!" Kaylee openly guffawed. She was appropriately dressed in a micromini and cheetah-print top. Leave it to her to fit in with the regulars. Mina, on the other hand, did not blend. She wore a conservatively cut suit, trendy at some point a few decades ago, in a dingy beige. "You look like my aunt Phyllis. Did you have to go so thick on the nose?" Her fellow agent leaned closer, inspecting. "The hair's not bad, even though red clashes with your skin tone. And honestly, those glasses make you look cross-eyed."

"Exactly the look I was going for. Cross-eyed, big-nosed, dour Aunt Phyllis. And it's working, because no one here is giving me a second glance. And yes, I had to go with this nose. My 3-D Face File got corrupted somehow. I didn't find out until I opened it tonight. This nose was all that I had left. It's from the Smith assignment. Remember when we had to dress up as old ladies to bust that embezzler?"

Kaylee slapped Mina's shoulder, snorting. "How could I forget? That's why the schnoz looks so familiar. I used my aunt Phyllis as the face swap for that op. She had the unusual talent of looking a spry sixty-five in her forties. Now she looks ninety." Kaylee eyed the set points. "That's an awesome application, however. I honestly can't tell it's a prosthetic. That skin cement is a godsend. Matches your coloring perfectly."

"Thanks." Mina picked up her pink drink, which happened to be frothing. Quinn had assured her she'd like it. That was, after she'd convinced him it was her under all this goop. She was having only a single alcoholic beverage tonight. Mina wasn't interested in taking another spin in her medi pod or making any more bad decisions. She nodded at her brother as she lofted her drink. He stood at the far end, busy with the evening crowd, seeming like he was made for this job. He waved, then made a fist, encouraging her to take a taste.

It was their *be brave* sign.

"Your brother is seriously adorable." Kaylee picked up her own glass, which contained blue liquid and was also frothing. "Those gray eyes and that sun-kissed, tumbled hair. Delicious."

Mina took a sip. The froth tumbled down her throat. Not bad. Subtle fruit flavor wrapped in delicious rum with a little citrus boost at the end. She gave a thumbs-up to Quinn, then addressed Kaylee. "Don't you dare think about it. He's too young for you."

"He's exactly three years, nine months, and ten days younger than me. That's nothing." She waved off Mina's rebuttal as she took a taste of her own beverage, flashing her own quick thumbs-up to Quinn, who waved back enthusiastically.

"How very specific of you," Mina replied. "He may not be too young agewise, but he's still in school, taking his sweet time earning his advanced degree. You, on the other hand, moved out of your family's home at thirteen, pursued your advanced degree by sixteen, and had a job nailing bad guys by nineteen. Now, at twenty-five, you're more seasoned than a Southern meal printer. You'd be bored of him in five minutes—and that's being generous. And once you called it quits, his heart would be broken into a trillion fragments. He adores you, and you know it."

"He would not bore me. After all, he's related to you, and I find you endlessly fascinating. But if you put it that way, yeah, I guess he's no Vincent Kramer." Sarcasm dripped like thermal plasma off a chemi reaction. "What the actual *hell*? I can't believe you haven't said anything yet. And me being me, I've given you ample time. We've been sitting here for at least fifteen. You come in looking like my old but spry aunt with no explanation whatsoever and make me wait like a chump. So you better spill, and spill good, because I'm pissed I had to catch you on-screen with that total hunky heartthrob of a specimen before I got the details firsthand."

"I'm sorry."

Kaylee was completely unmoved by Mina's apology, head cocked, fingers tapping, still waiting.

"I apologize. Truly. I've had zero time to fill you in until now. I swear. And to tell you the truth, I sort of forgot about it after my long day trying to mop up the spill that being out with him caused, especially after the effort it took to force myself into this ridiculous costume."

"You *forgot?*" Kaylee's head moved to the other side, her hair swishing. "You had dinner at a *real* restaurant with the colonel-in-arms of the French Protectorate, and it just"—she flipped her wrist—"slipped your mind." Kaylee picked up her drink and took a swig, eyes compressing. She set it down with a hard *clack.* "Yeah, you know, that happens to me all the time. Last week, I went on a fornicating date with the ambassador of Greater Scandinavia. Then we went back to my place and did the deed a couple dozen times. But I forgot to mention it to my *best* friend, because, you know, it was just another *day* for me."

"Fornicating?" Mina giggled. "And we didn't do the deed! It was just dinner. Planetary Seeker's honor."

Mina placed three fingers next to her temple and gave a salute. Plus, doing the deed would've been etched in Mina's mind forever, front and center. Forgetting that wouldn't be a possibility. "And who on earth can do the deed a couple dozen times in one night?" Kaylee was not amused. Mina dropped her hand. "Okay. I really am actually, truly sorry. It was a scoop, and you deserved to hear it straight from me right after it happened. Please believe me when I say I didn't have time to tell you before now. But I can assure you my meeting with Vince ended up being a crater-sized mistake. It's a massive headache that's going to take time to unravel." Mina understood her friend's pique. It was a big scoop, and Mina hadn't made it a priority to tell her.

"*Vince?* You're on a nickname basis with the CIA of the French Protectorate?" Kaylee crossed her arms.

Mina took a fortifying gulp of her pink froth. "Do you remember me telling you about my friend Vince growing up? I probably mentioned him a few times. He was the one I used to play my favorite collection games with."

"The mop-headed geek who liked to hunt holos with you is *the* Vincent Kramer of the FP?" Kaylee's tone couldn't have been more skeptical.

For the first time, Mina scanned the area. "Yes. And you yelling about it isn't helping my situation." It wasn't very agentlike either.

Kaylee's sleek bob executed a few smart whips against her shoulders as she glanced around. "Calm down, there's nobody around except your cute brother. Now back on topic. I'm having an incredibly hard time believing your

Vince is *that* Vince." Her voice dipped to a whisper-yell. "And if that's the case, how did you *not* know the press would be after him like vultures on a hot carcass?"

Mina shrugged, a single finger sliding idly around the rim of her almost gone cocktail. "I have no excuse other than I was completely shook when he showed up. I couldn't believe it was actually him. Even though I keep up with current events and know the names of the individuals in the top tier of the French Protectorate, it never occurred to me that Colonel-in-Arms Vincent Kramer was my childhood friend Vincent Kramer. I mean, why would I? I haven't seen a recent picture of him, and even then, I'm not sure if it would've sparked my memory. The kid I knew and the adult look incredibly different."

"You mean, incredibly *on fire combustible.*"

Mina grinned. "My Vince grew up here and pursued his advanced degree in banking. I haven't spoken to him in over seven years. He chatted me up out of the blue last night, and we met an hour later. Doing a lifecheck on him didn't enter my mind." The perks of having a government database at her voice command. "Again, why would I? He was my friend from long ago, nothing more. Then, once the shock wore off that it was *actually* him"—and Mina had been satiated with delicious champagne and oysters—"I didn't factor in the consequences. It's incredibly irritating that I misjudged the situation to such a large degree. Even if I'd had a second to think it through, I don't think I would've thought we'd be discovered. I mean, jeez, he's a colonel in the French

Protectorate. Can't a guy like that figure out how to get somewhere covertly? You'd think he'd be a pro at sneaking into places because he doesn't want to create a fuss." It was easier if Mina didn't have to shoulder the *entire* blame.

"He *is* the fuss. I bet everyone in that fancy eatery was gabbing into their cuffs the moment he stepped through the door. I'm even more certain screencasters give good credit for juicy tidbits when a visiting regime is in town. It happens so rarely. And you're lucky the statute of personal libel protects your image from being snapped by civilians without your permission. If Ambrose had been there with him, the place would've been shut down by gawkers in the first ten. Those two are like the electric duo of Team Female Hormones. Ovaries would've exploded on sight."

Mina chuckled. "He's not *that* cute. I mean, I realize he's eligible, and that makes him even more attractive to the masses, but honestly an uproar of that magnitude didn't enter my mind." Quinn winked at her from down the bar and jutted his chin up. Mina gave him the okay sign, letting him know they were good. "It was a stupid mistake. One that makes me think I could be slipping."

"You're not slipping. It didn't enter your mind because you don't pay attention to what you consider gossipy nonsense. But this is real life. You're going to have to keep your eyes open, or it's going to cost you. Did anyone buy it wasn't you? The pics I saw were blurry, but come on, it was clearly you."

"There was skepticism, but I was pretty convincing. I

played the down-on-my-luck gal who needs a job and couldn't possibly know Vincent Kramer, or why would I be there? It helped that I'd only been on my classified for a single day. Most hadn't gotten a good look at me or paid much attention. But to quell it further, McAllister's going to feed the media that a woman named Wilhelmina was out with him. That should shut it down for the time being. But now I'm on an incognito order, which is why I was forced to come out tonight looking like this." Mina drained her glass. "I could lose my job if the higher-ups get wind. I screwed up badly."

"You won't lose your job. You're too valuable. You bring ops down in less time than the rest of us. You're a shining star."

"My last op was eighteen months. And I won't be closing ops if I'm forced to do it looking like this."

"There are worse things than walking around looking like Aunt Phyllis."

"Name one."

"Looking like Uncle Pete."

MINA ENTERED TOTAL Enhancement at eight twenty-one the next morning. Babs was busy straightening things in the waiting room. No customers and their human companions had arrived yet. Mina lifted a hand in greeting. "Hey there," she called. "I'm here a little early to get a jump on things." Mina hurried toward the door so she wouldn't get caught in an unwanted convo.

Babs responded, "Did you see? The woman's name is Wilhelmina. It wasn't you after all!"

"I did see." Mina had tuned in to the screencasts this morning, like everyone else. The program had ended with Melissa Socorro vowing to track down the mystery lady named Wilhelmina, whatever it took, a heartfelt promise to all her avid viewers. *Good luck, Melissa.* There were three thousand Wilhelminas in the immediate area alone, and without DNA they would be hunting for a very long time. Everything attached to Mina's real identify had been expunged, other than a few boring, unflattering photos of a very young Wilhelmina Kandy Kane taken in her elementary years. Her job as a linguist was not exactly newsworthy. This was why she wasn't a social networker. Thank goodness. "That Wilhelmina is one lucky gal," Mina added as the interior door slicked open.

"Don't I know it," Babs called as she tugged a chair across the room.

Mina headed straight for the locker room.

The bot behind the counter greeted her in her succinctly modulated voice. "Welcome, your shift doesn't start until nine o'clock. You are thirty-seven minutes early."

"I know." Mina hurried to her locker. "I want to greet the animals before I start my shift. I've developed quite an affection for them." Mina had learned that the majority of owners dropped their pets off after work for convenience. That's why the kennels were always full in the morning. Mina was going to use the tracker that had been waiting for her in the craft this morning to see if microdata had been planted on any of the animals. Then she'd do the same thing at closing. It was her priority. As Mina grabbed her uni out of her security box, she casually asked, "Do you know if Ruth is here yet?"

"Ruth Donnelly arrives promptly at eight thirty each and every day."

"Good to know." Mina gave a quiet thank-you to the LiveBot's excellent capability of keeping track of absolutely everything and being unable to lie about it.

That meant Mina realistically had six or so minutes before Ruth arrived, plus the few extra minutes her manager would take to change into her outfit for the day. That should be enough time to do a quick scan of the animals.

A minute later, Mina zipped out into the main workroom. When she arrived at the kennels behind the glass wall, she found one of the bots, Heidi, standing there. Mina affected her normal stance. "Hi, Heidi. I arrived early hoping to greet the animals this morning. Is that allowed?"

Heidi smiled. "This is a unique request, but it's not forbidden. From time to time, workers do come in and greet some of their favorite clients. You may enter." The bot tapped a code into the pad beside the door. Things like door locks had to be amended for bots, since they didn't have DNA to do an automatic swipe.

Once the door opened, Mina slipped through.

The animals were extremely excited to have a new guest in their midst, and the barks, meows, and oinks wound up accordingly. Mina had the customized drive tracker in her pocket. It'd been formulated to the exact frequency of the device that had been recovered from the fur of the animal that had previously been discovered. McAllister had said the encryption itself had been no longer than a grain of rice. Because of that, it would be almost impossible to get a visual. Mina set the ping to low so as not to advertise what she was doing.

Hurrying toward one end, and to be completely thorough, she started with the reptiles. There weren't very many, and thankfully they were quiet, just a lot of forked tongues and bobbing heads. Mina passed the division into the rodent area. Nothing chimed. Once she arrived at the cats, she moved in a little closer to the kennels. Still nothing. The cats were relatively passive, but she got an especially big hiss from an orange tabby that she'd sprayed down the other day. "I don't blame you, pal," Mina muttered. "I can't believe you're back again so soon. Or maybe you never left. That's got to suck."

Mina passed the adorable pigs, stopping to stroke some of their cute snouts. They squealed in delight. The device in her pocket stayed quiet. As she entered the canine area, she palmed the tech, pretending to scratch some of the dogs behind the ears to make sure she got up close and personal.

Nothing chimed.

In the very last row, Mina turned, scooting the cylindrical, six-centimeter-long tracker back into her pocket. Everything was clear. No animals wore an encryption at this time. Now it was time to get out without being spotted by Ruth.

"Did you enjoy your visit?" Heidi asked as Mina stepped clear of the door.

"I did. Thank you for allowing me in."

"It was my pleasure."

"I'll probably be back again after shift. I'd like to say goodbye, since I'm only going to be here for a few more days." All the animals wouldn't be here, as the owners picked them up throughout the day, but she'd scan the ones that were left and hope for the best. Getting a ping soon would be excellent.

The bot didn't bat an eyelash at Mina's request. Of course she didn't. "Someone will be here to let you in."

No one was in the work space yet, though she had spotted a few workers heading into the locker room. Mina checked her cuff. It was eight thirty-one. Deciding it would be better to avoid Ruth on the floor, Mina cut her way through the stations, taking the hallway toward the meal room.

She paused at the door she'd broken through yesterday, giving the lever a turn. Locked. She pressed her ear against it. Nothing.

Mina ducked into the waste room, the easiest place to wait until her shift was ready to start. She entered a stall at the far end and shut the door. She tapped her cuff, wishing she'd been able to bring her compucase to this op. So much easier than working off a cuff. But nobody here worked on a computer—and most certainly not on a fancy supercomputer. It would've been completely out of place for her to be carrying it around.

Impatient for the data results she'd ordered last night on who'd purchased bots for Total Enhancement, Mina whispered into her cuff, "Display results in holo form of Total Enchantment Pet Center data search on LiveBot purchases ordered yesterday at eighteen hundred." Mina didn't want to have to read the words flowing across her wrist.

A second later, her cuff replied in its low feminine tone, "Results are inconclusive. No data found. Recommend refining search parameters."

Mina had performed the data query using a G10-level

government clearance only to find there'd been a higher-level government block in place. She'd then tried a G10-plus, hoping it would clear, but it seemed it hadn't. That meant it was going to take her more time to crack. And if she wasn't successful, she'd have to ask a specialized tech to break it. "*Damn*," she whispered. She was about to exit the stall when the waste room door banged open.

Ruth's voice reverberated clearly through the small space. "The bots are getting sloppy," she grumbled, her voice bordering on ragged. Mina assumed she was talking on her cuff or a handheld, but she didn't have eyes on her from behind the stall door.

Mina engaged *record* on her own cuff, thankful Ruth wouldn't be able to see her, as the bottom of the door went to the floor. At the top, there was a meter of clearance. Mina lifted her wrist to make sure she captured every bit of this interaction.

"Bots don't get sloppy." The male voice sounded grainy and far away. "They're programmed to do a job, and they do it. They don't make mistakes."

"The hallway door was unlocked," Ruth complained. "How do you explain that?" Ruth had already locked it back up, as Mina had just checked it. Mina hadn't had enough time yesterday to relock it after her run-in with Greta and Robs. There'd been too many people around, and she'd had to keep the feeling-sick act going.

"Sounds like human error to me," the man replied. If Mina had to guess, this guy was in his fifties or sixties, as his voice held the vibrato of age. She'd heard enough old people at Cullen to have it etched in her brain forever.

"If I can't trust you on this, I'm going to have to get someone else."

"It wasn't *human* error," Mina's manager sneered. "I'm the only human involved. And I didn't unlock it. These stupid bots are the ones who move everything around at night. It had to be one of them."

"Maybe the lock is faulty. Electronic locks fail after a few years. Let's get a locksmith in to fix it."

"Maybe we should have the same locks installed as we have on the doors inside." Ruth was pacing. The woman wore quiet-soled shoes, but she was stomping in her agitation. Ruth apparently hadn't noticed that Mina's stall door was closed, which was a good thing. "You promised the merchandise would be shipped out already. Why is it taking so long?"

Merchandise usually meant illegal goods, particularly in this context. That meant whatever was behind those doors would carry a prison sentence if the perpetrators were caught.

"The last of it is getting moved tomorrow night. New merch should arrive in a few days."

"You promised this was the last shipment." Ruth's complaint ended on a whine. "When I agreed to move to this location, you said no more than four shipments. We're on our sixth. I won't agree to harbor any more goods. It's too risky. This place is not secure enough."

"Is that a threat? Are you threatening me?" The voice held malice. The man was unhappy and knew he held the power. "Because if you are, you can be replaced very quickly. You do as I say, or your livelihood is gone. You'll be living in the outskirts within a week, if not shut up in a box like you should've been the first time I met you."

"Fine." Ruth's anger echoed off the walls. Mina could almost feel tiny waves of it pinging against her door. "But when the feds come calling, it'll be your own damn fault." A second later, a furious gurgle rippled through the room. Ruth had cut the man off, likely hanging up on him. "You think you can threaten me, Conny boy? I don't think so."

She stormed out.

Mina changed her cuff setting and eased out of the stall. She couldn't risk Ruth coming back in here and seeing her, so she had to quickly decide what to do. It was still early to hit the workroom. If she wanted to blend, she should wait until other workers arrived to provide an adequate distraction, especially since she would be coming out of the hallway instead of the uni room.

She settled her ear against the waste room door. She couldn't hear any movement, but that didn't mean Ruth wasn't out there. Mina took a deep breath and swung it open.

All clear.

Mina darted left and took the hallway to the meal room, the only logical place to go. She pulled up short as Ruth turned from a printer, holding a cup of steaming coffee. Mina calmed her breathing in an instant, flashing a bright smile. "Oh, hi. I was hoping for one of those, too." With two fingers, Mina hooked her hair behind her ears, her eyes darting to the ground, then she clasped her hands in front of her. "I woke up a little later than usual today," she explained. "So I decided to come in sooner in case there was any traffic. I missed breakfast. I think company policy allows for a coffee, right?"

Ruth assessed Mina, her frown deeply furrowed. But now Mina knew why. Ruth was involved in something that could land her in a box, and boxes were devoid of any kind of creature comforts, designed to make those who committed crimes feel isolated and lonely. It was the government's way of trying to deter crime, but it didn't work. Not when people were desperate enough to do anything to get ahead of their borrows. Most people, if given the chance, would take the box over the outskirts any day.

"As long as you're in your station when the day starts, take what you want." She turned her back on Mina.

A pang of sympathy reared up for her cranky manager, but it would evaporate quickly if Mina found Ruth was involved in trafficking young girls. However, Mina didn't think so. From the conversation she'd just overheard, it sounded like Ruth was being coerced into doing something, and that something had to do with what was behind those locked doors. They could indeed be connected, but Mina's hunch was she'd stumbled onto something else entirely. Time would tell.

"Thanks." Mina moved to the printer. "What duties do you have in store for me today? More clipping and dyeing? Or back to the sprayers?" Mina wanted to add a hopeful request for doing a massage, but knew nobody was doing that and didn't want to pique Ruth's ire further.

The manager wandered over to a single window situated on the far end of the room. The view was the side of an office building. Without glancing over her shoulder, Ruth replied, "Cube thirty-three. It's bioblast day. Be prepared for your hands to feel the burn. The gloves don't keep everything out." She'd uttered the directive listlessly and without her usual fervor.

Mina's eyebrows rose, but she kept her eyes locked on her coffee. "Got it."

CHAPTER 14

MINA'S HANDS WERE on fire. Ruth hadn't been kidding. The application itself was easy. Just another sprayer. But in order for the solution to sink into the fur and provide the best possible glow, Mina had to rub it in and wait two minutes before rinsing. The compound was organic, made from some sort of luminous algae, so at least it wasn't toxic. But it seeped through the gloves right into her skin. Mina had been concerned about the dogs, but had been told the animals got a conditioning treatment before coming to her that protected them, and being exposed to the application for just a few minutes was much different than handling the solution all day.

All the dogs seemed happy enough, and thankfully there had been no sharp-clawed felines, but Mina was glad her shift was over.

After rubbing some recommended gel on her hands from a container set in the wall in the uni room, Mina hitched her satchel over her shoulder. It was the same color as her compucase, a chocolate brown, but was made of a cheaper grade of eco-leather.

Mina had already changed into her street clothes, a basic red tunic and razor pants in a deep blue. Her hair was swept back from her face in a high tail, since she was still trying her best to distinguish herself from the blurry images of her with Vince still floating around on screencasts. It wasn't full incognito, but it was all she could do when she was still at work.

Everyone around her was getting changed into their normal clothes and moving out.

Feigning a worried expression, Mina headed into the large workroom again, veering toward the kennels. People passed her, but didn't comment that she was moving against the flow of traffic without her uni on. Ruth was nowhere to be seen, which made things much simpler.

The women at lunch had all heard about the mysterious Wilhelmina, so there hadn't been much Vincent Kramer discussion.

Candace stood in front of the kennels this time, the first LiveBot Mina had encountered on her first day. "Hi, Candace," Mina said. "Can I say goodbye to the animals? I started the day by greeting them, and I'm only here for two more days." She held up two fingers and waggled them. "I've become quite attached. Heidi said it wouldn't be a problem if I said goodbye."

"Workers may enter the kennel until six p.m.," Candace recited.

Mina glanced at her cuff. "Great. That means I have three minutes." More than enough time. Candace nodded and reached over, punching the appropriate code. As the bot's shirtsleeve fell back, her cuff was exposed. It was a snazzier model than she'd worn a few days ago. "I see they've finally updated your cuff. Good thing, huh? That one you had before was pretty beat up. It didn't make sense that they'd give you old tech."

The door unlatched, and Candace pulled it open. "Oh, no, we share cuffs. It's my day to wear this one."

Share cuffs? Why in the world do they do that?

Mina entered the kennel area, and the animals whipped into their usual frenzy at the sight of a new visitor. Rampant barking and whining filled her ears.

She headed straight for the canines. She wouldn't have enough time to scan every animal, and the tag that had been discovered had been on a dog, so she was making an educated guess.

Her mind went back to Candace's cuff. There was no reason for the bots to share.

Tech was personalized for a reason. Cuffs literally ran your life. Even bots made them their own. Every LiveBot was created with a different voice sig, even those who were made identical. A cuff was set up to recognize that particular sig. Reprogramming cuffs each day so that the bots could share would be a hassle. What would be the point? *Extremely counterintuitive.*

Mina hurried through the cages, greeting some of her customers with a scratch as she ran the check. In the very last row, her tracker emitted a soft ping and vibrated.

"Got you," Mina murmured. She wasn't sure which animal had caused the alert, so she squatted, palming the tracer and inserting her hand through the bars to rub the ear of a curly poodle with tan fur. No tone. "It's not you, but you're such a good boy." The dog tried to lick her hand.

She moved to another. This one was a yippie terrier mix.

On the third, she hit her mark.

The sweet Lab was at least ten years old, black with a graying muzzle and currently taking a snooze. She hadn't met this dog yet. Mina slid the tracker back into her pocket and eased open her satchel. From inside, she removed the thumb-sized scanner she'd used at her station to tag pet collars. It'd been risky to smuggle it out of her work space, but she'd had no other choice. She had to know how this dog had spent its day.

"Come here, love," she coaxed the dog in a low tone. "Look what I have. Would you like a nice, tasty treat?" The dog lifted its head lazily off of the comfort of its gel-molded pad. "Can you cooperate a wee bit more? I need to see your collar." Mina offered the pooch a soft protein chew between the bars. The dog edged forward, its nose twitching, but it was taking its own sweet time. "Come on, I know you can do it." Just as its snout eased closer to get the yummy incentive, the door behind Mina swooshed opened.

Mina turned toward the interruption, shielding her hand with her body as she slid the scanner back into her bag and stood.

Ruth stalked forward, followed by Candace behind her. "What are you doing in here?" the manager demanded in an irritated, accusatory tone.

Mina casually dusted off her pants, rearranging the strap of her bag. "Oh, I came to say goodbye to the animals. I've kind of gotten attached. This has been such a great job. I really wish I could stay." She added in some gushing pretense. "But I'm sure Pauleen is excited to get back to work. Who wouldn't be at a place like this?" Mina gestured down at the dog, who was already nodding off again. "I couldn't resist giving this sweet dog a treat, and I realized, silly me, that I left my jacket in my cube. So, I'll"—she moved forward, brushing past Ruth—"just stop in and get it on my way out." To Candace, she said, "I'll be back in the morning to say hello."

Ruth followed her out, practically stepping on her heels. "Those cubes are temperature controlled. There is no reason to need a jacket." More accusation, but also mild confusion. The woman's radar was up, as people's often were when they were involved in illegal acts. But a temp worker returning to a station to get a jacket and stopping to pet a few animals shouldn't raise any alarms. But Ruth was still suspicious.

As much as Mina would have preferred to have blended in more and taken her time, such a short op made that impossible. "I know the temperature is controlled. Most of the time, it's very nice," Mina agreed in an affable tone. "Unfortunately, I have very poor circulation, and after mealtime today, I was a bit chilly. You know, now that I think about it, it may have been whatever's in the bioblast concoction. I think I might've had a reaction to it." She shot Ruth a glance over her shoulder. Her manager's mouth was set in a firm line, no hint of a smile or frown. "My hands are pretty chapped. Anyway, I went and got my jacket. I hope that's okay. I didn't think I was breaking any rules. Was I?"

Ruth stammered for a moment, clearly at a loss, wanting to punish Mina, but finding no just cause. "No, I guess not." The woman huffed a few times. "Nobody's ever needed more clothes before. Other people work bioblast and don't have reactions." Her eyes narrowed. "I didn't see you with a jacket on today."

Mina was prepared. "I only needed it for about thirty minutes, until I warmed up. When the B workers were supposed to go on their break, I took it off. I remember, because right after the meal announcement, a bot came to get my animal, so I had time to take it off."

Ruth was always gone during B workers' mealtime, which was a mystery because there weren't any B workers.

They were nearing cube thirty-three. "There it is," Mina exclaimed brightly, gesturing toward the station. "Sitting right where I left it. I can't believe I forgot to grab it when I left. I set it on top of the readout so I would remember. Honestly, I'd lose my head if it wasn't firmly secured. Let me fetch it, and I'll be out of your way." The jacket was strategically draped over the digital device for a reason.

If Ruth stayed outside, Mina would get what she needed.

Without waiting for her manager to reply or follow her inside, Mina whipped open the door, walked briskly to the pedestal, and plucked up her coat as she placed the scanner she had palmed on the way in back into its slot.

It took only a second for the results to display.

Glancing down, she smiled.

Everything she needed to know was right there.

———

"The owner's name is Lambert, Mark S. Dog's name is Nancy. She's an old, bordering-on-lethargic Labrador. The dog wasn't encrypted this morning. Sweet pup was in her kennel sleeping. I think it's her number one favorite thing to do. That means the drive was attached sometime today. This animal was marked for a spray, a dry, and something called a tidy-up. That means general maintenance, nothing fancy. Nails clipped, but not dyed. No scent. Just the basics. I think they do some teeth cleaning, too, but I'm not sure. There're only a few cubes dedicated to tidying, and they're located on the far side of the room. I'll try to get that assignment tomorrow, if Ruth is feeling magnanimous." Mina also almost laughed. She knew she would get whatever assignment Ruth decided to give her. Ruth had been miffed by the jacket thing and likely happy that Mina's hands were irritated. If Mina had to guess, she would probably give her another day of bioblast. "Even if I don't get the tidy-up rotation, my gut is that this is more about the bots and their cuffs. There's definitely something there." Mina balanced her compucase on her lap, typing as she spoke to McAllister from her living room, reviewing the search she'd run last night that'd come up blocked. Her boss was at thirty percent, the data she was accessing from her computer displayed next to his image at forty so she could easily read the text on the wall. "I need to break through these G11 stops that are concealing the information about the LiveBot manufacturer. We need to know who ordered them for Total Enhancement and where they came from. Somebody doesn't want that information out. If the bots sharing cuffs are the ones that are attaching the encrypted devices, they are simply following orders. Depending on their programmed restrictions, it will be either painfully easy or extremely difficult to gather that information from them."

"Time is of the essence, and as you only have two days left on this op, I'm sending someone over to help you hack those G11's tonight."

McAllister's tone was firm enough that Mina looked up, surprised. "You mean, like, to my residence?" Unusual, but not unheard of. When ops got down to the fuse, other agents were often brought in, especially on a classified. Those ops were top priority.

"Yes. I'm sending Lee over. I want it finished tonight."

"Lee?" It came out as a pitiful squeak. "I thought he was reassigned to Kaylee." The two Lees together. Mina felt like giggling, but then, Lee was coming over to her residence, so she didn't.

"He is, and he's doing a fine job. But he can spare a few hours tonight. The kid is eager to prove himself."

McAllister's expression shifted slightly, one eye creasing. "He told me about hacking Cullen Industries and refunding borrows. He also told me you knew."

"I did know," Mina agreed, continuing to work, her eyes focused like a pair of lasers on her compucase. "But I figured he would tell you. It's not my job to be a snitch." Well, technically, since Lee broke the law, she could've—possibly should've—said something, but there was a lot of gray there. "I mean, elderly people getting their borrows back from a legal-should-be-illegal fraud company is kind of sweet justice if you ask me—it's the reason we do this job. To protect people from government corruption and big banks—"

"He compromised the mission." McAllister's tone was edged in anger. "If he'd been detected, he would've put the entire case in jeopardy. Not to mention, Cullen would've pressed charges. The op comes first, always."

"Well, he didn't get caught, because he's a Level XIII. His blatant inexperience in the field could've put the case in jeopardy just as easily." Mina hastened a glance up from her computer so she could judge exactly how mad her director was. He seemed to be simmering, but not flaring. Smartly, she decided to switch the topic. "By the way, did we happen to get an indictment on Cullen himself? And if we did, is it going to stick? And while I'm asking, please tell me Rick the Rat is already stuffed in a box someplace nibbling on some printed cheddar." Mina did not miss monitoring that sleazeball every day. She'd rather do a thousand bioblasts, chapped hands or not.

"Indictment is pending on Cullen. He's slippery, with a lot of powerful connections. But we're doing everything we can to make sure it sticks. We handed the case off to the fraud department. They're connecting the dots. Rick is in holding. Judge sees him end of this week. You did a thorough job, so there's no reason to believe he won't be escorted into a box shortly." McAllister had his superboard out. "Now, getting back to your evening plans. Lee will be there within the hour. I'm declassifying your interactions with him. Fill him in on what you know."

Mina held her tongue. McAllister cleared his throat, reaching a single hand up to loosen his tie. Mina's boss was old-school classy. Ties went out at least twenty—if not thirty—years ago. But Mina had to admit that suiting up made him look fierce and determined. People didn't mess around with people who continued to wear ties.

"Just so you know," McAllister said, "I threatened to put Lee on probation after the borrows incident, and he has assured me that he will follow orders down to the exact digital point. If he messes up, it's on him, and he'll pay the penalty."

"Okay. Noted. What's the plan with old Nancy the dog and her owner, Mark Lambert?"

"I'll put a tail on the owner and dog after this briefing. When that pup makes it to the delivery point wearing the encrypted device, the FPIU will take action. We now believe the person who is plucking the drives off these dogs is just a middleman. He's a known trafficker, but he's not the kingpin. This guy is enticing dog owners to the meet with the claim that they won a free gift. Once the middleman is taken off the streets, people will notice, so we're on a strict timeline now. No mistakes."

"Understood," Mina said. "I'll get it done. I'll have more nailed down by tomorrow. The imaging tech wasn't in the craft today, although I wouldn't have had extra time to do a scan of those rooms. It's a lucky break I overheard Ruth and the mystery man. We now know there's something stored there, which makes the search easier."

"The imaging equipment will be there tomorrow. It's small but efficient. Find out what's behind those doors. There is a slim possibility it's connected to the trafficking, but whatever is happening there is illegal."

"I will do my very best." Mina glanced at her cuff. Fifty-six minutes until Lee arrived. Having him in her home was going to be interesting. "I'll report at the same time tomorrow unless I get a hit on something juicy."

McAllister nodded. "Screen off."

Chapter 16

MINA FORCED HER mouth into a smile that felt only half fake as she opened her door. Veronica had announced Lee had landed a few minutes ago, and Mina used the public code to allow him to take a tube up from level twenty.

The tube doors opened, and Lee stepped out.

His hair was combed, although slightly tousled. He clutched his compucase, a somewhat shiny, brown affair, under one arm. He looked younger and even more innocent than Mina remembered, even though it'd been only a couple of days since she'd last seen him.

"Uh, hello," Lee offered.

"Come in, Lee," Mina managed in a fairly magnanimous tone, gesturing for him to enter.

"Whoa." The statement came out in a rush of air ending on a hard wheeze. "This place is positively *flaming.*" He made fast tracks to the windows. They were a showstopper. Floor to ceiling, covering the entire southern exposure. It was dark outside, and the city was laid out like a glittering, multistrand necklace full of rubies, diamonds, and emeralds blinking intermittently in the night. "I've never been in a unit this high up. You can look *down* on hoverbuses. *Whoa.* They look huge from up here." His eyes widened. "You forget how crowded the city is when you're inside the hustle, but man, this is spec. Totally spec."

"Yes, agreed. It's a spectacular view." Mina walked into her meal-prep area. "Can I offer you anything? I'm still fighting with my meal printer, but it surprises me with some pretty good eats. If you want, you can punch the button and take it for a spin."

"Oh, no, thanks." He glanced toward Mina's wall, where she had her data displayed at fifty. "Is that the site you're trying to hack?"

Mina appreciated that he wanted to get down to business. "Yes. I'll hook you into my home unit so you can have access from your comp. Veronica, allow new user to access data files displayed on-screen for the next four hours. Airmeld connection to personal computer registered to one Agent Lee Adams. Allow him to make commands. Voice imprint required." She nodded toward Lee. "Tell my house your name so she can work her magic."

Lee cleared his throat, and Mina resisted a smile. "Lee Timothy Adams."

"Locating computer registered to one Lee Timothy Adams and linking data," Veronica replied smoothly. "Voice commands activated. Termination in four hours."

"That's super tight." Lee took a seat on the lounger, opening his compucase. "My home program is ancient. It barely turns on the lights. I wired in my own upgrade, but it sapped too much power. Management made me disconnect it."

Mina crossed her arms, impressed. "Is there anything you can't do when it comes to tech?"

Lee looked unfazed. "Not much. At least I don't think. One of my earliest memories, before I could even walk, was fiddling around with an old board. I remember it captured all my attention. I could do almost anything I wanted with my little fingers, then my voice. It was incredible. That was before boards were thin and made of crystalline. It was an old clunky one, too heavy for me to carry on my own, but I cried every time my mom took it away." He began to type. "Veronica, display my comp on the wall next to home data."

Mina watched in fascination as the kid began to work. She took a seat next to him, picking up her own computer. "Make sure your hack is quiet," Mina told him. "If anyone finds out we're looking into this info, they could shut the operation down before we figure out the source. I'm not sure how much McAllister told you, but we're working to bust a trafficking ring. Young girls. It's classified, highly sensitive."

Lee's head popped up, and he peered at her like a baby owl. His coloring was even right on—brown with tufts of gold. "Like in sex? That kind of trafficking?"

He was so incredibly innocent.

"Yes, that kind of trafficking. Usually, the Sex Squad

takes ops like these, but they needed a quiet worker on the inside, which is where we come in. Someone at the pet enhancement center is placing encrypted drives onto dog fur. Then said dog has a run-in with the middleman, who takes that information to the right people. I'm closing in on who is placing those encryptions. My best guess now is the LiveBots that work there. The owners, or someone else, have purchased eight of the same model. All that's different about them are their hairstyles, names, and voice sigs. Today, I found out they swap cuffs for some reason. One is totally upscale. All the others are old and scuffed, barely useful except to tell the time and scan for the next pet pickup. I only caught a quick glimpse of the newer one, but it resembles the one Director McAllister wears, except it's crystalline banded in black. How a bot was given access to a government cuff that's not available to the public is the question of the hour."

Lee nodded along as he typed. It would've been easier for him to use voice commands, but it seemed he was well practiced in using his fingers. A second later, the image of a cuff popped onto the wall in front of them. "Does it look like this?" He used voice command to order, "Rotate cuff three hundred and sixty degrees in XZ plane, one revolution every ten seconds."

Mina watched the device turn, sitting back in her seat. "Yes, it looks similar. I didn't see the interior buttons set into the black titanium, but that looks about right."

"That's a government-issue XR794. It's the only one I know banded in black titanium. I try to keep up with the latest tech, and since I became an agent, I have full access to restricted sites, so I don't have to hack them." He grinned as a flutter of guilt flicked over his face. "I mean, when I hacked before, I just browsed. I didn't compromise any secrets. I swear! I just find new tech so interesting. I can't help myself." He gestured to the graphic. "Those buttons on the side are actually sensory nodes specified for LiveBots. They can work on humans in a similar way, using the neurosensory pathway, but it wouldn't be as seamless. The human body is much too complex, and no two people are exactly the same. So mainly, they're specified for bots."

"Sensory nodes? So a handler can better control the bot?" Everyday people used nodes to heighten many sensory experiences, like taste, hearing, sight, and sexual pleasure. Mina hadn't heard of using nodes with bots, however.

Lee was back to typing. A list of XR794 attribute specifications filled the screen on his side. "As you can see, the sensory experience is meant to work in tandem with a specific command. If you want a LiveBot to act more like a real person in certain areas, you trigger a compatible sensory impulse with the directive, and hypothetically the LiveBot responds in a more humanlike way. There's actually a lot of research happening now with a program called SymBot. They want to make this all a part of LiveBots' internal programming someday, to make them more empathetic and less threatening to people. But it's in its early stages yet."

Mina read through the list of attributes, nodding absently.

"Do you think this cuff would be handy if a person wanted a bot to act contrary to its internal programming? Say, an owner purchases a retail bot, and they want to override the nice disposition that comes standard on those guys. Maybe, occasionally, they want the retail bot to disagree with a customer, maybe when said customer is being a pain in the ass. Could that happen? If it's a brief interaction?"

Lee looked thoughtful. "Yeah, I guess it could. I don't think the nodes alone would be enough to fully adjust encoded behavior, however. It would only be enough for a momentary reaction. For example, if the owner of the retail bot linked a specific voice prompt to a specific sensory-node trigger—let's say they chose 'this is stupid' as the prompt—it would work. Whenever a customer said that phrase to a retail bot, the sensory node would act in tandem with a coded command, thus allowing the LiveBot to tell the customer to leave or give some other response that would be counterintuitive to what they're programmed to do." Lee shook his head. "But while this brief command would work based on that specific phrase, the customer would likely be agitated and begin to argue and say words that weren't in the command sequence. Then the LiveBot would go back to doing what it's programmed to do—bending over backward to make the customer happy. So in that situation, it would be ineffective and a waste of time. The owner would have to come up with hundreds of phrases, along with the specific sensory effects, to have a retail bot continue to operate counter to its internal coding."

Mina stood and walked toward the wall, hands on hips. She turned back to Lee. "But it might be enough for someone to give a bot a command to affix an encrypted drive onto some dog fur." She came back to her compucase and sat. "I like where this is going. I see a pattern here. I'm absolutely certain that whoever ordered those bots for Total Enhancement has a connection to upper government. How else could they have gotten their hands on a noded government cuff to give to their B workers?"

Lee was confused. "What's a B worker?"

Mina swiped her hand in the air. "I'm just rotating gears here. I mean, B workers could be what they call the bots, and they're supposed to take a break, maybe that's when they do the encrypting. Or switch up cuffs." Mina made another impatient gesture. "Never mind. Those details aren't important. What's important is, I believe someone at the pet center is using these bots, coupled with a handy sensory cue, to place encryptions on these dogs. Now I just have to find out who it is and prove it. They're likely using a different bot every day, possibly with a different prompt, to make sure that the sensory nodes stay in working order. Without them, these bots would likely not defy their internal programming." Mina chewed her bottom lip. "Possibly because these bots are being ordered to do something that might be considered harmful to the animal, even if it was just for a moment. Bots are hardwired not to cause harm to anyone or anything." Mina pondered further. "If bots try to go against their internal programming, they experience full-system failure, right? That would be costly. And come to think of it, Ruth told me on my first day that some of the previous bots hadn't known their own strength and had hurt a few animals. I bet that's not what happened at all. I bet they were trying to get these bots to do something they weren't programmed to do, and some of them shorted out. That would make more sense." Mina narrowed her gaze on the glittery sprawl of the city below her window, thinking. "I see it now. It's coming together."

"I love watching you work." Lee had uttered the words almost imploringly and then looked scandalized that he'd spoken them out loud. The blush started low, but quickly reached his hairline as his owly eyes, rimmed in their long, dark lashes, blinked a few times.

Mina spoke quickly, diffusing the awkwardness before it could grow. "My way is no different than how any agent works. We use our brains to connect the dots, or in this case the bots." She snorted. "You provided a big dot with the cuff. I'll pay more attention to government tech from now on. If I'd been in the know, I would've recognized it from the start." Mina hunched over her case. "Now let's get to work. I want to figure out who ordered these bots and where they came from."

"Yes, ma'am."

Mina grinned. All Lee needed was a Southern twang.

Chapter 16

"WE'RE CLOSE." MINA ordered, "Go back two clicks. Enter an X instead of a C." She stood a meter away from the wall. They were an hour and a half in. "Veronica, enlarge lower quadrant by eighty percent." That was the area that was giving them the most trouble. Mina leaned forward, peering at the code, watching as Lee changed the letters from his position on the floor next to her.

"You're right," Lee said. "That's the second time you've been right." He angled his head up, hair flopping over his forehead. "Are you sure you aren't a hacker?"

"Well, I'm no Level XIII, but I know my way around code. When I was a kid, I had fun with it. Spent time breaking into low-level stuff like most kids do. It was a point of pride to crack and hack." She circled her finger in the air around the data point. "The reason we're hitting a wall with this is that this language is old. This is from my parents' era and hasn't been updated, likely on purpose.

Whoever set the blocks figured the slick new hacks wouldn't know how to access old language." She smirked down at Lee. "It seems they'd be right. Xs used to be Cs, but only if the line starts with a two-one-one combo."

"Yeah, yeah, I know. But that line also ends with a hyphen star. So that means it reverts back."

"Not always. Look here. At the midpoint, there's a capital letter—"

Veronica's smooth British lilt announced, "Incoming vid chat request from Vincent Kramer. Do you wish to accept?"

"What? No! I mean, wait!" Mina was caught completely off guard. "Veronica, hold for a second. Don't answer until I say so." Mina tugged Lee up by the shoulder, grabbing a fistful of his shirt and yanking him off the floor. The poor kid scampered up as fast as he could, his compucase almost tumbling out of his lap. "Move, move. I need you out of camera range. Head down that hallway, past the utility door. You should be in the clear there. Don't make a peep. I have to take this call."

As Lee scooted down the hallway, Mina turned Eggie on. "Veronica, accept the chat. Video at thirty percent on-screen, twenty percent camera." She didn't feel the need for a gigantic view of Vincent Kramer and was letting him see only twenty percent of the area around her. The cameras were triangulated and motion sensitive, so they would track her as long as she didn't make any sudden movements.

As Vince popped onto the screen, she casually glanced over her shoulder, the most casual stance she could think of on short notice. "Oh, hi. You caught me in the middle of fighting with my meal printer. Sorry to keep you waiting. This thing doesn't work right." She gave the Magnito a firm slap, which seemed to reverberate a little too loudly.

Eggie responded with, "Order received. Printing the works."

"*Now* you're choosing to listen to me?" Mina feigned a soft chuckle, sidling up to the counter, resting her hip against the cool granite. "Dumb machine." She swished a wrist. "I'm pretty sure it's broken." She was coming across as weird, edging toward ridiculously ill at ease. Time to tone down the casual, which was tricky because her heart was beating a few beats too fast. She took a steadying breath.

Ease it down, Mina. It's just your old pal Vince.

Her old pal appeared as though he'd just stepped out of a dryer stall, temp at half. He was dressed in a pair of dark blue comfort pants with the waist tie dangling freely and a shirt of the same color hugging his chest to an unfair degree. His hair had been fingered back in a messy style. He looked tired, but happy.

Mina instantly regretted her thirty percent decision. One hundred would've been so much nicer. But she couldn't order it up now without being conspicuous. She wondered what percentage he had her at.

"What are 'the works'?" Vince asked with some humor.

Mina shot a wondering glance at Eggie. "I have no idea. I guess we'll see. The majority of the time, this thing doesn't comprehend a thing I say, but then manages to make me delicious things I had no idea I was craving."

She shrugged, offering a small giggle that she assumed a man like Vince Kramer was used to hearing from the ladies. Less weird, but not ideal. *Mina, get a hold of yourself.* "Unfortunately, I think I'm going to have to return it and get something that follows proper commands. Potato soup for breakfast is entertaining only up to a point."

"Potato soup...sounds interesting." Vince leaned forward, shoulders flexing, arms braced on his knees. "Listen, I called because I want to apologize to you in person. Your name somehow got leaked to the press, but I want you to know it didn't come from me." Mina knew exactly where it'd come from. "I'm not sure how they got hold of it, but as it stands, they don't have your surname. I was forced to confirm that I was, in fact, out with a woman named Wilhelmina, as I was being pressured by both American and French journalists. I acquiesced because I didn't want them to keep digging." He raked fingers through his slightly damp hair, leaving a new trail.

The man had no right to look as beautiful as he did. He looked better in lounge clothes than he had in full uniform at a lux restaurant. Mina was still distracted that this Vince was her Vince. It was strange and otherworldly.

"I also wanted to apologize for putting you in that position in the first place," he went on. "I should've given you fair warning from the start and let you make your own choices. When we talked before dinner that first night, I thought you knew about my FP position. But I think there was a part of me who wanted to impress you if you didn't already know." He shrugged, looking a little sheepish. "I have no better excuse than that. You have to know I idolized you back when we were kids. All those games we played, the ones you always won, were a blast." He chuckled. "We always had such a great time together. I think the little boy in me wanted to wow you after all these years."

"Well, you can tell that boy I was duly wowed." Mina tucked a piece of hair behind her ear, flashing a sunny smile, crossing her arms because she didn't know what else to do with them. Vince had thrown her off. Again. She had to get her head back in the game. She had a job to do. McAllister had given her a directive to develop a relationship with him, which she was going to do. But it would help if she could diffuse the constant fluttering in her stomach. "You've done very well for yourself. And I appreciate your face-to-face apology, but it's not necessary. I'm sure the press will leap off the scent as soon as the next big story breaks." Mina tried to frame the next part so that it sounded as if it'd just entered her brain. "Speaking of stories, I saw a screencast tonight about one of the big banks in France having a major problem. What's going on with that?"

Before Vince could respond, Eggie dinged.

Damn finicky food printer.

"First course finished. Please slide cover back and remove contents."

Crappy timing, Eggie. "Okay, okay, I'll do your bidding." Mina walked over and retrieved a bowl of delicious-smelling soup and a plate of what looked a lot like bacon-wrapped dates. A soup spoon and a small pronged fork lay next to the dishes.

"What did it make you?" Vince seemed genuinely curious.

Mina lifted the bowl up to her nose and took a sniff. "I think it's bisque. It might even be lobster bisque." She hoisted the bowl toward the screen so he could see. "And I'm pretty sure these are bacon-wrapped dates, which I adore. I'm not sure how this printer doesn't understand what I say, yet totally gets me." Then Mina remembered she didn't need any more food. For dinner, Eggie had made her pot roast when she'd ordered tacos. Fiddling with Eggie had been a ruse to get centered before she took Vince's call. Which hadn't worked nearly as well as she'd hoped. She set the dishes aside and addressed the manic printer. "Eggie, you can stop printing now."

Eggie replied stodgily, "Printing in progress. Please wait one moment."

Laughter rang out. "Eggie? It's just like you to name your meal printer after one of your favorite food groups. I think I'm going to have to get one of those. A mystery meal sounds extremely interesting."

Mina brought a spoonful of the bisque up to her lips, blowing on it before taking a small taste. "Yum. It *is* lobster. Honestly, if the food wasn't so good, I would've already thrown this thing out the window. And believe me, it's a long way down." Mina set the spoon to the side. She wasn't going to eat in front of him, but had to keep up the pretense that she'd been waiting for her dinner. "Anyway, so what were we talking about? Oh, yeah, the banking crisis in France. Do you know anything about that? It seems to be big news." Clunky. She *must* do better.

"'Crisis' is too big of a word," Vince replied easily. "More like internal strife."

"The cast I saw said all borrows from Colossal Bank are on hold while an investigation is pending." It was lucky Mina had caught that particular piece of news. She wouldn't have if she hadn't ordered on the craft screen during the ride home.

Vince shifted in his seat, his hands momentarily gripping the sides of the chair before he settled them on his lap, giving the indication he was relaxed when that clearly wasn't quite the case. "You know how the press gets. They've ramped up the drama considerably."

Interesting.

Mina lifted a bacon-wrapped date and took a bite. It was tricky tearing the bacon off cleanly without having it pull apart and snap like elastomer, but she managed. She needed a moment to think. "*Hmm.* I've never heard of a bank suspending its borrows. Without them, and the interest they bring in, they lose money like a rain catcher with a hole blasted in the side. It must be a little bigger than you're letting on. Certainly, the French Protectorate knows what's happening in its own country."

Vince's gaze narrowed, no more than a millimeter. If Mina hadn't been watching, she might've missed it. Then he was all smiles. He shrugged, crossing his legs, leaning back in his seat. "It doesn't really have much to do with the Protectorate. Banks are their own entities. Listen,

I actually don't have much more time to chat. I have an early morning meeting, and I'm cashed." Vince's time zone was six hours ahead of Mina's, so it was already early morning there. "What I wanted to do was apologize." He ran his fingers through his hair again, which was very distracting. Mina popped the rest of the canapé into her maw so she didn't make any moaning noises by mistake. "And, I guess, to see you again." He flashed her a grin that appeared sincere. "I'm not due back to the States for another couple months, but I could make it happen sooner, you know, if you wanted to get together."

He paused as Mina politely coughed into her fist. "Sorry." She thumped her chest. "A piece of bacon slipped down the wrong pipe."

"I didn't mean to put you on the spot." Vince grinned, this time with an edge that reminded her of a cat batting a toy. "You know, on second thought, it's probably better to go slow. How about a few more vid chats, and then we can discuss seeing one another again?"

Go slow? Were they going somewhere?

"That sounds like an excellent plan." A lame response, but once again Vince had completely knocked her off-balance. Flirting with a slimeball hacker had been an airglide compared to flirting with this formidable, good-looking man from her past. But even if they were going nowhere, Mina knew gathering information from the French Protectorate was necessary to combat crime and fraud in her own country. The big banks were all connected. "You know what?" Mina focused on being bright and cheery. "I'd love to chat again. I'm home at this time most evenings. How about I call you next time?"

"Sounds wonderful." He stood, the cameras on his side automatically tracking upward. Damn, he was tall. The lounge pants were stretched tightly across his thighs, giving the shirt hugging his chest a run for its currency. "I'll look forward to it."

So will I.

Would she? She guessed she would.

"Until next time, then." Mina waited until Vince canceled the program on his end, which was the polite thing to do, since he was the one who had initiated the call.

"Is it clear? Can I come back in now?" Lee called a few beats later.

Mina had temporarily forgotten all about Lee. "Yeah, come in."

"Was that..." Lee left the question hanging for a moment, his mouth opening and closing in a goofy fish gape. "Was that...Vincent Kramer?"

"Yep. We're childhood friends."

Lee looked incredulous as he leaned forward. "You're the Wilhelmina they're all talking about!"

"Yes. Wilhelmina is my birth name. But this is on a need-to-know basis, meaning that now that you know, you can forget it. I can't afford this getting out. We had to leak my first name so it wouldn't interfere with any of my aliases, and so far it's working."

"That's totally spec." His voice held awe. "I won't say anything. I didn't know your full name was Wilhelmina."

Because they hadn't shared much. "That's why it works." Mina faced her screen, scanning the data that had zapped back into place after Vince's call had disconnected. "You got in." She was duly impressed.

"Yep, that configuration you mentioned worked, and I added some padding so we can dig a bit deeper without getting flagged."

Behind them, Eggie announced, "Second course is finished. Please slide cover back and remove contents."

Mina walked over to the printer, grumbling, "Eggie, I'm begging you, please cancel printing. I don't need any more food." Inside sat a large plate of what looked to be some sort of elaborate pasta dish containing mounds of thick noodles dotted with a variety of plump shellfish. It smelled amazing, white wine mingled with something floral, or was that herbal? Whatever, it was an olfactory revelation. Mina carried it to the counter, along with a large fork, addressing Lee who had come over to inspect the dish. "I have no idea what this is, but I've already had my dinner. This thing won't listen to me. It keeps making me food. I'm going to have to get rid of it."

"That looks really good. I've never seen a Magnito in person. But I think I can help you with your problem." Lee grinned. "What language setting is it on?"

"What you mean? It's set to English, like everything else." The universal commerce language was English. That meant all technology was programmed to be consumed in English first. Mina had never had to adapt a language setting in her life.

"Magnitos are manufactured in Upper Scandinavia,

and those guys have a reputation for being...well, peculiar. The Magnito is speaking to you in English, that's true, but my guess is it's programmed to process one of the Scandinavian dialects first, English second. So it's picking up the tail end of your directions in English when it doesn't detect its given language. It's their little joke on the rest of the world. But there's an easy way to fix it."

Mina tossed her meal printer a dirty look. "Are you saying it's been messing with me on *purpose*? That's just all kinds of wrong."

"Like I said, it's their little joke. It's a well-known issue if you spend any time on siteboards. The techies think it's hilarious, especially when people like yourself complain that their meal printer isn't making them what they want."

"Fix it," Mina growled.

"It's coded to your voice. Simply ask it to process all orders in English."

"That's it?"

"Should be."

"Eggie, process all my orders in English. If you fail to do so, you're hitting the recycle heap."

Eggie replied, "Processing all orders in English. How may I serve you?"

"You can start by canceling any orders in the queue and shutting yourself down. It's the least you can do."

"Orders canceled, shutting down."

The machine went dark.

That had been ridiculously easy, and Mina felt silly,

but she was equally pissed that some Scandinavian manufacturer had been making her eat delicious pork chops and potato soup for breakfast. Mina handed the aromatic plate of pasta to Lee. "You deserve this. Thank you for solving my problem."

Lee took the dish. "I didn't do much, but this sure looks delicious."

"You just ensured happy eating for the foreseeable future. Investigating the Magnito was low on my to-do list. The mega rep who sold me this place should've mentioned something about the printer's fickleness for the English language. But maybe she didn't know. These are new on the market. Anyway, I owe you."

Lee took a gigantic bite of pasta, smacking his lips. Immediately, a moan formed on his lips. "Holy eats. This is payment enough. Completely flame."

Mina tugged out both stools so they could sit at the counter while they parsed the data Lee had just unblocked. She grabbed her compucase, her butt sinking down comfortably into the seat's perfect contour. Mina didn't think she'd ever get tired of this residence. An agent could request a new residence every five years. Her last place had been serviceable, but had been scheduled for a tear-down so a new, shiny mega could be built in its place. They were all the rage these days.

Lee sat next to her, gobbling up his feast in big energetic forkfuls.

Mina studied the information on the screen, popping a bacon-wrapped date into her mouth. Why not? "According to what you've uncovered, the bots were purchased by one Radcliffe, Conrad." The computer trail showed this man had purchased eight service bots, all the same lot, size, and shape. The shipment was delivered to Total Enhancement Pet Center. "I've heard that name, Conrad, before." Other than Ruth calling him Conny. "The purchase was made six months ago. Computer, list details of one Radcliffe, Conrad as pertaining to Total Enhancement Pet Center and any government jobs or affiliations."

Her supercomputer, linked to her wall, responded, "Working."

Setting down his fork and grabbing his own case, Lee started typing. "I'm going to check the business details of Total Enhancement. When it started and by whom."

Mina sat back, considering. "I have that data. It's registered to a woman named Gertrude Malestrum, age fifty-seven. It was incorporated in 2098. That makes it seven years old. But I haven't dug down deep on Gertrude. My guess is she has ties to Radcliffe. Why else would he purchase those bots for the company?"

A man was calling the shots, according to Ruth's conversation that Mina had overheard in the waste room. Her guess was Conrad Radcliffe—Ruth had called him Conny after all.

"That's strange," Lee commented after studying his screen. "These records should be public, but after a single layer, they're blocked." He glanced up, blinking. Kaylee was right. If he weren't so irritatingly juvenile, he might've been cute, in a little-brother-type way. But Quinn had him by a solid few points on both height and overall boy-next-doorness. "But lucky for us, it's blocked with the same olden-days coding. I should be able to hack it in three minutes by a simple transconfiguration subroutine."

"I'm giving you two and a half," Mina joked.

Her computer began populating the results she'd asked for, relaying in a crisp female sim, "There are forty-seven Conrad Radcliffes in the immediate area, 2,314 in the surrounding one hundred kilometers. Any Radcliffe surname connection to Total Enhancement Pet Center is unknown. Records are blocked."

"Working on it," Lee murmured.

Mina's computer continued, "There are two Conrad Radcliffes registered in a government capacity. The first one works as a clerk in the state health offices. The second is a judge in the Second Circuit, Fourth Division."

"That's how I know you," Mina murmured. "Judge Radcliffe. We've crossed paths before." Not all ops came out clean. Mina had been summoned to court a few times for private statements with various judges. "He's an ornery guy. Didn't strike me as a trafficker, but you never know with those types."

"Records are now hacked," Lee chimed. "Took me less than a minute."

Mina wasn't going to congratulate him on a job well done, even though she was secretly impressed. Cracking a hack in less than sixty seconds was a true gift.

"There's no listing of any Radcliffe affiliated with this business. Just Gertrude, like you said, and someone named Mason Bright. Looks like he became a co-owner last year, which is not highly unusual. When a business is failing, they bring in donors. Age listed as thirty-one. There's no other data. Strange." Lee tip-tapped on his keyboard.

"The business is robust," Mina stated. "No downward trends. Not sure why Gertrude would want to bring someone in. Computer, cross-check Bright, Mason with any LiveBot purchases made within the last year, delivery for Total Enhancement Pet Center. If found, further cross-check for government affiliation of any kind."

Her supercomputer replied quickly. Mina was surprised, because she figured the intel she'd requested would require a deeper search. "Data found. One LiveBot, female, purchased by Bright, Mason at the cost of three thousand world currency from The Bot Specialists. Delivered four months ago to Total Enhancement Pet Center. The same Bright, Mason who made this purchase is registered as a federal representative in the Northern District."

"What kind of bot did he purchase?" Mina already had a hunch.

"Instructor."

Chapter 17

"WHO'S A GOOD boy?" Mina crooned to a large brown-and-white-spotted dog with big, floppy ears. He had two hanks of slobber swinging from his droopy jowls. He gave her a slurp through the bars as she handed him a protein chew. She was at the tail end of her morning greeting. No animals had triggered the tracer, and Nancy, the old Lab, was gone. Nancy was now being monitored by CIU, and the middleman would be picked up soon, so that put her mind at ease somewhat. There would be an end to this trafficking ring even if she didn't solve which bot was directly responsible for applying the encryption. They had the names of the players, and that might be all she would get. Mina stood, clapping her hands to dust them off, heading toward the exit. "Thanks, Elsa," she told the bot as she passed through the doorway. She paused and asked, as if it was an afterthought, "Hey, is it your turn to wear the nice cuff today?"

The bot smiled amiably. "No. Today, Kari wears it."

"Good to know."

On Mina's agenda today was to find out what was behind those locked doors, and there was no better time than right now since she'd arrived forty-five minutes early and headed straight to the kennels with no uni, her satchel slung casually over a shoulder.

Mina crossed the room quickly, buzzing by all the empty stations, trying to keep her profile as low as she could. She was pushing it with possible discovery, but with only a day left to complete the mission, there was no other choice. Nobody here loved their job so much that they'd show up forty-five minutes early.

Mina had arrived at the same time as Babs, who had been unlocking the front doors and had been genuinely surprised to see her. Mina had managed to convince the bubbly attendant that she was just *so sad* she had only a few days left with the animals and wanted to spend some time with them. After all, she *just loved* animals, especially the mini pigs, which Babs heartily agreed were adorbs.

Reaching her mark, Mina paused in front of the last of the locked doors facing the work space, as far away as she could get without actually leaving the room. She glanced over her shoulder as she drew out a handheld NeuDAR system, which was disguised as a personal auditory journal. Elsa was busy doing something with the reptiles, and the other bots were nowhere to be seen. Must not be powered up yet.

The scanning system was no bigger than the pork chop Eggie had printed for her the other night, but it was heavy. The ability to see through objects using neutrons had been transformative, developed more than a century ago, but recently honed to exactness. Once opened, the "journal" broke into three panels, mimicking the popular devices people often carried around with them to document life events. It was loaded with mini and macro lenses, high vid capacity, and thought-synapse capabilities—meaning the journaler could attach a neural receiver "thought catcher" if they chose. The catcher was a head covering with sensors dotted all over it, which converted energy pulses into transcribable words. That particular tech was highly glitchy if you didn't have an implant, though, so the user had to clean it up later. Otherwise, anyone reading it would think the journaler had actually eaten titanium in a meadow filled with fungus, rather than eating treats at a mecca with friends. Too much work, not enough reward, in Mina's estimation. The only people she knew brave enough for a hardwire into their skull these days were ult-geeks, who walked around with a data plug sticking out of their foreheads like it was a badge of honor.

No, thanks. Honestly. No need for thought collection when vocal-to-text commands worked flawlessly.

Mina knelt on one knee. "Hurry up. Power on," she encouraged the machine while expanding the panels. "There you go." A neutrino laser was inset in the middle with receptacles on either side. The readout was on the main panel, graphics on both sides.

She activated the scan button and began to drag the tech in sweeping motions back and forth as she slowly stood. Images began to form immediately. The graphics were grainy on this handheld, but visible. The data would be airmelded to her supercomputer, as well as recorded on a chip, so she could go over it later. The best viewing would be done on her wall screen.

Mina raised the device over her head. Once she was certain she'd scanned the entire room, she squinted at the display. "What is that? That looks like…"

"Hey, whatcha doin'?" The voice sounded from behind her.

Mina spun, closing down the gadget. "Oh, hi! I'm just feeling a little sad I'm leaving and wanted something to remember this place by." Kelly, Mina's lunch partner, was walking toward her, giving her an inquisitive look. "I was recording a few thoughts and taking a few photos in my journal." She shook the tech in her hand. "This has been one of my favorite temp jobs of all time. I really hope I can come back someday." She slid the faux journal back into her satchel. "I'll be sorry when it's over."

Her sentimentality must've been on point, because Kelly's face eased into understanding. "I get it." She stopped in front of Mina, reaching out to rub Mina's arm in shared sympathy. "I love this place, too. Even though Ruth puts me on dye most of the time, the animals are such a stress reliever. I can't afford one of my own, so I get my fill here." Kelly gazed around, her eyes landing on the kennels across the room. "It's hard not having a permanent job. I hope you find something soon."

"Me, too." Mina began to walk toward the uni room. Kelly fell in step with her. "What are you doing here so early?" Most of the time, Kelly rushed in at the last minute.

The woman's face brightened, highlighting the small enhancements she'd applied today—cheek shadow and light lip cream in a conservative pale nude. "My son won an award for his music academia. He creates guitar and piano music flawlessly. He even knows how to play the real instruments. He has an ear for it, but he didn't get it from me." She chuckled. "The ceremony's at five. Ruth said if I came in early and did some cleanup work, like mucking out some of the kennels, she wouldn't dock me if I took off a little early. I'm sure she'll make me handle the lizards." She shivered. "I'm not a fan of the cold-blooded types. I saw you standing here, so I came over to say hi first."

"That's wonderful about your son. Music is not my forte either. You should be so proud. Glad you came to say hi," Mina told her. They stopped near the uni room. "I'm going to get changed. I'll see you at meal break."

Kelly nodded, turning toward the kennels. "Okay. Wish me luck. I hope the bot has instructions to go easy on me."

Once inside the locker room, Mina enacted the second item on her agenda as she leaned against the industrial counter. "Hi," she said to the bot positioned there. This bot didn't have the same brown hair and features as the other LiveBots. Her hair was jet-black, her features sharper, intended to slightly intimidate, which was standard for instructor bots. "I don't think I've properly introduced myself. I'm Marjorie Wilcox, the temp worker." She stuck out her right hand.

The bot mimicked her movements, extending her own hand, replying, "Hello, I'm Diana."

Mina brushed her finger lightly over the bot's shirtsleeve, revealing a black-banded cuff. She wasn't surprised to see it, given what she'd uncovered so far, but that told her there were two fancy cuffs in play. "I like your cuff. It looks high-tech."

The LiveBot gazed down at it like she'd just noticed she was wearing it. "It is a standard cuff. But thank you for commenting on it."

It was far from *standard.*

"So, you hang out with the other bots, right? I mean, you're in charge once all the humans go home?"

"Yes," Diana replied smoothly. "I am an instructor bot. Therefore, I'm programmed to organize, teach, and supervise others. Here, that applies to LiveBots instead of humans."

"Who was in charge before you arrived?" According to the data she and Lee uncovered last night, this bot had been here for four months, while the other bots had been here for six. The questions Mina was asking were likely a shot in the dark, as this instructor bot would have no memory of anything she hadn't experienced herself, unless she'd been specifically told.

"There was another bot in charge before I arrived. But a defect was discovered."

"What kind of a—"

At that moment, Ruth burst through the door, drawing up short when she spotted Mina chatting with Diana.

Mina eased away from the counter quickly, casually

waving, telling the bot, "Okay, I'll drop my uni off with you tomorrow." She smiled enough to show a good amount of white as she addressed Ruth. "Silly me, of course you guys are going to recycle the uni. I think I'm secretly hoping I get to come back. I mean, there's always a possibility another worker will take a vacation. You never know." Mina was careful not to formulate anything into a question the bot might try to answer. If not asked anything directly, Diana should stay quiet. But hard to know with an instructor bot. Mina hadn't met many of them.

Ruth's gaze narrowed to two slivers as she darted a quick look between the two of them. "What are you doing here so early?" she all but barked at Mina.

Mina made a show of glancing at her cuff. "It's not that early." *Anymore.* "I came in to see the animals, like I told you last night." Mina took a few steps toward her locker. "Anyway, I'm just going to go get dressed, then I'm going to give those dogs some yummy treats." Ruth had no idea Mina had already been on the floor, so she'd just loop through the kennels a second time so Ruth didn't get suspicious. "Thank you for your time," she said to Diana.

The bot replied, "You're welcome. Would you like me to answer—"

"No, that's okay. I have everything I need." Mina turned her back, avoiding any more conversation.

Mina took more time than necessary getting into her uni and heading back out. She went over in her mind what she thought she'd seen on the NeuDAR as she made her way toward the kennels. Elsa was still at the kennel door, but she let Mina through again with no questions asked.

Once Mina was done with her second greeting and had located Ruth handing out assignments for the day, she decided to head to the waste room. She needed some privacy to get a hold of McAllister.

Inside a stall, Mina engaged her cuff, choosing to type rather than use voice even though she was alone. Someone could walk in at any moment.

She typed quickly with two fingers on a holo keyboard:

NEUDAR SUCCESS. APPEARS TO BE PRINTERS OF SOME KIND.

Mina had immediately recognized the shape, along with the buttons and nozzles. Figuring out what they were programmed to do would be a harder task to decode from the images alone. If they were illegal, which was highly likely, their programming would be altered, likely for weapons printing, but nothing would look overtly conspicuous from the outside.

Mina didn't wait for McAllister to respond. Instead, she hurried back to the main workroom, seeking out Ruth for her daily assignment. As she got in line, she noticed the bots filing in from a door that led to the back of the building. Diana was in front, ushering them out. Mina had never seen her do that before.

Ruth barely gave her a second glance. "Bioblast. Station twenty-one." Mina was about to engage in some back-and-forth to try to wrangle herself a tidy-up station, but one look at Ruth's face and Mina changed her plans.

The woman not only appeared haggard, but she was ready to snap. Whatever was going on with those printers and shipments had her on edge. "You got an issue with your assignment?" the floor manager asked out of the side of her mouth.

"No. Bioblast is fine."

"I want you to do seventy-five today. If not, this can be your last day. I'm certain we can find someone better to do the job."

Mina was about to argue, but instead she met Ruth's heated stare head on.

Challenge accepted.

"Seventy-five. No problem."

Chapter 10

"THEY'RE DEFINITELY PRINTERS, but I can't make out any labeling. The NeuDAR isn't sensitive enough in this compact form to capture the finer details. We'd need a neutron generator as big as a barrel to get a precise look." Mina stood in front of her screen, absentmindedly rubbing together her sore hands. Not only had she managed to blast seventy-five animals, she'd done seventy-nine. It'd been an epic day.

Now Mina was at home examining the data she'd taken this morning. It was displayed on one side of her wall, McAllister on the other side, sitting at his desk at headquarters with his own copy in front of him.

"What do illegal printers have to do with sex trafficking and encryptions?" The question wasn't directed at her. He was thinking out loud.

Mina pondered the same thing.

She took a seat, still contemplating. "My guess is we're looking at two different crimes here. Ruth, and likely

Radcliffe, are involved in the printers. This guy Bright and his instructor bot are involved with the encryptions and trafficking."

"What about the other owner? Gertrude Malestrum? Where does she fit into this?"

"She's not involved as far as I can see, but we can't rule it out." Mina studied the images again. "That might be something the Sex Squad will have to determine when they dig deeper. Right now, we have a recently encrypted dog and two bots wearing highly specialized sensory-noded government cuffs." Mina had verified that there were two. "If both bots were purchased by the same man, I would have you call the FPIU squad leader and tell him this is our guy. But we have Mason Bright, new co-owner of Total Enhancement, purchasing one, and Judge Radcliffe buying eight others, with two government-issue cuffs in the mix. It doesn't add up. Are the two men working together? Maybe Radcliffe purchasing the bots was a nice coincidence for Bright? It took the pressure off a single bot performing all the tasks. So, then Bright buys an instructor bot to take care of delegation so he doesn't have to be on the scene. He gets his hands on two cuffs, gives Diana one and programs her to alternate giving the second one to other bots. That puts Radcliffe in the dark about what's going on because he's too busy smuggling illegal printers." That didn't feel exactly right. "Why do it that way? More could go wrong for Bright involving all these bots, because artificial intelligence can't lie when questioned, unless they are illegally altered." Mina stood, her brain switching gears. "Lee did a thorough lifecheck last night on all the players involved, and Radcliffe didn't come up connected anywhere near this business. Bots are expensive. Those eight would've set him back at least twenty thousand borrows. He wouldn't simply just give them away. We're missing something."

"But you're certain the manager, Ruth, is working with Radcliffe, and not Bright." McAllister made a sound, a murmur mixed with a sigh, his *working on it internally* mode. "If that's the case, Ruth's and Radcliffe's backgrounds should cross at some point. Let's compare them and see what we find. Without Ruth's DNA, it will be tougher to do a full lifecheck on her, but we can get a historical timeline based on her current employment."

Mina grinned, heading to her satchel, which she'd set on the lounger. "That won't be a problem. I managed to get some DNA off of her today in anticipation of a deeper dive. When she begrudgingly congratulated me for bioblasting so many animals today, I reached out to shake her hand. Then I causally settled another arm around her shoulder, surprising the hell out of her. I plucked a few strands of hair off her head as we parted. It was a highly uncomfortable encounter for both of us, but it was successful." Mina pulled out a vial containing three pieces of wiry auburn hair. It was illegal to snatch another person's DNA if you didn't have a badge. Hair was the least effective way to collect DNA, as the carbon elements rapidly disintegrated once the hair was removed from the scalp. For public sensors, the timeframe to enter hair into a receptacle was less than ten seconds from the time plucked to the time submitted, to avoid the potential for identity fraud. If it was longer than that, the sensor would deny you.

Mina's government helix recorder could accurately cull DNA from hair for up to two months. If it was a wig or implants, Mina would be out of luck. But it was worth a try.

"Good job," her boss told her. "Run it, and see what you get, then cross-check with Radcliffe. The judge's files should be public. If they're blocked, I'm sure you can hack them. If your hunch is right, there will be some connection between them."

"Will do. Once Lee started digging on Bright, he didn't get very far. His information is heavily blocked. If we dig, we're bound to set off alarms."

"Hold off on burrowing on him for now. I'm going to relay everything we have up to this point to Commander Ellison of the FPIU within the hour. They can assist on their end. Tomorrow is your last day, and we need to seal up as much as we can. We have to assume those printers are illegal. The conversation yesterday between Ruth and the mystery man indicated the merchandise would be moved tonight. I think it's a good idea to get eyes on that. A midnight surveil of the area is the plan. They won't act before then. The skies and the streets will be too crowded, and the pet center is located in a prime retail area. Do not engage, surveil only. Whatever you gather tonight should be enough to make an arrest. That floor manager isn't going anywhere, and neither is Judge Radcliffe. There is no flight risk. Figure out what they're hauling as best you can, and I'll inform the proper channels once you're finished."

"Got it."

"The Labrador was grounded as of fifteen twenty-one this evening and the encryption confiscated. By tomorrow, everyone involved will know the ring has been infiltrated. By this time tomorrow, the FPIU will have already taken Bright in for questioning and impounded the bots and the cuffs. It's very close to being locked down. Since time is of the essence, I'm sending both Kaylee and Lee to you tonight for the surveil."

Mina's brows arched. She wasn't going to refuse help. "Kaylee, too?" She tried not to sound too pitifully hopeful. She missed working with her best teammate.

"She finished her op today with the help of Adams." McAllister grinned. "That boy is proving to be well worth the trouble. I thought the prospect of working with your old partner would make you happy. Am I wrong?"

"You're not. I'm ecstatic."

"By the way, your next op is coming in now."

"You're being deliberately mysterious again. Is this standard procedure now?"

"It is. I'll expect a report tomorrow a.m. If anything of grave importance comes up tonight, contact me. I'll be waiting." He signed off.

Not even twenty seconds later, Veronica announced, "Incoming vid chat request from Kaylee Poston. Do you wish to accept?"

"Yes," Mina answered. "Visuals the same."

Kaylee popped up where McAllister had been. She was sitting in her favorite chair. "Looks like we're going to be working together tonight. Did McAllister fill you in?"

"Yes, just." Mina walked over to Eggie. The first thing she'd done when she arrived home from work, as always, was contact her director and give an oral report. Now it was time to eat. "I could use the help, even if it's just for a few hours. This op ends tomorrow. Eggie, power on." The Magnito sprang to life. "Print a BLT on sourdough with a cup of tomato soup. Provide appropriate utensils."

Eggie replied promptly, "Printing BLT on sourdough and tomato soup, single serving plus utensils."

"Impressive," Kaylee crooned. "You wrestled the beast and won. Makes a lady proud. I have a little tear to prove it." She gave a fake swipe.

"Actually, Lee fixed it. He said Magnitos are manufactured by a bunch of Nordic jokesters. It wasn't processing my orders in English."

"Lee, huh? Having a little tryst I should know about?" Kaylee tilted her head as a full-throated laugh tumbled out. It was a great sound, reminding Mina of wind chimes in a gale.

"Yeah, you caught us. He's my lover. We're super hot and heavy now." Mina rounded the island as she waited for her food, leaning back, crossing her arms.

Kaylee's mouth snapped shut, her eyes showing alarm. "Really?"

"Of course not!" Mina giggled. "McAllister sent him over to do a hack last night. I hardly thought it was a secret. I figured he'd squeal first thing this morning."

"Nope, the kid was nothing but professional. Didn't breathe a word. And seriously, without him, that bank bastard wouldn't be in a box today. Lee figured out a conversion in about ten minutes, and we were able to track the first wire transfer that asshole put through. That's all I needed. Guy's going to spin for a long time."

"That's great. I'm assuming McAllister gave you clearance on my classified?" She had to ask. It was protocol.

"Yep." Dag wandered into camera range, and Kaylee obligingly started petting him. "Those traffickers are going to burn. I can't believe with all the legal pleasure options we have in this world, kidnapping girls still exists. It makes me completely ragey."

"Agreed. It's rage-worthy. Surveillance for tonight, however, is for illegal printers just discovered, likely for weapons, but unknown. Likelihood of a connection to the trafficking ring is small, other than it happens to be going on in the pet enhancement center. Do you want in on the lifechecks, too? I'm going to do a little digging before midnight rolls around."

"Whatever you need. I can be there in thirty. Just need to take Dag out to stretch his legs first."

"Super. Deal with that good boy, and I'll see you soon." Dag gave an enthusiastic bark, and Kaylee laughed. "Transpo hub's on twenty. They'll ping me when you arrive. Floor three-twenty, unit three-two-eight."

"Got it. Kaylee, out."

Mina's pal disappeared, and Eggie beeped a second later. Mina happily went to get her precisely made meal.

"This place is hands down, off-the-charts lit up like the night sky right out this epic window." Kaylee had arrived and was examining every square centimeter of Mina's new residence. "I can't believe you scored this place. It's completely flash with a heavy side of lux."

"When your lease is up, put in a request. I'd love to have you here. It's flush."

Kaylee was dressed in her usual chic—a pair of black suction pants, a long tunic, and ankle-high point boots with an exaggerated dagger heel. The polar opposite of a puffboot. Kaylee had come carrying a large duffel of gadgets, along with her compucase containing the same supercomputer as Mina's, the covering mimicking green alligator skin with a high sheen. Style looked good on Kaylee.

"Yeah, we'll see," Kaylee replied. "As much as I'm complaining, I do love my residence, and Dag is happy there." She marched past Mina, who was grinding her dishes after her delicious meal, which had included a slice of strawberry cheesecake. Kaylee's heels made clacking noises as she proceeded to complete her thorough exploration of the residence. Mina watched her pal head down the hallway toward her bedroom. A moment later, there was a shriek. "Look at that soaker! Holy *shit.* The things you could do in there. It's actually big enough for three or four. Honestly, the ways in which pleasure could be achieved makes a girl blush."

"Since when have you ever blushed?" Mina met her coming out the door. They entered Mina's bedroom together.

"You're right, I don't blush. But maybe I would if I had a man to entertain me on this enormous platform bed." Kaylee crawled on top, making exaggerated motions, dramatically dropping onto her back, arms splayed, short hair fanning in a compact halo around her face. Then she aped making a snow angel, the covers bunching up nicely. Something Mina had done as a child.

"Somehow, I don't think that's how it works." Mina smirked. "Sex is sort of a different motion. A little more grindy, less flaily."

"Oh, believe me, I know. I was just enjoying myself on this impressive gel-foam masterpiece. Half my body is submerged. But if you'd like to see my sex moves, I'd be happy to demonstrate—"

Mina chuckled, holding up a hand. "Um, no. Really. I'm fine without seeing that."

"You sure? Because my technique is a solid A-plus-plus. If you arch your back a little like this, your ass goes down as your ti—"

"Stop," Mina begged, accompanied by a few short snorts. "I've got decent moves of my own, but this bed won't be seeing any action for the foreseeable future."

"Don't sell yourself short." Kaylee took a fistful of sheeting into her hand, bringing it in for a closer inspection, then rubbing it against her cheek. "Jeez, is this micro-modal? Feels like it. And the color is dyno, totally in fash right now. Who doesn't love gold? It's the color of the money of our dreams." She shot Mina a look, followed by a not-so-subtle wink as she purred, "Little ol' Vincie would feel right at home here." She patted the bed next to her. "I bet you two could work up quite a sweat tumbling around in these juicy micro-modal sheets—"

Mina stopped her right there. "I can assure you that's not anywhere near the cosmos of happening."

Kaylee climbed off the bed, reaching to brace her hand on Mina's forearm for support, careful not to catch a pointy heel on the fabric. "Oh, really? Has that boy vid chatted you yet?"

Avoidance was preferable, but Mina answered truthfully. "Yes. He called last night while Lee was over. But only to apologize for my name getting out to the press. It was no big deal."

"Sure. I believe that. But that streak of red creeping up your neck says otherwise. Did he say anything about chatting again soon? Or seeing you in person?"

Mina started for the living room. "Maybe he did. Maybe he didn't."

"See!" Kaylee stomped behind her, her steps becoming more animated as she accentuated her point. "I happen to know how these things work. You're just rusty. It's been, what, a year since you've seen anyone seriously? And, I mean, it's Vincent-*ovary-popping*-Kramer. Of course you're wondering why he would choose you. But it seems to me he's been harboring a current for you for quite a while, so it makes sense."

Mina spun around, offended. "You think I'm wondering why he would *choose me*? Like I'm not a worthy choice? I'm not wondering why... Well, not exactly. Maybe. But..." She trailed off. "Never mind! Honestly, I can assure you there's no current of anything between us." Maybe a small volt? In the two range? "We're a couple of adults who knew each other as kids, reminiscing about our childhood. That's it." Okay, if Mina were being honest, there'd been a teensy bit of electricity. The guy had worn formfitting lounge pants for their second interaction. But Mina wanted to keep that tidbit to herself for the time being. If there wasn't anything there, she didn't want to make it into something it wasn't.

Mina's cuff chimed before Kaylee could respond. She hit a button and said, "Clear Lee Adams for entry to three-twenty-eight after DNA swipe."

Kaylee gave Mina a pointed look from under the fringe of her perfectly aligned bangs. Even after a roll around on Mina's platform, Kaylee didn't have a hair out of place. "You and Vincent Kramer will be pleasure seeking by the end of next month. Mark my words."

"We will not."

"Oh, yes, you will."

"WE'RE OUT IN fifteen." It was eleven forty on the dot. Mina was finishing up packing a duffel in synth-silk, an extra-strong material made to withstand the weight of heavy equipment, with long-range lenses, amplifiers, mics, and everything else they would need.

Lee had joined her and Kaylee to do some lifechecks before the spying began. They'd researched the area around Total Enhancement and found that the business had one loading dock, with ample viewing from various positions. Surveilling should be a snap.

"This Radcliffe guy won't be sitting up on his high bench for long." Kaylee flung the bag she'd brought over her shoulder. "That judge is going to tumble down hard. I can't believe what we uncovered during that search. I almost feel sorry for your floor manager, but Ruth Donnelly has quite a history herself. I'm going to go with she deserves what's coming."

"Agreed." Even though Mina thought Ruth did deserve

what was coming, it didn't make her feel any better. Ruth hadn't had much of a choice. She either went along with the judge's plan or she went in a box. "The day she faced that bastard in court for petty misdemeanor, her life was sucked down the waste tubes. She hasn't been free of him since."

Ruth had been caught falsifying her identity. Her case had been seen by Judge Radcliffe six years ago. She had a checkered past, which included petty theft and a few delinquencies. Surprisingly, she'd been exonerated for the identity theft and had taken a job soon after at a custom-printed furniture store co-owned by one Conrad Radcliffe. She'd worked there for two and a half years, undoubtedly monitoring the transfer of illegal goods. Then she landed the managing job at Total Enhancement, perfect for more illegal deeds because it had more space and a better cover, based on Lee's quick schematic comparisons of the two businesses.

All of this was speculation until they got a confession. But it made sense.

They hadn't found much on Bright, even though they'd tried. Total Enhancement's owner, Gertrude Malestrum, had handed the reins of the company to him and had promptly retired to Boca Raton, Florida. After that, the trail had dried up. They couldn't even confirm she was still alive.

"Bright is going to be hard to pin down." Lee stood next to Mina as she stuffed the last few things into her bag. "He's kept himself well cloaked."

"Slimy bastard," Mina grunted. "When the circuits

fizzle on this, which he knows they will at some point, he wanted to make sure he stayed clear and undetected. But that instructor bot was a big mistake. It shows him as primary owner. And I'm fairly certain that bot hasn't been officially restricted, because she doesn't wear a government seal." It was illegal to restrict public sector bots' communication or wipe them clean without official approval. A sticker had to be placed in a prominent location, usually on the back of the neck. "So if I, or the Sex Squad, asks the instructor bot the right questions, she should relay what we need to know. That's why choosing a nonhuman to do this kind of work is going to backfire on Bright. He can't wipe her internal programming without triggering the feds. He can only use the sensory nodes to manipulate certain, short-term behavior. He should've found an air breather to do his dirty work. Now that Babble is highly regulated, he might've gotten away with it."

Babble was a truth serum that had been used for decades. Only recently, since a growing number of people had taken their own lives after being injected, had massive reforms hit. Babble wasn't choosy. It uncovered every memory you had. If you were found to have broken any laws, no matter how long ago, you could be tried for them. New laws restricted its use to only suspects of high crimes, like murder.

Kaylee sat on a stool, waiting for Mina to finish packing. "Once the illegal printers are out of the shop, we should take a look-see inside. If this instructor bot is powered up, you can interview her right then and there."

"Breaking and entering without a right to search would throw a titanium rod into this plan. We have to step carefully." Mina zipped up the duffel. "Sex trafficking is a grade A crime. We don't jeopardize anything. We stick to the legal codes so nothing slips by."

"I'm not saying we should risk the op," Kaylee argued. "I'm saying that all you need to do to close this case is to get a recording from that bot, and we can acquire it tonight. We can unlock with a disengager and summon the bot to us. It would be easy enough to claim the door was unlocked when we arrived, especially since we'll have vid evidence of the transferring of illegal goods. Weapons printers are a class C-1 felony, minimum fifteen years, and once they're located on the premises, we get instant rights to search and seize."

"I'm aware of the laws." Mina wore all black, but had opted not to go in full disguise, since they were going to stay out of sight. She hoisted the heavy satchel over her shoulder. "Let's see what comes out of that pet center first. If we can't identify the merch, we hold off. If it looks like everyone's working together, we go in. But we decide nothing until we have a visual."

"Deal." Kaylee followed Mina to the door, Lee close behind. The young agent hadn't brought any equipment other than his compucase, as he hadn't been assigned any. Toys came with rank. But the kid had done most of the digging on the lifechecks over the last few hours. He'd been an asset. There was no denying it. Much to Mina's chagrin.

Mina shut the door behind her and ordered,

"Veronica, lock up, level four. Fingerprint required for reentry." Mina always shored up her residence. Her unit had several tactical upgrades, including her door handle smudger, which captured any fingerprint applied to its surface, whether the visitor wanted it taken or not.

A craft was waiting for them on twenty. Once they were inside, it took them less than four minutes to reach their destination. Since this was a last-minute op, they were going in cold, more so than Mina would've preferred. It wasn't optimal, but it was certainly workable.

The craft set them down two blocks north of their destination in one of the only public lots in the entire city. Print It was a household retailer that could print anything you wanted in dozens of styles, from art frames to lampshades, towels to vases. You could even bring in your own designs. There weren't many places that could accommodate custom orders, and because of that, Print It had become the world's largest home store, with a huge landing lot for just about every type of vehicle on the planet. Land was at a premium. The cost of securing so much of it was mind-boggling.

Access lanes for crafts and pedestrians ran between all the buildings and were still crowded, even at this time of night. People conveyors whisked eager shoppers uninterrupted for blocks at a time on land. Airchairs, hoverboards, jetties, and anything else that was deemed legal single-passenger transpo ran three meters above it, occupying four interior lanes, two heading in one direction, two in the other. Hoverbuses held the airspace six meters and above that and had docking stations every six blocks. Their vertical takeoffs had a three-story height minimum and didn't impede human traffic or personal airspace below. Private crafts flew higher and were restricted on where they could take off and land.

All in all, people got where they needed to go, and everyone was happy. This was how the majority of the people moved around the city. If you were going farther, you used the mag-lev trains below or took private transpo.

"Follow me," Mina ordered as they cut through the lot. At this time of night, almost closing time for Print It, most of the occupied spaces had cleared out. Trying not to look overly conspicuous, the three of them ducked down a small passageway between two large buildings. These tight lanes allowed only for commercial delivery and disposal craft. A fair amount of buildings still lacked fully integrated recycling systems, so city disposal units came to collect, usually in the early morning hours, after the pedestrian traffic died down. Five years from now, in 2110, every building and residence would be required to be compliant with a closed system, and there would be no need for pickups. Since space was at a premium, Mina had no doubt these small lanes would be turned into retail space soon enough.

"We should have eyes on the back of Total Enhancement in half a block." Kaylee had donned her macro-lenses.

"If the landing area behind Beautification Benefits isn't freed up," Mina said, "we'll need to search elsewhere." Beautification Benefits shuttered around midnight, but everyone who used the spa might not be cleared out, including staff. "The treat kiosk might be another option, but we won't have much room for cover. It closed at ten, so it should be empty."

As they eased closer, sliding between two more buildings, Total Enhancement came into view. "Looks like there's a few spots open at Beautification Benefits." Lee gestured upward. That location would give them the best bird's-eye view. A railing ran around the landing area, with ample slots for viewing. They just had to find a way up.

"Can you smell that?" Kaylee took in a deep breath. "You didn't tell me this kiosk specializes in maple sweets. I'm dying. I haven't had a fix in too long. We should've come earlier."

Mina chuckled. "And what? Tried to appear normal in our black recon outfits and synth-silk duffels filled with espionage equipment while we ordered some pancakes or a doughnut? You'll have to get your fix tomorrow."

"I'm never over this way," Kaylee groused. "That kiosk is the only one in the city that makes decent maple-flavored treats. I had to buy real maple syrup the other day, and it set me back a hundred borrows. My account can't keep taking that kind of hit."

"Sounds like you need to get that sweet tooth checked." Mina stopped, glancing up. Their proposed spying place was cantilevered a meter over the flight lane they were standing in. "We should've just had the craft land here and been done with it. Then we'd already be up there."

"It's coded parking," Lee said. "No appointment, no landing."

"The roof next to it is fairly close. We can jetty-leap, no problem." Kaylee started for the building next door.

"Let's do a loop first and see if this is the best location," Mina countered. "I want to drop a mic in the back at Total." As of right now, all was quiet behind the pet center. Mina had discovered that pet owners could drop off animals until ten.

As they began to assess the area, a craft entered the lane behind them. Without communicating, each of them blended into the scenery. Mina faded behind a bush, Kaylee around the corner of the building, Lee behind some signage.

The craft was industrial, recognizable by its steel-gray color and thick, banded yellow stripe. It flew high enough not to be a danger to pedestrians, and it was cruising fast. It passed overhead, continuing down the block, where it stopped behind a nondescript building.

Once it was out of sight, the three of them completed the search for the best surveillance spot. After their assessment, they decided Beautification Benefits was it and that climbing to the roof next door, then leaping onto the landing balcony was the best way to get there.

Luckily, the building next door had a fire stair attached to the outside, which was mandatory for any building that housed activities for children. Other buildings had other safety measures, like inflatable slides and compact jetties, that adults were expected to know how to use.

"Stairway is locked," Lee announced. "I can hack the code. As kids, we spent a lot of time on roofs when we were supposed to be studying."

"We all did," Kaylee grunted. "I broke my first stair gate at age seven. Just hurry up and get it done." Kaylee's impatience was evident.

"Not all rosy in the land of Lee," Mina muttered to her pal while the rookie got down to hacking.

"He's just so...inexperienced," Kaylee whispered back. "I mean, he's a total genius and kind of cute with all that hair tumbling into his eyes, but good *Lord*, he needs to keep his mouth shut. I haven't talked that much since I was eleven."

"I told you." Mina chuckled.

"Done," Lee announced as he stood, the gate swinging clear.

They made their way up, careful to shut the latch behind them so it wouldn't trigger any alarms. Once they were on the roof, the landing pad next door was less than two meters. "I'll go first. Once I'm over, toss my bag."

Mina pulled out her mini jetty and strapped the small contraption around her shoulders. Then she grabbed her lamella gloves to ensure a good grip. The small jetty wasn't robust enough to keep her in the air for long, like a full jet pack could, but if she fell, it would slow her descent enough to provide a soft landing.

Mina engaged the motor and walked to the edge. She tilted the turbines outward so she could use the airstream to help propel her and leaped. She snagged the railing on the next building seconds later and hoisted herself over.

Kaylee tossed Mina her bag.

Her fellow agent and pal already had her jetty on. She

tossed Mina her duffel almost at the same time as she leaped. Once over, Kaylee and Mina both glanced back at Lee, who stood there with his compucase, staring at them like this had all happened too quickly for him to comprehend.

"Shit," Kaylee said. "He should've jumped before me."

Both Mina and Kaylee were fiercely independent, used to pulling their own weight and making quick decisions, thinking identically most of the time.

It was clear Lee hadn't yet honed those skills.

"That's okay," Lee stammered. "I can just...jump. I don't need any help. If I'd known we were going to do this, I...I would've brought my hoverboard. I don't have a mini jetty, but my hover would've worked..." He trailed off.

Mina already had her straps undone. She tossed Lee her jetty, causing him to almost drop his compucase as he fumbled to grasp the unit before it disappeared between the gap and crashed to the ground.

"Lob us your case," Mina ordered. "Strap the jetty on and get over here. We're at the point of being too conspicuous as it is."

"Sure. Yes, sorry." Lee tossed his case. It arched a little wildly, but Kaylee managed to snatch it before it bashed into the side of the building.

Lee looked awkward and unsure as he donned the jetty. Mina crossed her arms. "Lee, you can do this. Take a deep breath. Use the thrust the jetty produces to propel you. Making a jump like this is a printed piece of cake. Something cadets learn on the first day. Don't look down, and you'll be fine."

"Ten borrows he does a face-plant into the building," Kaylee muttered.

"If anything, he misses the distance and goes straight down. We don't want that. He won't have the wherewithal to reach back and redirect his turbines to cush his landing, and instead of completing our surveillance, we'll have to call in a medi-unit." Mina took a step back to clear the way. "As soon as you make the jump," she called, "you're going to put in a requisition for some real gear. McAllister can't expect you to come into the field with nothing. Just think of all the cool stuff you're going to get."

His face brightened, the jetty wound up and ready. "Do you think I'll get one of these?"

"Absolutely. But you have to get over here first."

The kid jumped.

Both Mina and Kaylee leaned over the railing simultaneously, grabbing on to his wrists as he came in short, just as Mina predicted, and hauled him up. Lee was out of breath. "Thanks. I guess I need some practice."

"You mean your friend hasn't written a VR program for this yet?" Mina teased. "Sitting in a chair hacking all day makes you weak. I'm going to get you in touch with my trainer, Mack. He's an animal, and he'll get you ready for outside ops, but it's going to take work on your part."

Lee nodded vigorously, huffing and puffing as he unstrapped the jetty. "I'll do it. I want to be a good agent."

"A good agent unpacks the bags and sets up the tech." Kaylee gestured behind her. "We need the heat screen up a-sap. They could arrive any minute, and anyone with half a brain and a pair of chromes can pick up body heat." When Lee simply gave Kaylee an owlish blink, she ordered, "Get on with it."

"Yes, ma'am."

Chapter 20

IT WAS TWO thirty. Mina was giving up hope anything was going down tonight. Radcliffe could've changed his mind. The three of them were still crammed behind a compact, one-way heat screen.

"We're going to have to start a sleep rotation soon." Kaylee yawned. "What time are you going to call it? Crooks usually hit between one and three. Bad guys are a predictable bunch."

"Let's give it another hour," Mina replied.

"I think I hear something." Lee had his back against the side of the building, his compucase out. The kid hadn't stopped working since they'd settled.

The three of them turned toward the sound of incoming props. The craft hovered lower than usual, creeping along. Anyone piloting wouldn't make them at this vantage point, as their current surveillance area was higher than the flight path. They watched as the large drone turned toward the back of Total Enhancement, moving at airchair speed. Whoever was at the helm was taking their sweet time, trying not to draw attention.

"We got you now, assholes," Kaylee murmured, coming up onto her knees, fatigue replaced by a hefty dose of ass-kicking adrenaline.

Mina donned her macros and pushed a sensor into her right ear. She'd amplified the area around the loading dock, so everything would be recorded. The props were loud as the craft slipped toward its destination, but the amp was filtered for human voices, so the volume wasn't too bad.

"That could be a sanitation craft," Lee commented. "It's the right size and the right colors."

"No sanitation craft I've ever seen moves that slowly. Workers want to get in and get out," Mina said. "But I have to hand it to them, using a city utility craft is smart. It's large and unassuming. I bet that's how they've gone undetected all this time. Nobody notices a craft that's expected to be there."

City and governmental drones, for the most part, couldn't be purchased by the general public. In the rare instances they were sold, the owner was required to repaint them and remove all government markings.

"Kaylee, are you recording visuals?"

"Yes, vid documentation is in process and confirmed."

"Lee, start running the ID numbers on that craft. I want to know exactly where it came from."

"On it."

"Let's see how this operation begins," Mina said. "I may have to go in for a closer look. Identifying all the players involved will be mandatory for arrests later. We're not letting anything slip."

"The accordion doors are rising on the back of the building," Kaylee informed them. "Nobody's emerged from the craft, at least that I can see from this angle. The back end of the craft isn't open yet."

Mina shifted her position so she could get a better look, peering around the screen. "They're waiting for something or someone." Mina eased all the way out, needing a better vantage point, as the craft hadn't parked in the middle of the docking station as hoped, but rather unhelpfully to one side. The darkness should be enough to keep her cloaked. However, if anyone down there had infrared chromes, it'd be another story. But Mina didn't think so. The attention of everyone involved seemed to be focused on the back of the pet enhancement center.

Movement came from inside the pet center, and the back end of the craft began to rise. Two figures exited from the front—one male, one female. From Mina's location, she couldn't get a good look into the building and didn't have a definitive lock on the people. Nobody had spoken yet.

She had to get closer.

"The female suspect who exited the craft is not Ruth Donnelly. Too tall, too skinny," Mina commented, plugging another sensor into her left ear. "I'm heading in. I need to get a confirmed visual. We communicate via mic as needed from here on out."

"I'm on the prowl, too." Kaylee plugged in her own sensor and placed a mic on her lapel. "I want to make sure we get full vid coverage. I'll pretend the drone parked behind us is mine. If they detect a body up here, they'll assume it's a worker heading home for the night."

Mina nodded. "Lee, stay behind the screen. Stick this in your canal and secure your mic." Before Lee could respond, Mina had her jetty out, along with her gem laser, which she hooked to her waist. She switched the turbine on the jetty so it faced down. She was going to have to max out the rpms to ensure she didn't break a leg, but the large craft at the pet center was still idling, so the prop wash should mask the noise of the motor.

Mina leaped over the railing, bending her knees as she hit the ground. It was a hard landing, knocking most of the breath out of her, but she was up and moving quickly. As she rushed forward, she unstrapped the harness and lobbed it under one of the ornamental shrubs dotted like buoys of green throughout the city. Time was not in her favor. Whatever they had in there, they were going to load quickly and move out.

As she eased closer, the props on the craft began to power down, and she began to pick up a conversation.

"Just get it done," a familiar voice ordered, causing Mina to lose her footing. Luckily, she caught herself. The voice was young, and it'd come out short and clipped. Nothing like how the woman had spoken on the mornings she'd greeted Mina. "This is too risky. Why did we have to bring them here?"

Them?

"Damn," Mina muttered. "I missed it."

"What? What's going on?" Kaylee hissed in her ear.

"The female is Babs. Works the front desk. Nothing in my gut told me she was involved. Huge mistake. She's indicating people, not product." Mina crept closer, staying low. "Lee, drop what you're doing. I don't know her surname, but her first name is unique, Babbettlyn." Mina spelled it. "Age range between twenty-three and twenty-six. I want to see if she has links to Radcliffe, Bright, or Donnelly. Give me her connections."

"I'm getting interior visuals, but they're partially blocked by the craft," Kaylee said. "They are moving something. It's girls. Young ones. They're blindfolded. They're moving girls!"

"This op just took on an entirely different mission." Mina's voice was as cold as graphene as she drew her gem. "Lee, contact McAllister on your cuff, mic off, and fill him in on what's going on. The FPIU needs to be on scene. Kaylee—"

"I'm already on my way. Nobody leaves until we have those innocents under our protection."

Sometimes, things went off script in a case. This was one of those times.

"We need a body count before we move," Mina said. "I've got eyes on Babs and a male approximately thirty to thirty-five, too young to be Radcliffe. This could be Bright or just a helper. They don't seem alarmed. They're moving slowly. No nervous twitches, no looking over their shoulder. They think they're in the clear."

A male voice sounded in Mina's ear. "We had no other choice but to bring them here." Irritation and a fair amount of disdain rang through his words. "The feds are on to us. They picked up Benny this afternoon. I knew that asshole was going to get us caught. Your low-life brother is completely incompetent. We should've hired a professional like I told you."

"He *is* a professional," Babs answered crisply. "You're the incompetent one. You were supposed to be this incredible mastermind, able to turn borrows into currency like magic. But here we are, schlepping product around in the middle of the night."

Product.

Mina fumed. It was an insult to humanity, and Babs was going down as hard as Mina could feasibly take her. She would make it sting.

"Radcliffe owes me," the male said. Mina felt he had to be Mason Bright, based on Babs' familiarity and that she'd called him a mastermind. "I've given him the run of the shop. These girls go out with the stupid printers he's peddling and disappear forever. Nobody's the wiser. No bodies, no crime."

Yeah, that might be true if we didn't have your confession on audio and vid. You're as good as boxed.

Mina eased around the corner, placing her within two meters of the craft on the pilot side. It was still dark enough to keep a decent cover, and nobody was looking for an agent lurking in the shadows.

Because no one was anticipating company, it proved beyond a doubt that Bright was no mastermind—he was barely competent. He'd just said the feds were on to them, and he still thought they were in the clear. He was the worst kind of idiot. The moment Ricky had known they were on to him, he'd run like his puffboots were on fire—and rightly so. And that still hadn't helped that sleazy jackoff.

"How long do we have to wait?" Babs whined. "I hate it here. The bots give me the creeps, and the animals are irritating. You promised we'd be on a tropical island by now. You said all the money we made from this would put us beyond borrows. It's just one delay after another. I could've netted more on *Win Big*!"

"Radcliffe should be here in fifteen. He sent his lackey to meet us. She should be inside already."

Cries of distress from the girls as they were jostled sent Mina's hackles all the way up. Way, way up. There were at least four girls, by the sounds of it, and their fear was palpable. "Lee," Mina murmured into her mic at the lowest possible decibels. "Tell McAllister to contact the local PPF. I want interception on the craft that's due here in fifteen. Radcliffe never makes it. The printers are inside. So is Ruth, but our only priority is the girls."

A new voice entered the mix in Mina's left ear. "You make me sick." Ruth's voice dripped with disgust, the kind Mina knew she was capable of delivering but hadn't experienced firsthand. "I'm being forced to help you, but I hope you rot in the depths of Hades. This is despicable! These are innocent human beings." Surprisingly, newfound respect blossomed for Ruth. "How dare you bring them here like this!"

"Stick a rod in it, you slimy piece of rotted kelp," Babs snarled. Mina imagined Babs' finger boring into Ruth's chest, a poke for each word she uttered, but she could only assume since she had no visual. "The only reason you're not decomposing in a box is because you're useful. Once you're not, back you go. If my uncle hadn't given you a break, you'd be calling the outskirts home by now. Get these girls out of my sight and wait for our mark. If you ever talk about this to *anyone*, I'll see that your entire family pays dearly for your indiscretion."

Uncle? This was turning out to be quite the family affair.

A big holographic map began to form in Mina's mind, with Babs at the center and her brother, uncle, and Bright all connected through her. Not suspecting the eager-eyed desk attendant had been a big mistake. Though Mina had never seen her and Ruth in the same room together. There would've been tension, and Mina hoped like hell she would've picked up on it.

Mina got her first clear view of Babs as the former receptionist marched to the end of the docking platform. She was dressed decidedly differently tonight in all black. Her syn pants molded to her legs like dye on fur. Her bright pink hair was slicked back into a high tail, her makeup dramatic. Her eyes rimmed in kohl, lips a vibrant and reflective red, her stilettos exceedingly tall, colored to match her hair. She was all about the details tonight.

It seemed this was the real Babs, and she'd been playing a role as the "innocent clerk" before. "Damn rookie mistake."

"What?" Lee asked in her ear.

"Nothing." Mina skirted to the other side of the craft.

"Looks like it's only these two and Ruth. No muscle. They think they're still hovering under the radar. I'm giving them two minutes to get the girls situated, then I'm going in."

"McAllister is sending FPIU reinforcements," Lee told her. "They're due to arrive in less than five."

Mina heard a ding of feedback ring in both ears.

"Oh," Lee added, "and he gives you free rein to take the suckers out. He said it a little more forcefully than that, but those girls and their safety are your top priority."

"Good to know we're all operating on the same readout." Mina glanced around, spotting Kaylee a few meters away. They both eased a hand up to their mic. But before Kaylee could speak, Mina whispered, "I get Babs." She could almost taste how good it would feel to bring that piece of biowaste down. "Your target is Bright. Ruth won't be an issue. The bots might be a problem. Set your laser to sear and go for the chest. They might be programmed to protect."

"I know how to take down a bot," Kaylee replied. "We go in like we did on the Brewer op. Stealthy, invisible, and hit them hard enough to make their heads spin."

"Shouldn't be difficult. These guys are focused elsewhere. We go on my count, so wait for it. Lee, we're logging out. Too much feedback this close to the amps and each other. I'll keep my mic open so you can hear us. Let's hope we finish this up before the FPIU arrives."

"Got it," Lee said. "Go get those assholes."

Mina kept her smile under wraps as she pocketed

both ear sensors. Kaylee did the same, deactivating her mic as they both slid closer to the back entrance.

Everyone had gone inside.

Mina hopped onto the small platform, level with the craft, positioning herself to one side of the open doorway, her gem at the ready. Kaylee moved to the other side.

Mina slashed an arm down, and they both ducked inside.

Chapter 21

No one was there. Mina hadn't been in this space before. It was a storage and staging area piled high with extra crates, supplies, and food printers for the animals. Mina nodded to her partner as she made her way toward a door she was confident led to the interior of the building where she'd spent the last four days tending to animals.

She eased the door open, listening.

Inside, less than half of the overhead lights were activated. Because of the recent ruckus, the animals that had been left overnight were barking and generally agitated. It provided nice cover. Mina slipped through the doorway, followed by Kaylee, both of their lasers up.

No one was in this space either.

That left several places Babs and her partner could've taken the girls: the uni room, the front lobby, the meal room, and where the illegal printers were stored. Mina's vote was with the printers, as the girls were supposed to go out with them.

Mina led Kaylee toward the kennels, ducking behind a large crate of protein chews. Her voice low, she said, "My guess is they took the girls into the rooms where the printers are being kept, down an adjacent hallway across this expanse. Since we don't have eyes on the bots, we need to do recon first. No surprises, nothing left to chance." A surprise could end this mission in all the wrong ways. "We head to the uni room first to see if the instructor bot is there. That's her usual hangout. The government cuff she's wearing could provoke her do something she's not programmed to do. She doesn't get anywhere near the innocents."

"Got it," Kaylee whispered back. "Once the FPIU shows, they won't tread lightly. They're going to storm in here full-on SWAT, and if they do, these dicks could use the girls as hostages or human shields." Or worse.

"Agreed. We get to them before the Sex Squad. Let's go." Mina led the way, racing up the aisle toward the uni room, where she set her ear to the door a second before pushing through, bracing her foot for Kaylee to slide in after her. The minute they entered, automated lights tripped.

Diana, sitting and likely on standby, brought her head up, eyes opening. "May I help you? You are five hours and twenty-one minutes early for your shift." She rose from the chair.

Kaylee had her laser up, ready to toast her circuit board. Mina stilled her partner with her hand. She had a hunch she wanted to confirm before they brought the bot down, though she'd never interrogated a bot before.

"Diana, what does your programming say about aiding an officer of the law?"

Without hesitation, the bot replied, "I am programmed to be of service to any officer or agent of the law."

Mina tapped her wrist. Her holo badge popped above her cuff. She held it out. "Scan this immediately. No time to waste."

The bot did as she was told. In less than two seconds, Diana clasped her hands in front of her, head bowed. "I am at your service, Agent Kane. Your ranking supersedes any primary within my system."

"Come around the corner," Mina directed. "Take off your cuff and hand it to Agent Poston." The bot unhooked the cuff from her wrist. Kaylee had her badge in holo as well and took the proffered tech. At least Mina knew the bot wouldn't be manipulated by a sensory node now. "Come with us. Follow my directions exactly."

They exited the uni room. The animals were still agitated, which meant they could keep their dialogue at a low volume for the time being. "Where are the other bots?"

"They are powered down in their holding area. None has been activated, or I would know."

"Where is the holding area?" Mina asked.

"In the back, near the loading dock." Mina hadn't noticed a door, but that didn't mean there wasn't one.

"If they get activated, can you shut them down remotely?" Mina asked as they crept toward the hallway that would lead them to the area where the printers were stored.

"No, I am not licensed as a remote coordinator. To power them on or off requires a physical switch."

"Is your primary Mason Bright?" Primaries set the license and programmable data for their bots. LiveBots were supposed to follow the primary's voice commands above all others, as long as the commands didn't counter their fail-safe programming.

Mina was that fail-safe at the moment.

"Yes," Diana replied.

"My authority supersedes anything he might command you to do?" No reason not to double-check.

"Yes."

"If I command you to restrain Mason Bright, will you comply?"

"Yes."

"That's good enough for me," Kaylee muttered from behind them. "And by the way, I'd pay good currency to see that."

They were close to the entrance to the main hallway when Diana stopped, her head making a tight, succinct turn to the right. The motion had been extremely nonhuman. "Two bots have just been activated."

"By whom?" Mina demanded. The person activating them had to be authorized, as the average layperson couldn't activate or deactivate a bot, or customers would be doing it in every retail space they could and making off with merchandise.

"The code is muted."

"Explain," Mina said impatiently. Bots didn't pick up on every human nuance.

"Whoever activated them has used a general code that is not person-specific."

"How many people are authorized to handle those bots?"

"Five," Diana answered.

Mina would bet her life that three out of those five authorized users were in this building. "How many ways are there to get to the bot holding room?"

"Two. You may enter through this area or through a single door accessed by a short hallway that leads to the main lobby."

Kaylee gave Mina a look. "We can't let these bots wander around activated," she said, nodding toward the back of the building. "How many did you say there were again?"

"Eight. And no, we can't." Mina gritted her teeth. They should have scoured the entire area before entering the building. "We can't risk the one wearing the cuff being in Bright's control. No harm to the girls. Let's go."

It took them less than twenty seconds to reach the door they'd originally come through. They slipped back into the loading area, and Mina inclined her head toward Diana. The bot, understanding her meaning, gestured to a nondescript wall surrounded by storage bins and boxes. As Mina moved closer, she noticed the seamlessly inset door.

Her gem was up, both hands steady on the grip. Mina motioned for Diana to move ahead, knowing a security bypass would be required to get inside. As Diana reached the door, Mina whispered, "Open it quickly, then step aside."

Diana did what she was told as Mina met Kaylee's gaze.

Kaylee gave her a firm nod. "Chest-high."

"Chest-high on three."

The door zipped open, and Diana stepped back.

Mina whispered, "Three."

They moved as a unit.

A surprised woman, her face surrounded by an unkempt tangle of auburn hair, stared back. Her shock was quickly replaced by anger. "What the hell are *you* doing here?" Ruth demanded, ignoring the lasers pointed directly at her heart.

Mina didn't answer, doing a necessary sweep of the room, making tracks to the far side. No one else was here, and the door on the other side was sealed.

Three bots were awake and stared at Mina without speaking. She lowered her weapon to knee level. She wasn't taking chances as she patiently asked Ruth, "The better question is why are you here? Have anything pressing to share with us, Ruth Donnelly?"

"I don't answer to you—"

Mina held her wrist aloft. Her holo badge gleamed like a muted star in the dim lighting. "One of these bots is wearing a government cuff that can cause it to do something contrary to its programming. We need to remedy that situation immediately."

Kaylee was already ordering the powered-up bots to show her their wrists.

Over her shoulder, Mina ordered, "Diana, come in here."

For the first time, Ruth showed fear. "What's going on? I'm just... I'm just here doing maintenance. I haven't done anything wrong. I—"

"Stick it in the recycler," Mina snapped. "We know exactly why you're here, Ruth Patricia Donnelly, formerly Renner, of Saskatchewan, colony of the Canadian Republic, immigrated to the US at the age of five in 2066, busted repeatedly for petty crimes since the summer of '94. We know all about you, and I know who's back there." Mina jutted her chin toward the interior of the pet center. "This can go two ways. You can cooperate, and I'll inform the feds you're only involved in the transfer of illegal goods. Or you can fight and go down hard, face first, with lots of ugly, and spend a lot more time in a box than you ever imagined. Your choice." Mina set her jaw, almost daring her beleaguered manager to pick the second option. "Kaylee, find the other cuff. Diana, activate the remaining bots." It seemed Ruth was in no shape to do it now.

"How do you know all this?" Ruth asked lamely, her shoulders sagging. In about sixty seconds, Ruth Patricia Renner Donnelly had aged about ten years, her face going slack, her eyes dimming, hands shaking.

"I know because I'm a government agent. I was sent here to figure out who was attaching encrypted devices to pet fur for a large, high-level trafficking ring. I stumbled onto your side printer ring with Radcliffe. Illegal printers aren't my priority. Getting those girls out is. If you cooperate, things will go much better for you. Accessory to the transfer of illegal goods is five to ten. Accessory to sex trafficking is twenty-five to life. As I said, it's your choice, but you have to choose now."

"Trafficking?" Ruth's voice was hollow. Her hands came shakily up to the sides of her face, rubbing absently at her temples. "I had no idea this was going on. I swear to you. I only saw those girls for the first time tonight. It's repugnant. I...I..."

"Why were you activating the bots?" Mina asked, cutting her off. Ruth was no use to her if she continued to spiral down into shock. "Did Babs and Bright order you to gather the bots? What's their plan? I need answers, Ruth." Her former manager continued to shake. Mina moved, her expression disgusted. "If you want to help those girls, answer me. Do it quickly. Did they order you back here to gather the bots or not? Will they hurt those girls before they load them in with the printers?" For good measure, she shook Ruth's shoulder, raising her voice in command. "Answer me!"

"No. No! I don't know. I swear I don't know." Several of Ruth's emotions fought for control. "I told them my cuff beeped...and...and I had to go meet Radcliffe for the delivery. I didn't have a plan. It was a lie. I couldn't look at those girls one second longer. I thought...I thought if I came back here and turned on these bots, maybe we could...fight them...I don't know." Her voice trembled with misery. It was good to know Ruth had a soul rolling around in there someplace.

"A noble thought, but it wouldn't have worked," Mina told her, pacing over to the far door, settling an ear against it and wishing she'd set amps inside earlier.

Then she'd know exactly what was going on. "Those two would have no problem taking you out. You're collateral damage, Ruth. A pesky obstacle in their flight path. Once the FPIU arrives, things are going to get complicated. We need your help. We have to isolate Babs and Bright away from the girls. You can help us do it easily by summoning them." Mina glanced over at Kaylee. "Do you have the second cuff?"

Kaylee nodded. "Yes. We're ready to go. The bots have scanned my badge, and I'm the top kahuna."

Mina's cuff vibrated twice, sending up an amber star. The call was meant to be answered if she was able. She was. "Kane here," she said.

"We're outside, less than fifty meters from the back and front entrances," McAllister asserted. "I took lead. With my agents inside, I have priority. FPIU is unhappy, but holding. I didn't want to come in hot knowing all those bots are in there with orders that go against their programming. What's your status?"

"We're here with civilian Ruth Donnelly in a closed room with the bots. Both government cuffs have been confiscated. She's going to help us isolate Babs and Bright away from the girls." Mina directed a pointed look at Ruth, who was listening to her conversation with her director. "Once we have them down, I'll send up an alert."

"Agent Adams and Agent Poston are with you, correct?"

"Poston is, but not Agent Adams. Isn't he with you?"

"Negative. There's been no sign of or communication with Agent Adams since he first contacted me. Turn on your locators. I want full intel. We monitor every step from here on out."

Mina activated her homing button and nodded at Kaylee to do the same. Any hackers searching for a government signal would pick up on them, which was why they weren't activated at all times. No one had found a permanent block for locators yet, as every time they tried, a hacker looped a satellite feed and sold it to the highest bidder. But when innocents' lives were on the line, it was necessary to be transparent.

Mina didn't have time to worry about where Lee was. She was busy formulating a plan. "Did the PPF commandeer Radcliffe's craft?"

"Yes," McAllister asserted.

"Bring it quietly to the back. Park it next to the craft there and leave it idling, the agent piloting on standby. If Babs and Bright think everything is on schedule, all the better. I'm going to send Ruth to them with a message that their ride is here. We'll go from there. We need them separated from the girls before we take them down."

"The craft will be on its way in less than sixty seconds," McAllister replied. "Do you need assistance on the inside?"

"Negative," Mina replied, thinking of Babs' skintight outfit and shitty attitude. "Bright might be armed, but the woman isn't. We have all the bots in compliance. We have more than enough power in here to get the job done with less risk to the girls."

After a short pause, McAllister said, "I don't have to stress to you the importance of getting those vics freed without harm, even if the two assailants get away. We have their profiles. They won't get far."

"Copy that," Mina said. "I'll leave my comm open. If things get out of hand, send in backup."

Kaylee commented, "We have to move. Those two are for sure getting restless back there. We don't want restless."

Mina nodded. "I have a plan."

Chapter 22

MINA DIDN'T DWELL on how her plan rested squarely on the shoulders of her hanging-on-by-a-tattered-carbon-thread former manager. Mina had seen the advantage, and she'd taken it. It's what she'd been trained to do.

Babs and Bright weren't going to suspect Ruth of anything. Yet. All Ruth had to do was not fall apart and let them know their ride had arrived. Once the craft had puttered into view, Mina sent Ruth on her way.

"What odds are you giving this?" Kaylee whispered from her spot behind a stack of guinea pig food, her nose curling. "This smells horrific, by the way. They actually feed this stuff to living creatures?"

"I'm giving it one hundred if Ruth does her job, ninety-seven-point-five if she doesn't. We outnumber them in this building alone twelve to two," Mina told her partner behind her own stack of food, which must be for the reptiles. The stench of pond scum was overpowering.

"If animals weren't living, they wouldn't need this crap-ass food."

"I don't see why they just don't print on demand instead of storing it. Nobody stores food anymore."

"The printer would be running all day, every day. You saw how many animals they have in there. The turnover is amazing. This place must reap currency."

"*Hmm.* Ninety-seven-point-five is on the high side, dontcha think?" Kaylee said. "I'm not sure that manager of yours has it in her. Her knees were knocking pretty hard when she stumbled through that door."

"It doesn't matter. It's two of them against us and the bots. We win."

"I'd agree with you if those girls weren't in there. They can use them as pawns fairly—"

A clatter came from inside, followed by a sharp, high-pitched squeal and quiet weeping. *Damn.*

"We know you're in there," an angry male voice called. "Let us by, and these girls won't get hurt."

Ruth, it seemed, hadn't done her job. Mina refused to recant her percentage of success. This was hers to win.

A second later, the door bounced open, crashing back on its hinges. The shoe that had kicked it open was a custom euroboot in dark charcoal. Euros weren't the only thing to enter. Scuttling in front—more like being swept along—were a pair of ballerina slides in light purple.

Mina had eyes on the guy from the waist down, not a clear view of his top half. It didn't matter. He had to move past Mina to get to his getaway craft, which was under the control of a federal agent.

Without showing herself, Mina called, "Let the girl go, and we can talk."

The male replied, "No deal. We're going to walk out of here, or else—"

"Hey, I know that voice." Babs stepped through the doorway, clacking into the room with two girls wearing pastel shoes on either side of her, softly whimpering. "It's that temp! What's her name? Marjorie something. Hey, Marjorie, what are you doing here? Came to see the animals one last time?" She was full of confident snark.

Bright argued, "Christ, B. It's the feds. They're here to take us in, and you think it's the temp?"

"Look around. There's nobody else here. No sirens outside. Just our ride, right on time like my uncle promised. It's her. My aural skills are top-notch. I told you I'm good at remembering things. That's why I'd scoop top tier on *Win Big*. I swear on my mother's ashes, now floating in space, may her soul rest eternal, it's that temp who said she wasn't out with Vincent Kramer. The one I told you about. She's always early." Like it just dawned on her brilliant mind that Mina's behavior was suspicious, Babs sputtered, "Hey! I bet she's mixed up with Ruth and those printers, and she's just trying to cover her ass. That's probably what Ruth was trying to tell us before you stunned her. You didn't give that lady a chance to speak before you dropped her like a bag of bones."

"I already told you the feds are on to us. We're not taking any chances. And that lady was trying to get us to leave the girls behind with her and come out here alone."

Bright was on a razor's edge. His voice was staccato and tight.

"It's not the feds. It's Marjorie something or other. Somebody has to fly us out of here. Like I told you, this girl's way too good-looking for this shit job, and she's slick. Ruth's been giving her the primo jobs. I've been watching."

Primo jobs? Babs had been watching?

Mina had checked for surveillance cams the first day and had found none. They wouldn't risk running an illegal operation with vid surveillance that could be used against them. "Hey, Marjorie, show yourself. We're not going to hurt you. We know you're working with Ruth. Everybody has to make some scratch, we get it."

Mina caught Kaylee's expression, a mix of amusement and annoyance. Her partner gave her a quick nod, encouraging Mina to go along with the light-on-smarts Babs.

"Okay, you got me." Mina holstered her gem out of sight behind her back as she stood, her hands up, holo badge no longer floating around. "I don't want any trouble. I'm only here to pick up the printers." She mocked surprise as she took in the scene, pretending she'd had no idea they had hostages, even though she'd already mentioned it. "Um, I'm not sure what you were told, but humans aren't part of the deal. Radcliffe runs printers and small-time stuff only."

Babs' expression was downright manic as she realized she'd been right and that it was actually Mina after all. The girls she held on to were terrified. It gutted Mina to see them in that state. They were gagged and restrained. They accounted for only three out of the four girls Mina had assumed were here. The other one better not be hurt. It was time to finish this.

"See, I told you!" Babs sneered at Bright, who looked stunned that Mina had actually popped up from behind a crate. That made two of them. "She's in it with Ruth." Babs yanked the girls along as she pounded over to where Mina stood. As she moved, her pink tail swayed back and forth like a pendulum counting down her remaining seconds of freedom.

Kaylee slid behind another stack, staying out of sight, so she could slip into position behind Bright. Mina was going to have to placate this nitwit until Kaylee was ready. Babs narrowed her gaze. "How long have you been running goods? You didn't strike me at first as the type to grift. Too clean-cut. But I see it now. Lots of attitude."

Mina crossed her arms, hip out, pretending she was upset about the delay. "Like you said, we do what we have to do, and I'm a good actress. I could say the same about you." Mina matched Babs sneer for sneer. "At least what I'm dealing in lets me sleep at night. Girls? You can't be serious."

"So what?" Babs' tone sliced like a hot laser. Mina had hit a tender spot. "They're a means to an end—an end where I get *rich*. Then I'll be one of the lucky ones. But I didn't get to where I am now from luck. It took *skill*. Who cares if these sniveling chits have to pay the price?" She shook their arms, and the girls' terror instantly ratcheted up, their eyes imploring Mina to help them.

Mina ached to send her booted foot into Babs' sickening smile, cracking her enamel right out of her head. But she needed to give Kaylee a little more time.

"There's always a price in our world," Babs continued, "and someone has to pay. This time, it's them."

No, actually, it wasn't going to be them.

"That kind of payment seems a little steep to me." Mina shrugged. "But who am I to tell you how to do your job? I'm just here to pick up the merch. Where is it, by the way?" She glanced behind Babs, searching for a signal from her partner, pretending to look for Ruth.

"How should I know?" Babs sent a withering look at Bright. "Ruth was babbling about something, so he stunned her to shut her up. She's in charge of the goods."

Bright clambered forward, finally rising out of his stupor, dragging the girl in front of him, settling a knife to her neck.

A blade wasn't part of the plan.

Now that he'd moved, Kaylee was going to have to expose herself to get to him, thereby giving Bright time to stick the tip of the knife into this little girl's neck.

That wasn't going to happen.

"Don't believe this bitch," he bellowed. "She could be a cop, easy. We need to get the girls on that craft and get out of here. *Now.*"

Mina held up her hands, both as an indicator to Kaylee to stay back and as a show of submission to Bright. "Whoa there. I don't think sticking a blade to a child's throat is necessary. That kid is in no position to hurt you." Now McAllister knew what was going on. "I can get you guys where you need to go. I can drop you in my private transpo—it's parked right outside—then come back for the goods. When Ruth comes around, she'll get it handled. She's efficient like that." To seal the deal, Mina gave Babs a look. "You know what I'm talking about. Ruth runs the show. But we're going to need to take flight soon. Morning's breaking."

Babs glanced between Bright, who had come up alongside her, and Mina. She wasn't so sure anymore. She and Bright were in this together, and Mina was an outsider. "No, Ruth doesn't take any crap." Babs hesitated. "But she thinks she's more important than she is. She's a nobody and always will be. She should stop annoying people."

Mina didn't want to give Babs any reason to doubt her intentions. She took a step back, toward the idling craft, her voice placating. "You're right. I heard Radcliffe is done with her anyway. She did something recently to piss him off." Mina counted on Babs' uncle complaining to her about his call with Ruth. "Come on, let's spin out. Like I told you, I can get you where you need to go. At this point, the merch can wait until tomorrow. If you get caught with…" She nodded toward the girls. "Things will get sticky fast. Trafficking carries twenty-five to life in a box. There's no *Win Big* happening in there."

"How do you know that?" Bright demanded. "How do you know how long the sentence is?" He bared his teeth. If this man hadn't had a blade lodged at the base of a child's throat, Mina would've taken him as the mildly stuffy public servant he was. Boring hair in neutral brown, carefully shellacked around his bland face.

Clothing style was formal, not quite a suit, but close—a dress shirt and trousers, both an uneventful gray, shoes to match. Clean-shaven, face lightly enhanced so there were no visible blemishes, everything orderly. He was every bit a federal rep, and one who seemed to know his time was up, and he wasn't going to like where this ended.

No more lux life. Public judgment, in the form of scorn and fury, would be dumped over his head like a bucket of biowaste. There was nothing in the universe elected officials loved more than being idolized. His base was going to have a fit once they discovered what he'd been up to while spending their precious currency.

But for now, Mina's only job was to keep him steady. The girl at knifepoint gave Mina a pleading look, but remained quiet, her eyes showing that she already knew too much. That was another punch to the gut.

Casually, and pointedly unfazed, Mina replied, "I know how long the sentence is because, unlike you, I research things that could get me into trouble. I only take jobs that carry less than five." Mina's voice was steady, even though her rage was climbing to stratospheric levels. "Why would I risk more than that? Unless it was for ten million borrows. For ten million, I'd do just about anything."

"These girls can net us more than that." Babs took a jaunty step forward, a ringing stiletto crack popping off like a hydrocracker. "We can cut you in." She gave Mina a shrewd once-over. "I bet you have a few hidey-holes. Let's say we take these urchins to one of them and wait it out.

Once we're in the clear, and things are back on track, we make the deliveries and take our cuts."

Bright sputtered next to her. "Are you *kidding*? The feds are on to us! Even if this one isn't a cop, we cut, bail, and get rid of the goods. That's the only plan we have right now. And we're doing it without this bitch. I don't care what she says, I don't trust her."

Mina focused on Babs.

Bright thought he was in control. He was wrong.

Babs had set this entire thing in motion. Mina was sure of it. The former desk clerk rang fully opportunistic and as greedy as a cat pawing a printer for nip. She was determined to win big, whatever it took. Babs had likely scouted Total Enhancement, deemed it worthy, had brought in her uncle first, then her brother and Bright. Encryptions on dog fur were an easy way to transport data right under the feds' noses. Or so she'd thought. She wasn't that smart, but that didn't make her any less conniving or dangerous. She'd dispose of these girls, ending their lives without remorse.

She was the worst kind of human—if Mina could even call her *human.*

Mina knew her director and the entire FPIU were listening in and were going to pounce if she waited much longer. She'd given them enough clues that these two were dangerous and that Bright had a blade. They could hear the children's whimpers. Mina counted on the fact that McAllister would hold off as long as he could, but they were at max time now.

"I don't care if you don't trust her," Babs snapped at

Bright. "You got us into this mess, and I'm getting us out. We're going with Marjorie, and I'll decide how we deal with the baggage. If we'd gone with my plan to begin with, we'd already be in the islands by now."

"If we'd gone with your plan, we'd be in a box," Bright growled, looking more and more wild-eyed, his knife hand quivering. "You don't understand how any of this works. You have to do what I say! I'm the elected representative, for the sake of the cosmos. I'm the one in charge of this operation, and we aren't listening to her—"

"Guys, I hate to interrupt your shitty argument." Mina's voice rang with annoyance. "But once the sun is fully up, it's going to be hard to slip by the masses with three freaked-out girls. You can finish your *discussion* in the craft. Actually, scratch that. I don't care what you do. Take my ride. It's better for me if I stay out of it anyway." Mina walked another meter backward. If she turned, her gem would be visible. She was close now. Once they followed her outside, she would have the pleasure of ending this, with the added bonus of getting physical.

Mina cleared the opening of the building, the craft right behind her, the cargo end open. Babs passed Bright, dragging the girls toward the waiting transpo, a pissy look on her face, which seemed her norm.

But before she could step over the threshold, Bright stayed her with his hand, snarling, "I go first to see if it's safe. Stay here." He went, distracted and muttering a string of obscenities as he passed into the hazy morning half-light, heading for the pilot side of the craft.

Mina was about to strike, fast and furious, ready to jam her upturned palm into the most sensitive part of this asshelmet's face. When, out of nowhere, Bright went down like dead weight in front of her.

The knife he'd been holding clattered to the ground, and the young girl spun free. All Mina could do for a full three seconds was gape.

LEE STEPPED OUT of the shadows, a grin on his face. He was clutching a high-tech stunner no bigger than his thumb in his right hand. "I got him. I didn't want to risk using a maneuver, so I stunned him instead." He held up his maxi. Turned all the way up, it was lethal.

It seemed Lee had a few toys in his arsenal after all.

"Good thinking," Mina murmured as she stepped over the completely unmoving Bright.

Babs started screeching as Mina came for her, clambering back into the building like a woman who'd been scorched by the impending daylight, yanking the two frightened girls along with her. "I will end them. Don't come near me! I will—"

Mina's booted foot shot out, connecting with Babs' jaw as Kaylee buckled her knees from behind. The boot-to-face contact made an awesome cracking sound, and as she flew backward, Babs let go of the girls.

She went down harder than Bright, which was

satisfying. Unfortunately for her, she was still conscious.

"Suspects are down," Mina announced, deactivating her locator, knowing the media and civilian gawkers would arrive soon. "I repeat, both suspects are down. Girls are safe."

Kaylee was already rolling Babs over, reading the former desk clerk her rights while snapping her into a pair of e-restraints. Lee was doing the same with the unconscious Bright. Mina gathered the frightened girls, who had converged together like they were magnetically charged, and gently guided them back into the loading area as FPIU agents descended like SWAT over the area, weapons out, full tactical on. Their first task would be to secure the entire area, which they did as they rushed by.

"I'm innocent!" Babs yelled. Mina heard fear. Good, it was about time. "Mason, he...he kidnapped me! He made me do things. I was his prisoner. I had no choice!"

"Give it a rest," Kaylee ordered. "We have you on audio and vid confessing to all your bad deeds. You're as good as convicted. All I need is a DNA swab to confirm your vocal signature and facial file. We recorded all this on an authenticated channel, so no jury necessary. The box you'll occupy will be small and sterile. No game shows for a thousand kilometers. Stop thrashing, or you're going to—"

There was a sharp hiss, followed by a pop, and Babs went still.

"She got herself sizzled." Kaylee stood, grinning. "I might've keyed in her body weight a tad off. She's about the size of a world-class ultralifter, right?"

Mina suppressed a smile as she untied the girls' gags and released their hands. All three promptly burst into tears, hugging each other. "You're all safe now," she assured them. "You're going to be all right." She wasn't sure what else to do. She was an amateur when it came to dealing with young girls, even though she'd been thirteen once. "Once we get your DNA, your parents will be summoned. Some medi-workers will be here soon to check you over."

One of them turned, a pretty blonde with seafoam eyes who looked very young and innocent. "What about Millie? Is she okay? The guy stunned her. He did it when he stunned that lady. I'm not sure he meant to, but she went down. He just left her there. On the floor! We don't even know if she's alive." Two fat teardrops tracked down both cheeks.

Another girl chimed in, this one with dark hair straight as a contrail and eyelashes longer than Mina's framing eyes the color of jade. "We were just shopping at a Mega Mecca. They...they grabbed us. We didn't do anything!"

"No, of course you didn't. None of this is your fault." She met each of their fearful gazes, making sure she projected calm authority. "You did everything right. The people who took you are bad people, and bad people don't win. I want you to remember that. I'll go check on your friend right now." Mina flagged down a female FPIU member and motioned her over. "Can you watch these girls? There's a fourth inside."

The woman gave a nod. The officer was decked out in

full graphene honeycomb armor, including a tricarbonate face mask and chest shield. These agents took their job seriously. "They have the girl back there." Her voice vibrated off the mask. "She's in with the older lady. Medis are on their way. So is social." The girls would have on-the-spot counseling and would be accompanied home by a social aide until they were ready to be on their own.

Mina made her way inside.

Ruth and Millie were seated on a short bench in the main room, each with a blanket draped over their shoulders. The interior was crawling with feds, and the animals were beside themselves. It made for a crazy, deafening environment.

Mina knelt by the young girl, who had her hand cupped inside of Ruth's. "Hi, Millie. My name is Mina, and I'm here to help you. Your friends are okay and in the back, waiting for their parents to arrive. Would you like to join them? They're worried about you."

Her brown curls swung up and down as she nodded. "Yes, please." She eased her hand out of Ruth's and patted the manager's shoulder. "I hope you feel better, and I'm sorry I couldn't help you more."

"No problem, kid. You did plenty," Ruth answered, her voice cracking. "Go see your friends. I have a feeling that life is going to be very good for you."

Mina's eyebrows arched as Millie stood, the blanket sliding off her shoulders. "What happened?" Mina asked Ruth.

"I was doing what you told me." Ruth rubbed the side of her face. "And the guy stunned me. And this one"—she gestured at Millie—"jumped in front of the stream, trying to protect me. We both went down. When we came to, we helped each other. She's got a spine of titanium, that one. Young lady, you're a hero," she said to Millie. "Don't forget it."

Mina settled her hand on the girl's shoulder. "I agree with Ruth. Anyone who steps in front of a stunner stream is clearly made of titanium. That takes guts." The girl gave them a weak smile as an FPIU officer approached with e-restraints. "I'll be filing a detailed report," Mina told the officer, "and I want it included in Ruth Donnelly's official statement."

"I'll pass that on to my superior."

Mina nodded at Ruth, letting her know she'd do what she could. Ruth returned the nod, weary and exhausted, not complaining as the officer restrained her.

Mina reunited the girl with her friends. Two socials had already arrived and were calming the girls, giving them treats and water, and assuring them that everything was going to be okay. Thank goodness for that.

McAllister walked briskly into the area, motioning for the craft to be taken elsewhere. It zoomed off.

He wore a suit of deep black with a silver tie and reeked of authority, more so than anyone else here, even in full body gear with weapons drawn.

"Job well done, Agents," he said to Mina and Kaylee, as well as Lee, who had joined them. "Where are the bots?"

Mina gestured toward the holding room. "I thought it best to keep them out of the fray. Diana was commanded to emerge if I uttered a specific phrase. I took her summoner for that reason." Mina reached into her pocket and dropped the small box into McAllister's palm. "But when Bright had his blade lodged near the kid's throat, I decided not to activate her or any of the others. Too risky."

"Here are the noded cuffs." Kaylee handed them over.

McAllister examined the units banded in titanium, angling them up to the light. "You've all done our department proud. These aren't the smartest criminals I've ever seen, but they could've done serious damage to the most vulnerable in our population." He placed the summoner and cuffs into a jacket pocket. "This Babs seems to be the connection point to both operations, which makes tracking down the rest of the players easier. She'll be simmering in a box for quite a while. The audio and vid are enough for a conviction, not to mention a dozen FPIU witnesses, including Commander Ellison. This should be nice and tidy."

"I'm glad it's done and the girls are safe," Mina said. "Ruth turned out to be an asset. I'm going to be completing a report that says same, including that she was coerced into transporting illegal goods against her will. After a thorough investigation of the manipulation by Radcliffe, an elected official meant to uphold the law and not endanger citizens, I'm hoping they'll be lenient on her. She's a prime case of hard knocks, but not a threat to society."

"Get it done, and I'll make sure it gets into the file." McAllister turned, narrowing his gaze on Lee, who'd been conspicuously quiet. "Good job taking the assailant down,

Agent Adams. But next time, I'll expect you to report to your superior agent before any decisive action. This is a team effort, not a solo job. You brought a violent assailant down, one who had taken a minor hostage, but it could've gone the other way, and said minor could have been harmed."

Lee blushed to his forehead and bowed his head. "Yes, sir. I didn't know my cuff was dead. I apologize. I wasn't planning on interfering, just acting as backup, but when the opportunity presented itself, I took it."

The makings of a good agent, Mina had to admit. Thinking fast on your feet was absolutely essential.

Lee fiddled with his cuff, and everyone's eyes landed on it. It was old and battered and clearly without power.

McAllister cleared his throat. "I'll be commissioning a new government cuff today, as well as several other essentials you'll need in the field. Appear at headquarters after you get some sleep to pick up those items." He gave the area another solid once-over. One set of parents had appeared. Their reunion with their daughter was sweet and emotional. "These girls were snatched within the last twelve. We believe they're just shaken, but they haven't"—he made an indecipherable sound in the back of his throat—"been subjected to anything more than being restrained and dragged around. The middleman, one Bennet Bandy, had all the encryptions stashed away. Apparently, he was using them as collateral. As of seventeen hundred today, eighteen girls have been recovered and reunited with their families. It's going to take more to round up the rest of them, but the FPIU is on it. Good work, everyone. New ops will be assigned tomorrow. Now, go home. Get some sleep. All of your equipment has been collected, and there's a craft waiting for you outside." He held up a hand to an agent rushing by. "Commander Ellison, I need a word."

A rugged man taller than anyone around him stopped. He had deeply inset age lines creasing his face like bunched fabric, offsetting jet-black hair clipped stubble-thin, and a set of piercing dark eyes. "Of course. Are these your agents?"

"Yes, Agent Kane is the one you heard on the audio. This is Agent Poston and Agent Adams."

FPIU Commander Ellison held out a hand. Mina shook first, followed by Kaylee and then Lee. "Nice job in the field. We appreciate your help. You've made a lot of families very happy today and help stopped corruption at the highest levels." He motioned to McAllister. "Follow me, Duncan. I need to check in with my team."

Once they headed off, Mina, Kaylee, and Lee walked outside to their waiting craft. "I missed the actual stun you gave that dickwad," Kaylee said to Lee, slapping him on the shoulder. "But judging by the way he went down, good job, rookie." She gave him a friendly elbow in the ribs.

"Thanks," Lee said. "Honestly, I didn't plan for it to go down like that. Well, I did, once he was in my sight. I mean, I had the stunner and everything. But it wasn't actually a conscious decision."

"It was good timing is what it was," Mina assured him. "Just like gauging correctly when Rick the Rat was trying to slip out. Your instincts are solid, Lee. Everything else can be learned."

"Director McAllister said he was going to issue me tech," Lee commented happily as they climbed into the government craft. "I love tech."

Mina chuckled. "Yes, we're well aware. McAllister also granted you a huge favor by not calling out your maxi, which is illegal for citizens to carry. Don't forget it." Lee was about to protest. Mina shot him a look. That make and model was at least three years old, so he'd had it long before he became an agent.

Out of the corner of her eye, she caught a glimpse of media drones dropping out of the sky. No way this story wasn't going to be splashed all over newscasts. It was time for them to get out. It was essential that their identities weren't linked to this story in any way, or they wouldn't be able to work their next ops.

Undercover was a lifestyle.

Chapter 24

Mina exited the craft—disguised as public transpo—at a designated landing pad in front of The Spire. It was easier than landing on twenty. The hub would be starting its commuter day in earnest, and she didn't want to deal with the commotion. Mina desperately hoped that at five in the morning very few souls would be moving about in the mega's massive lobby.

Once inside, she hurried toward a wall of tubes, relieved to see traffic was sedate, aching to get inside her residence. End-of-op fatigue had washed over her, the adrenaline rush subsiding as a wave of exhaustion took its place. She couldn't decide if she would take a quick soak or fall face-first into her silky sheets. Both sounded delicious.

"Wilhelmina! Wilhelmina Kandy Kane!"

Mina snapped her head around, wondering who in the space and time continuum would be calling her by her real name. She watched as Suzanne, her mega rep, hurried toward her as fast as her ice-pick sling-backs would carry her. These particular shoes were a sparkling shade of periwinkle—they literally *sparkled* under the ultras, like they were covered in hundreds of pinpoint crystals—perfectly matching her skirt-suit and her precise blue-tinted lip cream. Diligently applied hyperglo blinked on each nail.

It must be dizzying to have to figure out that level of matching every single day.

"I was hoping I would run into you!" This wasn't exactly *running into*. It was more like *accosting*. Suzanne huffed politely as she came to a stop, needing a brief moment to catch her breath after her mini-meter dash. As she steadied herself, she brought her hands up to check her updo, which hadn't moved so much as a strand. At least it wasn't hyper-dyed periwinkle. "I just wanted to check in with you and see how you're enjoying your new residence," she singsonged. In Mina's estimation, it was too early in the day for singsonging. Actually, any time of the day was too early, unless you were a NannyBot with an infant.

"It's very nice," Mina replied succinctly, pressing her thumb into the tube call button, making sure it caught her print, and trying to will it to descend quickly to whisk her away from any forthcoming chitchat. "Everything I wanted and more."

"That's wonderful to hear. We love it when our residents are happy. We think of you as our personal guest the entire time you live here!"

"That's...nice..." Mina trailed off. Where was the damn

tube? The cars were pneumatic and frictionless. One should be here already.

The door finally whooshed open, and Mina stepped inside, but not before Suzanne settled a grip on Mina's forearm, her hyperglo popping on and off like neon signage. The move stopped the door from closing as she gave Mina a conspiratorial wink. "I saw you with Vincent Kramer on the screen a few nights ago." She positively bubbled. "When they confirmed his friend's name is Wilhelmina, I just knew for sure it was you. How exciting! And you had dinner with him at our very own À La Carte. I've never met anyone that famous before." She appeared to be in danger of exploding with all the pent-up enthusiasm she'd accumulated. She was literally vibrating with it. She gave Melissa Socorro a run for her money as she rattled off, "Are you seeing him again soon? Is he as crushingly handsome in person? He seems like he would be." Her hands crossed over her heart as she moved half in, half out of the tube. "Are you two an item? You looked so good together. I can't believe it all happened here, right in our very own Spire!"

Mina barely refrained from banging her head against the side of the tube. So very few people had access to her real name, and she'd forgotten she'd given it to this rep. And then she'd met with Vince right under Suzanne's very nose—a highly sensitive lux-sniffer, at that. Mina was pretty sure Suzanne could sniff a borrow out of a dry husk if she set her mind to it.

Mina stepped out of the tube, guiding Suzanne in front of her. She needed to halt any gossip. She took Suzanne by her elbow to a secluded area, which was essentially a few trees spilling out of twin giant pots the size of her meal counter upstairs. Everything in this place was enormous.

"Listen, Suzanne," Mina said, hovering near the rep's ear and using a conspiratorial tone. "Before I tell you any sordid details, I'm going to need your complete attention and confidence on this."

"Of course," the rep breathed.

"I am, in fact, Vincent Kramer's childhood pal"—there was no denying it at this point, so why try—"but we weren't on a date." Suzanne's expression dived toward disappointment. "But the reason we met up is even better," Mina amended quickly. She had to keep this rep energized. "We met to discuss a *very* important topic, one you're going to be spectacularly interested in."

"Oh, really? What was it?" Her eagerness overflowed so much, she could've watered the trees with it.

"Vincent Kramer is considering securing a residence at The Spire."

A high-pitched squeak forced its way out of Suzanne's constricted throat.

Vince was in no way securing a residence here.

Mina continued, "It would have to be A grade first class, full of all the super lux and high-tech he's used to."

Suzanne's diffracted periwinkle eyes bulged as she nodded along.

"He's found himself commuting to the States more and more, and The Spire can provide exactly what he needs. He seemed very impressed." Mina's face became drawn, her tone dire. "But if word got out that he's looking, every megascraper in the city would be vying for his business, and you know how that goes."

The rep's lips pressed into a severe line.

Mina added the kicker—the thing that would keep Suzanne bottled up nice and tight. "But if you keep this news to yourself and don't let anyone know *anything* about our meeting, or that you know who was out with Vincent, when he's ready to lay down currency, I'll direct him to you." Mina had specifically said *currency*, since people like Vincent Kramer didn't deal in borrows like the rest of the plebeians of the world. Currency would double—or even triple—Suzanne's commission.

In general, the lure of getting sticky fingers on actual, physical money was like injecting a drug straight into the bloodstream, particularly with people like Suzanne. It was a pharma the user begged to take again and again, and it left them high for weeks.

"I won't say a word. Not a single, solitary word. You have my solemn oath." She held up three blinking fingers.

"Perfect," Mina told her. "That's just the way he wants it. He values his privacy very much." *And so do I.* "He has a soft spot for beautiful women, so..." Mina let that comment linger in the air for a moment. "You never know what could happen along the way." She gave Suzanne a saucy wink, not feeling the least bit guilty.

The rep tittered, clutching both hands and placing them under her chin.

"Vincent and I go back a long way," Mina continued, "but we're just friends. He asked me for help, so I gave it.

It's been years since he's lived stateside. It was inconvenient the media caught wind of it." She sighed, playing the put-out pal of an international heartthrob like a synthesized tuner. "Guys like Vincent Kramer like to keep things on the down low, especially when it involves *huge* purchases like lux residences."

"Oh, yes, yes," Suzanne agreed, nodding quickly. "I've dealt with a lot of wealthy individuals before. I know just what they want, and privacy is always number one. If you'd like, I can forward you all of my personal credentials. That way, when Vincent is ready—can I call him that?" She giggled. "Anyway, when Mr. Kramer is ready, he'll have no trouble getting hold of me." Suzanne clutched Mina's forearm with both hands, leaning in and whispering excitedly, "You can assure him I won't breathe a word."

"Yes, send your info, and I'll put it in a file. Thanks for understanding, Suzanne. You're the best." Mina headed back to the tubes, not giving the rep time to think of any more questions. She lifted her hand in a short parting wave as the door opened. "Have a great rest of your day! Oh, and next time, just call me Mina. No need for the entire birth name."

"Oh, I will! Thank you. Thank you for everything—"

The tube door slid shut, and Mina slumped to the side. She didn't think Suzanne would be a long-term issue, but it was irritating that the woman knew her real name and had connected her to Vince. She'd have to let McAllister know. But that could wait.

First came sleep.

The tube delivered her to her floor a few seconds later, and Mina emerged, walking the ten necessary steps to get to her door. She pressed her finger into the handle, glancing around the hallway at the six other doors that occupied the space. She'd never met any of her neighbors, which was fine by her.

Her door popped, ultras blinking on low. Veronica's greeting came next. "Welcome home, Ms. Kane. How can I be of service? Perhaps you'd enjoy a spot of tea?"

"No tea, however tempting. Close sleeping room shades, maximum blackout. Place all calls on silent, except from Director McAllister. Wake-up at fifteen hundred." Mina headed toward her room as the shades engaged. By the time she stepped inside, it was almost pitch-black. Perfect. She peeled off her clothes, not bothering to hit the utility closet, instead letting them drop on the cool, marble floor.

Climbing into her platform, she took a moment to relish the feel of the micro-modal sheets against her very cool, very bare skin. The Vincents of the world weren't the only ones who could afford decent comfort.

"Shades are secured," Veronica intoned. "Wake-up scheduled for fifteen hundred."

"Thanks, that's good," Mina mumbled, her head already semiburied in her eco-feather pillow. It was unbelievably soft. She'd be asleep in minutes, if not seconds.

"You have one vid message from Vincent Kramer. Would you like me to play it now?"

Sputtering, Mina hauled herself up, blinking in the darkness. "What? When did he leave a message?" She'd left the residence at nearly midnight. It was ten after five in the morning.

"The vid chat came in at twelve nineteen a.m. He intended to leave it as a message. It was not put through as a formal call."

Mina eased back, tugging the covers up to her chin, her heart thumping as a rush of adrenaline shot through her, making her tingly and a little buzzy. It would be nice if he stopped having that effect on her. "Um, okay. Play it. Bedroom screen, sixty percent." Why not get a good gander?

"Hi, Mina," a dressed-for-work Vince said. He was seated in what looked to be his sleeping area, but she couldn't tell, as he had himself at about twenty percent, obscuring any good background details. At sixty on her end, he took up a good portion of her wall. He wore a slim-fitted dark suit printed in the French style, with a curved open collar and tapered waist, so dark the midnight blue almost looked black.

More formal than anyone wore here, except, of course, Mina's director.

Vince flashed her a brilliant smile, then suddenly looked sheepish. "I know it's late there, so I didn't want to bother you. But I wanted to let you know something's come up. I'm heading out of the country for the next few weeks to accompany Ambrose on a mission. If you try to tag me at this vid address, I won't answer. The destination is classified, but if I can, I'll try to reach out in between duties."

Mina struggled up on both elbows. Did she detect

uncertainty? Was he nervous? He ran a hand through his hair, which was becoming one of his go-to gestures. This time, his hair wasn't wet, so the tracks weren't as well defined.

There. She saw it. His eyes creased at the corners, one side of his mouth tilted downward. It was quick, and then he was back to his normal casual demeanor—well, as casual as someone could look in a custom-printed French business suit. "By the way, I had a funny dream about you last night."

He'd dreamed about her?

Adrenaline surged forward willy-nilly, buzzing her right up.

"We were in your childhood room, about to play holo seek, when we were suddenly eating oysters, and I was dressed as Sir Servant of Seville." He chuckled. He had a very nice vibrato. "You picked up an oyster, examined it, and promptly proclaimed, 'These are fit for a queen.' I guess you never were a princess. Good night, dear Mina. I hope we chat again soon. Screen off."

Vince disappeared, and Mina felt empty, like a hologram sucked into the ether.

"Why do you have to be so bigger than life?" she lamented. "You had a mega rep twittering over you like a lovesick puppy. You had people at the pet center losing their minds. Kaylee's convinced we're going to go at it soon. It's nice to have my childhood friend back, but at what cost? At what cost, I ask you?" Mina plumped the pillow, giving it a couple of good whacks, before settling back in.

"Shall I send that voice message back?" Veronica asked.

"What? *No!*" Mina yanked the covers up over her head. "No, don't do that. I was talking to myself. It's time to get some sleep."

"Night sequence engaged."

"Thanks." Mina snuggled down. "What are the chances I dream about him?"

"Chances are high."

Mina snorted, pleased by Veronica's plucky answer. "You're all right, Veronica."

"You are, too. Pleasant dreams."

As Mina drifted off, a clear picture of Sir Servant of Seville formed in her mind. Immediately, he morphed into the current-day Vince Kramer of the French Protectorate offering her a plate of oysters in formfitting comfort pants the color of maple syrup. Mina made an unintelligible gurgling noise. Then Vince beckoned her, unstrapping a mini jetty from his back as he held up a single bacon-wrapped date. She glided toward him, weightless, wearing nothing but her nakedness. He popped the delicious treat into her mouth, asking, "Shall we play holo seek now? Winner takes all."

"Yes," she replied in a breathy voice. "I always win."

Vince flashed a brilliant smile as he held up a glass of real champagne, clinking it against hers. "Indeed. Drink up. We've got the entire day to ourselves."

Mina snuggled deeper into her silky modal.

It was going to be an excellent day.

Sneak Peek

PERFECT PLANT

A MINA KANE NOVEL
BOOK TWO

AMANDA CARLSON

Chapter 1

"HORTICULTURE?" MINA'S PRINTED spoon hovered above a bowl of crispy rice puffs bobbing in creamy dairy-sub the color of toasted walnuts. "Like a gardener? Someone who digs in the dirt?"

"That's correct," Duncan McAllister, her esteemed, suit-wearing CIU director, responded from his projected position on her wall. "In layperson terms, you'll be a personal gardener—appearing to dig in the dirt, while you're actually digging up incriminating data." He grinned, his sharp features relaxing for a second, his eagle eyes, normally fixed and concentrated, crinkling at the corners. The expression made him look younger than his fifty-odd years, but it wasn't any less weird. Mina's boss did not usually crack jokes.

"I see what you did there." Mina chuckled. She wasn't going to dwell on the fact her director's behavior had changed from just a few weeks ago. "Gardening doesn't sound too hard. I mean, it's just plants and flowers, right?

Not a lot there that can go wrong."

It wouldn't be the strangest op Mina had ever been assigned, but it was fairly unusual. Most people in the twenty-second century, particularly in densely packed urban areas, didn't have the space to grow ornamental flowers or vegetation, not to mention having the luxury to do so. And they certainly didn't have enough borrowing power to afford a horticulture specialist, i.e. a personal gardener to dig around in the dirt for them.

That meant whoever Mina was going after on this op was loaded sky-high with currency. On the whole, being flush above borrows wasn't much of a stretch from engaging in illicit activities. Contentment didn't come easy in this tech and byte world. Those who were flush wanted more. Those who had some sought lots. Those who had none had to make do with whatever they could scrounge. It was a never-ending cycle of greed coupled with basic survival.

Mina sat at her meal counter, eating breakfast at four in the afternoon. Her comfortable stool, a smooth white polymer creation with a wide circular base and a formfitting sink-your-backside-in gel-cush pillow, was one of the many perks that came standard in her new, lux residence. Eggie, her recently cooperative meal printer, had done well, serving her up a nice bowl of mocha-flavored crispy puffs in a dairy derivative that was super creamy and delicious.

She ate another spoonful.

Director McAllister was positioned at forty percent in her living area, which made him look enormous, since her new home came complete with floor-to-ceiling, flawlessly integrated, visual wall comm. In addition to ample screenage in every room, Mina had solar-catch windows with a spec view of the city from three hundred and twenty stories up, a lush sleeping platform with super-soft golden micro-modal sheets, lots of lux chrome and printed marble finishes, and to top it all off...the aforementioned top-of-the-line meal printer that could create a decent mushroom without the need for trace elements.

All in all, Mina was settling in just fine.

As far as hard things went, this ranked somewhere in the negative-particle zone.

"Yes, you're correct. Gardening won't be hard." McAllister leaned over his printed wood-grain desk in his compact office back at headquarters. His astute gaze missed nothing. His eyes narrowed, lips pursed in a steady line, no hint of a smile now. He reminded Mina of a hungry falcon sighting a tasty rabbit. She'd seen that look before. Her boss was a master at spotting the details. "Did you get enough sleep after we concluded our op this morning?" His way of noting the dark circles under her eyes without officially calling them out.

"Some." Mina busied herself, looking anywhere but at her wall, fighting the rush of blood she felt flaring across her cheeks as visions of a snug-comfort-pants-wearing Vince Kramer popped into her brain. They were the very same ones that had kept Mina from acquiring any good-quality REM. "Enough." She wasn't sure if she was talking to herself or McAllister. "Sleep, that is," she clarified.

"Yeah, I got enough." Her mouth felt like it was full of elastomer.

To compensate, she shoveled in some puffs. Honestly, it was rude to eat during a meeting, especially an official operative designation. But when McAllister had realized he'd interrupted her afternoon breakfast, he'd insisted she continue.

At the moment, she was happy to have something to do.

Mina freely chomped away, and as she did, she tried to scour the laser-hot images that had been seared into her brain from her last interaction with the colonel-in-arms of the French Protectorate. But comfortably clad Vince was being persistent. He gave her a lopsided grin as he raked his hands through his still-wet hair. The finger tracks were disturbingly sensual.

Mina coughed, covering her mouth with the back of her hand.

She'd slept only a few hours. Maybe one? But could she even really call it *sleep*? It'd been more like restless repositioning.

Her director seemed to be observing her like she was an atom splice under an electroscope. A toddler would be able to tell Mina hadn't slept a wink. A former, decorated FBI-CA agent would have no problem detecting it. And because of that, Mina's scorching-hot blush was in the process of creeping down her neck. The heat seared her like an ozone-free sunburn. She desperately hoped McAllister wasn't planning on continuing down his path of questioning.

To help things along, she squeaked, "Let's move on, shall we?" *Smooth.*

He raised a single gray-flecked eyebrow. "Indeed."

"Who, or what, am I going after?" Best to get right down to business.

McAllister reclined in his seat, crossing his arms. "The target's name is Franco Tedesco the Third, sixty-three years of age, native city dweller. His primary residence is the top floor of the first megascraper built in the city, aptly named The Mega, of which he owns a majority share. He has numerous hobbies, but his gardens are his pride and joy. They're lavish and encompass the entire roof of the scraper. A team of horticulture specialists tend to them daily."

Unlike Mina, McAllister looked well rested. The man was rarely ruffled.

"Franco makes the majority of his currency shipping goods all over the world in his sleek hydro-fleet, two hundred vessels strong. The Department of Goods and Services has suspected he's been dealing in illegal shipments for years, but they haven't been able to prove it. A recent delivery to a Greek island has been seized, and enough biowaste and chemis were found on board to configure several hive bombs."

Mina whistled. Hives could take out an entire city.

"They believe Franco himself not only ordered this shipment, but might be manufacturing the chemis at one of his facilities, and the records he keeps locked away in his private penthouse will prove it. He's claiming the goods in question were placed on board without his knowledge. That's where you come in."

Mina nodded. "A standard B&E. I go in under the guise of gardener and break into his residence to find the incriminating data. Are we looking for airmelds or confiscating the tech itself?"

"An airmeld is satisfactory. The DGS needs proof, and they can convict using an authenticated airmeld." Authenticated airmelds transferred the data wirelessly to a government-secured satellite. The trick would be hacking into Tedesco's system and setting up the sequence. "We will need complete files pertaining to all illegal activities. We're assuming there will be many."

"It's not going to be a printed treat getting in there," Mina said. "A man swimming in that much currency wouldn't skimp on security, especially if he's been dealing in contraband equating to chemi warfare on such a huge scale. He's going to have surveillance and blocks all over. His tech is likely vault-protected, and he'll have sensicams everywhere. If the blocks are above a Level X, I can't guarantee a break on the first day."

McAllister nodded. "That's why I'm sending you in with Agent Adams."

Mina kept her mouth firmly shut. No elastomer, no puffs. Lee Adams, her former telework partner on the Cullen op, had been an asset recently. Mina couldn't deny it. But he was still a sopping-wet rookie who could ultimately make things harder, even if his presence as a Level XIII hacker would be valuable. Level XIII was pretty much as high as a hack could go, only thing higher was the term *super.* Level XIII meant Brilliance Level when it came to untangling code.

Mina allowed for a tiny sigh. She wasn't perfect.

"We don't have specific intel on the exact layout of Franco's personal offices," McAllister continued, unfazed by Mina's reaction to his Lee partnering announcement, "but scanners placed in one of the residences below have given us some useful information. According to the readout, Tedesco keeps a concealed superunit behind a north-facing wall in what appears to be a study or a library of some kind."

Only people with currency to light aflame had a library. Physical books were considered collector's items, their borrowing price through the stratosphere, as paper hadn't been manufactured on a large scale in nearly sixty years.

"The barrier wall that protects the tech is made of a top-line composite, likely graphene mixed with chromium hardeners. It's thick enough to prevent an airmeld. You'll have to open it to access the data and set up a sequence, assuming that unit is where he conducts his criminal activities, which is likely, due to the heavy security surrounding it. The superunit is a quantum pico, but there is no bank vault behind the barrier, which is to our advantage."

"I'll say." Mina set down her spoon. Most people with currency like Tedesco usually went the way of old bank vaults to protect their wealth from hackers. Vaults, typically constructed of solid titanium ten centimeters thick, used a rotary handle with an old-fashioned numeric combination and were impenetrable without the aid of a hydro-bomb or barrel laser, which were not sanctioned gardening tools for even the savviest of horticulturists. If Mina entered the penthouse with a barrel laser slung under one arm, things would get messy fast.

McAllister kept going. "Records show that his son, Franco Tedesco the Fourth, identity-chipped Frankie Four, runs a security firm called Four Story Security. The son has been in charge of making sure everything is safe and secure, and it seems the father has put his trust in him."

"That'll either work in our favor or against, depending on how many illegal or unapproved security upgrades Four Story has installed."

It was against the law to add extensions to home security systems, but even so, it happened regularly. Folks with heaps of currency went to great lengths to protect what was theirs, especially if their predilection was to do bad things.

"Up front, Four Story Security is clean. No lawsuits, no criminal activity. But Frankie Four is another *story*." Maybe a clever McAllister was a better McAllister? Too soon to tell. "Under several layers, we've found a juvenile record. Frankie started out small with petty theft, DNA manipulation, identity misuse. Then he moved on to illicit pharma distribution and had a penchant for co-opting other people's transpo units."

"Let me guess. Each time he came before a judge, his daddy purchased his freedom."

"Correct." McAllister's solemn tone mirrored Mina's own feelings about the rampant corruption in the world.

Currency was king. And if you were king, you got what you wanted. Agents for the Corruption Investigation Unit, or CIU, the secret agency Mina worked for, did their best to take lawlessness out at the highest levels, but it was a constant battle. "Frankie Four appeared before a magistrate a total of nine times. Each resulted in max fines, no time spent in a box. The last craft he commandeered belonged to a well-known screencaster, which generated significant media buzz, but no incarceration. Shortly after, this prominent screencaster retired to the Colonies of the Bahamas, void of any debt. Since then, Franco Tedesco the Fourth has kept himself out of trouble."

"Daddy gave him an ultimatum. Stay above the cuff, or I'll laser you off, hot and fast."

"Likely. Then he gave him enough borrows to start his own company."

"And Four Story Security was born." Mina sighed. "I bet they service quite a few prominent individuals with currency-lined pockets in our esteemed community."

"They certainly do. No less than a dozen individuals investigated by various federal agencies use Four Story. That's gleaned from a Level I search. Go deeper, and I'll wager there will be at least a dozen more."

Mina rose off her stool, gathering her dishes. What was left of the toasty walnut-colored dairy-sub sloshed around in the bowl as she carried it to her grinder, where it would be diced up and recycled by weight into the bowels of the megascraper. "This op has the potential to net two crime-ridden extortionists for the low, low borrow of one."

"That's a strong possibility, and if you come across incriminating evidence against the son, so be it. But our prime objective is to take down the father. You're to find and locate any and all data pertaining to the purchase of chemis concurrent with constructing hive bombs with links to *The Blind Fury*, which docked in Santorini, Greece, yesterday at approximately twenty-three hundred."

"Wasn't that the name of a popular vid a couple years ago? Starring Jefferson Manor? *The Blind Fury* and its sequel, *The Blind Terror*? They were released in full holo, too, if I remember correctly. The critics ground them into biomatter and spit them out."

Full holo meant the production could be played in 3-D hologram in the room of your choosing, rather than being consumed strictly on a wall screen or in a pleasure theater—if you were so inclined to spend extra borrows and leave the comfort of your own home. Mina rarely did.

"Yes. It seems the senior Franco is a serious screen buff. He's been known to finance projects. Every one of his fleet of two hundred is named after a major vid production."

Mina sighed again with more oomph. "It takes all kinds." She refrained from engaging her grinder until they were done with the meeting. Instead, she rested her hip against the counter, crossing her arms.

"It does." McAllister cleared his throat, clasping his hands together in a decidedly formal way, which usually meant he was going to say something Mina wouldn't be excited about. "One more thing. You're going into this op with a semiperm alteration." He held up his hand as Mina began to sputter. "I'm giving you a direct order. Your mega rep recognized you this morning. She knows your birth name and has connected you to Vincent Kramer, which means this issue is still at the forefront. We aren't taking any chances that someone else will identify you as the woman who was out dallying with the French Protectorate's colonel-in-arms until this entire spectacle dies down."

Dallying? Mina didn't think she'd dallied. But maybe?

It was her own fault she'd been spotted with Vincent Kramer, so she would take her lumps. So what if she hadn't known at first that her childhood pal Vince was the high-ranking official Vincent Kramer? She should've jettied out when she'd realized who he was.

But she hadn't.

She'd stayed.

It'd turned out to be a Lee-sized mistake.

Because she'd opted to linger with Vince over dinner, her likeness had been captured and circulated through the media, generating a small fervor to uncover her identity. In an effort to quell the masses, McAllister had leaked her full first name, which no one besides family sworn to secrecy and her mega rep knew. The very same rep who had accosted her this morning, fishing for details about Mina's delicious date with the international heartthrob.

"I don't think Suzanne will be a problem," Mina stated. "As I already reported, I convinced her that Vince is interested in purchasing a residence here. She'll back off as long as she thinks there will be a currency commission involved. I can keep that fiber line taut as long as I need to."

"It doesn't matter. She has your name and evidence to associate you with the French Protectorate, and she might not be the only one. Until we get a better handle on this, you will go into your next op as Marilyn Leonard, expert gardener from Milwaukee, Wisconsin, who does not bear any resemblance to Wilhelmina."

Her director politely left out her surname, which was Kandy Kane.

Mina had self-named at the age of three after her parents had left her with no moniker to spare her the burden of accumulating debt, a loophole they'd discovered at the time of her birth. Her chosen name had been cute once upon a time, based on one of her favorite screencast heroes, but she'd identity-chipped herself as Mina Kane at the age of twelve.

"Chance recognition while you're undercover isn't something we take lightly." McAllister didn't exactly huff, but he came close. "Calling attention to yourself can be a career-ender as an agent in this department. An appointment will be scheduled for you at eighteen hundred with an enhancement specialist at head-quarters. Then you're to report to Perfect Plants at oh six hundred tomorrow. A craft will be waiting for you at oh five forty-five. All tech needed for this mission will be on board. From there, you'll accompany the other gardeners to Tedesco's. He sends a personal utility craft to retrieve the gardeners. Lee will be joining another group as a transport technician. This entire op has been aligned to coincide with a large delivery of vegetation that, by our intelligence, should take several days to get in order. You'll be on a communication freeze with the outside world while in position. All satellites in that designation are owned by Tedesco and are closely monitored. Once you find the pico, we will assign a government satellite to the area, timing it to arrive and leave again without raising suspicion. Any questions?"

Mina shook her head. "Another short but serious op. I got it." One that came with a semiperm alt. Even though Mina felt like complaining, as living under all that gunk would not be optimal, this fallout was hers, and she'd find a way to manage. "I'll contact Lee tonight and fill him in." Mina had to make sure the rookie kept his cool and his mouth firmly shut. "As well as read the file on Marilyn Leonard and consume enough horticulture techniques to make me competent. I'll be ready by morning."

McAllister nodded. "I'll expect a report tomorrow evening."

"Is there a plan in place if Franco remains at home for the duration?" Sneaking around under the noses of the other gardeners would be tricky, but if Tedesco was present, there would be no getting into his private sanctuary.

"As of last intel, he's booked for meetings at his business holdings for most of the day tomorrow. If that changes, you'll be informed via cuff before you take off from Perfect Plants. You only have two to three days on this, Agent. Make them count."

"That's the plan."

Nothing is completed without a great team.

My many thanks to:

Awesome Cover design: Damonza
Digital and print formatting: Author E.M.S
Copyedits/proofs: Joyce Lamb
Final proof: Marlene Roberts

Head to my website to sign-up for my Book Alert newsletter to receive new release info in your inbox so you don't miss a thing!

About the Author

Amanda Carlson is a graduate of the University of Minnesota, with a BA in both Speech and Hearing Science & Child Development. She went on to get an A.A.S in Sign Language Interpreting and worked as an interpreter until her first child was born. She's the author of the high-octane **Jessica McClain** urban fantasy series published by Orbit, the **Sin City Collectors** PNR series, the contemporary fantasy **Phoebe Meadows** series, the dystopian **Holly Danger** series, and the futuristic thriller **Mina Kane** series. Look for these books in stores everywhere. She lives in Minneapolis.

FIND HER ALL OVER SOCIAL MEDIA

Patreon: Patreon.com/authoramandacarlson
(Get my books early & for less than retail)

Website: amandacarlson.com

Facebook: facebook.com/authoramandacarlson

Twitter: @amandaccarlson

Instagram: @author_amanda